ZIPPORAH

Wife of Moses

ALSO BY MAREK HALTER

Sarah
(Book One of the Canaan Trilogy)

The Book of Abraham

The Wind of the Khazars

ZIPPORAH

Wife of Moses

A NOVEL

BOOK TWO OF THE **CANAAN** **TRILOGY**

MAREK HALTER

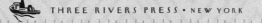 THREE RIVERS PRESS • NEW YORK

First published in hardcover in the United States by Crown Publishers, an imprint
of the Crown Publishing Group, a division of Random House, Inc., New York, in
2005. Originally published in France as *Tsippora: La Bible Au Féminin*, by Robert
Laffont, Paris, in 2003. Copyright © 2003 by Éditions Robert Laffont, S.A., Paris.

Library of Congress Cataloging-in-Publication Data
Halter, Marek.
[Tsippora. English]
Zipporah, wife of Moses : a novel / Marek Halter.—1st ed.
p.   cm. — (The Canaan trilogy ; bk. 2)
Translation of: Tsippora.
I. Title.
PQ2668.A434T7513   2005
843'.914—dc22   2004023889

ISBN-13: 978-1-4000-5280-6
ISBN-10: 1-4000-5280-7

Printed in the United States of America

Map by Sophie Kittredge
Design by Barbara Sturman

10 9 8 7 6 5 4 3 2 1

First Paperback Edition

I am dark but beautiful,
Daughters of Jerusalem,
Dark as the tents of Kedar,
As the tent curtains of Solomon.
Do not stare at me because I am dark,
It is the sun that made me so.

—SONG OF SOLOMON 1:5–6

If a stranger lives with you in your land, do not ill-treat
him. Treat him as you would your native-born, and love
him as you love yourselves, for you were strangers in the
land of Egypt . . .

—LEVITICUS 19:33–34

Moses failed to enter Canaan, not because his life was
too short, but because it was a human life.

—THE DIARIES OF FRANZ KAFKA, October 19, 1921

Are you not for me like the children of Cush, children
of Israel? says the Lord. Did I not bring Israel up from
Egypt, just as I brought the Philistines from Caphtor and
the Arameans from Kir?

—AMOS 9:7

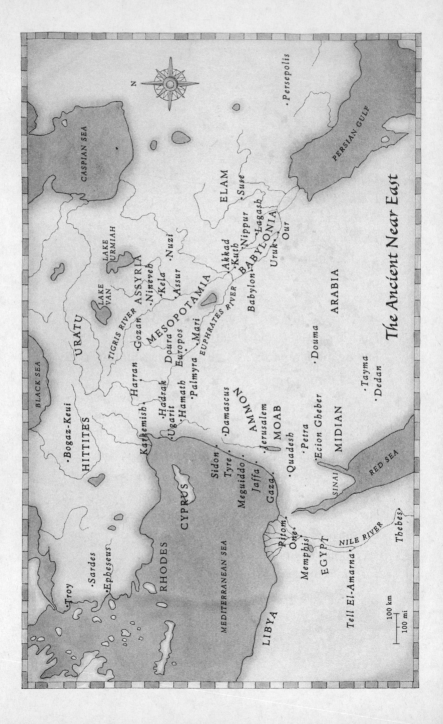

The Ancient Near East

ZIPPORAH

Wife of Moses

PROLOGUE

Horeb, god of my father Jethro, accept my offerings.

At the north corner, I place the barley cakes I have baked with my own hands. At the south corner, I pour the wine, made from grapes I picked myself.

Horeb, god of glory, you who make the thunder rumble, hear me! I am Zipporah the Black, the Cushite, who came here from beyond the Sea of Reeds, and I have had a dream.

In the night, a bird appeared to me, a bird with pale plumage flying high in the sky. I laughed as I watched it fly. It flew above me and cried out as if calling me. I understood then that this bird was me. My skin is as black as burned wood, but in my dream I was a white bird.

I flew over my father's domain. I saw his houses of white-washed brick, his tall fig trees, his flowering tamarisks and the canopy of vines beneath which he gives his judgments. I saw, over toward the gardens, the servants' tents in the shade of the terebinths, the palm trees, the flocks, the paths of red dust, and the great sycamore on the road to Epha. On the path that leads to your mountain, oh Horeb, I saw the village of the armorers with its circle of rough brick houses, its furnaces, and its pits of fire. I flew far enough to see the well of Irmna and the roads that lead to the five kingdoms of Midian.

And I flew toward the sea.

Its surface was like a sheet of gold, so bright I found it impossible to rest my gaze on it. Everything was blinding: the sky, the water, and the sand. The air through which I flew had lost its coolness, and I wanted to stop being a bird and be myself again. I touched the ground with my feet and my shadow was restored to me. I shaded my eyes with my shawl, and it was then that I saw it.

A canoe was swaying on the water, among the rushes. A beautiful, solidly built canoe. I had no difficulty in recognizing it. It was the canoe that had carried my mother and me from the land of Cush to the land of Midian, from one shore to another, keeping us alive despite the sun, despite our thirst and fear. And there, in my dream, it was waiting to take us back to the land where I was born.

I called to my mother to make haste.

She was nowhere to be seen, either on the beach or on the cliff.

I waded into the water. The sharp rushes cut my arms and palms. I lay down in the canoe. It was exactly the right size for me. The canoe set off, the rushes parted, and the sea opened before me. The canoe advanced between two huge walls of water. Walls so close, I could have touched the hard green water with my fingertips.

My stomach was tight with fear. I huddled in the canoe. Terror made me cry out.

Soon, I knew, the cliffs of water above me would come together like the edges of a wound and swallow me up.

I was screaming, but I couldn't hear my own scream, only the lament of the sea, like something broken and suffering.

I closed my eyes, sure I was about to drown. Just as the canoe was about to crash against the seabed, there, on the seaweed, wearing the pleated loincloth of the princes of Egypt, his arms laden with gold bracelets from the wrists to the elbows, a man stood waiting. His skin was white and his brow was covered with brown curls. With one hand, he stopped the canoe. Then, lifting me in his arms, he walked across the Sea of Reeds. On the opposite shore, he clasped me to him and put his mouth on mine, giving me back the breath the sea had tried to take from me.

I opened my eyes. It was night.

The real night, the night of the earth.

I was on my bed. I had been dreaming.

"Oh Horeb," I asked, "why send me this dream?"

Was it a dream of death or a dream of life?

Is my place here, beside my father Jethro, the high priest of Midian, or is it in the land of Cush, where I was born? Is my place among my white-skinned sisters who love me, or there, beyond the sea, among the Nubians, who are under the yoke of Pharaoh?

Oh Horeb, listen to me! In your hands I place my breath. I will dance with joy if you decide to answer me, you who know my distress.

Why was the Egyptian waiting for me at the bottom of the sea?

Why erase my mother's name, and even her face, from my memory?

What path was the dream you interrupted indicating to me?

Oh Horeb, may my call to you be answered. Why do you remain silent?

What is to become of me, Zipporah the stranger?

No man here will take me as his wife because my skin is black. But my father loves me. In his eyes, I am a woman worthy of respect. Among the peoples of Cush, what would I be? I do not speak their language, do not eat their food. How would I live there? Only the color of my skin would make me similar to my fellows.

Oh Horeb! You are the god of my father Jethro. Who will be my god if not you?

PART ONE

Jethro's Daughters

The Fugitive

 hat day, and all the days that followed, Horeb remained silent.

The dream lingered for a long time in Zipporah's body, like the poison left by an illness.

For several moons, she dreaded the night. She lay on her bed without moving, without closing her eyes, without even daring to touch her lips with her tongue for fear of finding the taste of the stranger's mouth on them.

She thought for a moment of confiding in her father Jethro. Who better to counsel her than the sage of the kings of Midian? Who loved her more than he did? Who better understood her torments?

But she said nothing. She did not want to seem too weak, too childish, too much like other women, who were always ready to believe their hearts rather than their eyes. He was so proud of her, and she wanted to show him that she was strong and sensible and held firm to all the things he had taught her.

With time, the images of the dream faded. The Egyptian's

face became blurred. A season went by without her thinking of it once. Then, one morning, Jethro announced to his daughters that young Reba, the son of the king of Sheba, one of the five kings of Midian, would be their guest the next day.

"He has come to ask counsel of me. He will be here before the end of the day. We shall welcome him as he deserves."

The news provoked a great deal of mirth among the women of the house. All of them—Jethro's daughters, the handmaids—knew what was going on. For more than a year, barely a moon had passed without Reba coming to seek Jethro's counsel.

While everyone bustled to prepare the next day's banquet, some preparing the food, others the reception tent and the carpets and cushions that had to be laid out in the courtyard, it was Sefoba, the eldest of Jethro's daughters still living in their father's house, who, with her usual directness, said out loud what everyone was thinking:

"Reba has had more counsel by now than anyone needs in a lifetime—unless, behind that handsome little face of his, he's the stupidest man Horeb has ever created. What he really wants to know is if he still appeals to our dear Orma. He's hoping Father will think his patience a sign of wisdom and agree to make him his son-in-law!"

Orma shrugged. "We all know why he's coming," she admitted. "But what's the point of these visits? They bore me. They're always the same. Reba sits down with our father, spends half the night chatting and drinking wine, and then goes home again, without ever making his mind up to say the necessary words."

"Yes, I wonder why," Sefoba said, pretending to be thinking deeply. "Perhaps he doesn't find you beautiful enough?"

Orma glared at her sister, unsure whether she was joking. Sefoba laughed, pleased with her teasing. Zipporah sensed that they might be building up to one of their customary quarrels.

She stroked the back of Orma's neck to calm her, and received a slap on the hand by way of thanks.

Although they had the same mother, Sefoba and Orma could not have been more dissimilar. Sefoba was short and round, sensual and tender, with nothing dazzling about her. Her smile revealed her lack of guile, the honesty of her thoughts and feelings. She was completely trustworthy and, more than once, Zipporah had confided to her what she did not dare tell anyone else. Orma, on the other hand, was like one of those stars that keep their brilliance even when the sky is already flooded with sunlight. There was no woman more beautiful in Jethro's house, perhaps in the whole of Midian. And certainly no woman prouder of this gift of Horeb.

Suitors had written long poems about the splendor of her eyes, the grace of her mouth, the elegance of her neck. In their songs, the shepherds, although they did not dare mention her by name, vaunted her breasts and her hips, comparing them to fabulous fruits, strange animals, and magic spells cast by goddesses. Orma savored this fame, never tired of it. But she seemed perfectly content to inflame others, without herself being inflamed. No man had yet been able to arouse in her an interest greater than the interest she had in herself. She was the despair of Jethro, who saw her fussing over her robes, her cosmetics, and her jewels as if they were the most precious things in the world. He had had no success in making her a wife and mother. Although she was the youngest daughter of his blood and he loved her dearly, there were times when even he, who rarely lost his composure, could not restrain his harsh judgment of her.

"Orma is like the desert wind," he would rage, in Zipporah's presence. "She blows first one way then the other. She's like a bladder that fills with air and then bursts. Her mind is an empty chest. Even the dust of memory won't settle in it! She's a jewel,

of course, and she grows more beautiful every day, but I sometimes wonder if Horeb is angry with me and is using her to
test me."

"You're too hard on her," Zipporah would gently protest.
"Orma knows very well what she wants and has a strong will, but
she's young."

"She's three years older than you," Jethro would reply. "It's
high time she thought less about making hay and more about
making babies!"

In fact, there had been no lack of suitors. But Jethro, having
promised Orma that he would never choose a husband for her
without her consent, was still waiting, just like the suitors. Now
new songs were being sung across the land of Midian, saying
that the beautiful Orma, daughter of Jethro the sage, had been
born to break the hardest of hearts and that Horeb would soon
transform her, as virgin as the day she was born, into a superb
rock on his mountain, caressed only by the wind. But now Reba
had decided to take up the challenge, and was endlessly coming
to pay his respects to Jethro with the impatience of a warlord
before a battle. Nobody doubted that his persistence deserved its
reward.

"This time, little sister," Sefoba resumed, "you really must
make up your mind."

"Why should I?"

"Because Reba deserves it!"

"No more than anyone else."

"Oh, come on!" Sefoba said, warming to the argument. "What
other man would you prefer? Everything about him is pleasing."

"To an ordinary woman!"

"To you, Princess. Do you want a man worthy of your beauty?
Ask any of the women here, young or old. Reba is the handsomest of men—tall and slim, skin the color of fresh dates, firm
buttocks! Who wouldn't want to give him a cuddle?"

"That's true," Orma chuckled.

"Do you want a rich man, a man of power?" Sefoba went on. "He'll soon be succeeding his father as king, and then he'll own the most fertile pastureland and caravans so richly laden they stretch from sunrise to sunset. You'll have gold and fabrics from the East, and as many handmaids as there are days in the year!"

"What do you take me for? To become a man's wife just because his caravans are so impressive—how boring!"

"They say Reba can sit on a camel's hump for a week without getting tired. Do you know what that means?"

"I'm not a camel, I don't need to be straddled every night— unlike you, squealing loud enough to stop other people sleeping!"

Sefoba's purple cheeks turned crimson. "How do you know that?" she cried, which merely increased the general laughter. "Well, all right, it's true," she admitted. "When my husband isn't running after his flocks, he comes to me every night and eats me up! My heart isn't dry like Orma's, I enjoy giving it nourishment. And doing it every night," she concluded, now joining in the laughter, "isn't as easy as lighting a fire to bake cakes!"

"The fact is, the seasons are passing," Zipporah said softly, when calm had returned. "You've already rejected every other suitor, my dear Orma. If you send Reba away, who else will dare to want you?"

Orma looked at her with a touch of surprise, a stubborn grimace creasing her pretty nose. "If Reba is only coming here to talk to Father, without declaring himself, then I shall stay in my room tomorrow. He won't even see me."

"You know perfectly well why Reba doesn't ask Father for your hand! He's afraid you'll refuse. He has his pride, too. Your very silence has become an affront. This may be the last time—"

"Tell them I'm ill," Orma interrupted. "Just look sad and worried, and they'll believe you . . ."

"I shan't say anything!" Zipporah protested. "I certainly shan't tell a lie."

"It won't be a lie! I will be ill. You'll see."

"Nonsense!" Sefoba exclaimed. "We know exactly what we'll see! You'll paint your face until you glow and, as usual, you'll be more beautiful than a goddess. Reba will only have eyes for you. He won't even touch the excellent food we serve him. That's really the saddest thing about being your sister. The proudest, handsomest men come here, and always end up looking stupid!"

The handmaids, who had been all ears, burst out laughing, and Orma laughed with them.

Zipporah got to her feet. "Let's take the sheep to the well," she said, decisively. "It's our day and we're already late. Forget about husbands for the moment—real or imagined."

THE well of Irmna was a good hour's walk from Jethro's domain. In the distance rose the great mountain of the god Horeb, its covering of petrified lava sparkling in the evening sun. Below it, between the folds of red rock, plains of short grass, sometimes green in winter, stretched as far as the sea. Such was the land of Midian, vast, harsh, and tender, a land of burning sand and volcanic dust where scattered oases shimmered like oil in the desert heat. The wells of abundant, miraculous water found at the oases were both sources of life and gathering places.

Every seven days, those who had pitched their tents less than two or three hours away by road, or who, like Jethro, owned gardens, flocks, and brick houses, were entitled to fill their goatskins at the well of Irmna. They were also allowed to let their flocks drink there, whatever the size of the flock, provided they finished in the time it took the shadow of the sun to move six cubits.

It was late summer, and the men had already left Jethro's domain with the livestock to sell it in the markets of the land of Moab, along with the iron weapons produced by the armorers. They would not return until the dead of winter. In the meantime, it was the women's job to lead the remaining animals to the well. This was where Zipporah and her sisters, with the casualness of habit, were taking their sheep. As they tramped along in their clogs, the dust rose off the road like flour.

The tall shaft of the shadoof was already in sight when Jethro's daughters noticed a herd of long-horned cows pressing around the adjoining drinking troughs.

Sefoba frowned. "Look, they're drinking our water! Whose animals are those?"

Four men appeared, pushing the cows aside with their staffs. They all had thick beards, and were dressed in old, patched tunics white with dust. They positioned themselves at the top of the track, and planted their staffs in the ground.

Orma and Sefoba came to a standstill, while their sheep went on by themselves. Zipporah, who had been walking behind, now joined them and shaded her eyes from the sun to get a better look at the men.

"They're Houssenek's sons," she said. "I recognize the eldest, the one with the leather necklace."

"Well, this isn't their day," Orma said, setting off again. "They'll just have to go."

"They don't look as if they want to," Sefoba observed.

"Whether they want to or not, this isn't their day, and they're going to leave!" Orma said, angry now.

The sheep had sensed water. It was too late to stop them. They began trotting toward the troughs, jostling one another and bleating.

Zipporah caught hold of Sefoba's arm. "Less than a moon ago, our father passed an unfavorable judgment on Houssenek. He and his sons aren't too keen on the law."

Sefoba, eyebrows raised, asked her to explain what she meant. But they were both interrupted by Orma's shouts: "What are you doing? Have you gone mad?"

Houssenek's sons had started running toward the sheep, yelling raucously. In a panic, the animals began to disperse. Within a few seconds, they had scattered in all directions. Zipporah and Sefoba tried in vain to stop them. Some ran down the slope, risking breaking their necks on the rocks. Houssenek's sons laughed and swung their staffs.

Sefoba stopped running. Out of breath, her eyes black with rage, she pointed at the scattered flock. "If a single sheep is hurt, you'll regret this! We are Jethro's daughters, and this is his flock."

The four men stopped laughing.

"We know perfectly well who you are," muttered the one Zipporah had pointed out as the eldest.

"Then you also know it isn't your turn to be at the well," Orma retorted. "Get out of here and leave us in peace. What's more, you stink like old oxen! It's quite disgusting!"

She underlined her disgust with a grimace, adjusted her tunic, which had slipped from her shoulder, and walked toward Zipporah. Heedless of her insults, the men watched her, fascinated.

"It's our day today," one of them said. "And tomorrow, and the day after tomorrow, too, if we feel like it."

"You animal!" Orma snapped. "You know very well that isn't true."

Zipporah placed a hand on her arm to silence her.

The one who had spoken before started laughing again. "It's our day whenever we like. We've decided this well belongs to us."

Sefoba let out a cry of rage.

Zipporah stepped forward. "I know you, son of Houssenek. My father passed judgment on you and your brothers for stealing a she-camel. If stopping us from reaching the well is some kind of revenge, it's stupid. Your punishment will be really harsh this time."

"We didn't steal any she-camel," one of the brothers exclaimed. "She was ours!"

"Who are you, black woman, to tell me what I can and can't do?" the eldest jeered.

"I am Jethro's daughter and I know you're lying."

"Zipporah!" Sefoba said in a low voice.

It was too late. Brandishing their staffs in the air, the men stepped forward, coming between Zipporah and her sisters.

The eldest of Houssenek's sons pushed her away with a blow on the chest, and laughed. "Your father is only your father because he kissed the arse of a black ox."

Zipporah slapped his cheek with such force that the man staggered. His brothers stopped laughing. Zipporah tried to take advantage of their surprise and started running. But one of the men was too quick for her. He threw his staff, aiming it between her legs. She fell headlong.

Before she could even try to get up, a heavy body, stinking of sweat and grunting with hatred, fell on top of her. She cried out, in fear as much as in pain. Rough fingers clutched at her chest, tearing the fabric of her tunic. A knee was planted between her thighs. Her head throbbing, she could hear Sefoba and Orma screaming in the distance. Nausea rose in her throat. Her arms felt weak. The man seemed to have a thousand hands, as he scratched her thighs and mouth and stomach and crushed her wrists and her breasts.

Then Zipporah, eyes closed, heard a wet sound, like a watermelon bursting. The man groaned and rolled over onto his side. All that remained of him on her was his smell.

She did not dare move. All she could hear was heavy breathing and the sounds of struggle and stamping feet.

Sefoba cried out. Zipporah finally opened her eyes. Sefoba was dragging Orma toward the well. Close to her, the eldest of Houssenek's sons seemed to be asleep, his cheek squashed up against a stone, his mouth red with blood and his arm strangely twisted.

Zipporah leaped to her feet, ready to run away. Only then did she see him.

He was standing facing the three men who were still on their feet, holding his staff at shoulder height. It was no ordinary shepherd's staff, but a real weapon, with a heavy bronze tip. He was dressed in a pleated loincloth, and his feet were as bare as his chest. His skin was very white, his hair long and curly.

Suddenly, he swung his staff, describing a perfect curve. With a dull thud, it struck the legs of Houssenek's youngest son, who toppled over with a cry of pain. The two others leaped back, but not quickly enough to escape the weapon, which came down on their necks, forcing them to their knees.

The stranger pointed at the eldest, who still lay motionless. "Take him away," he said.

His voice was sharp, and his accent made the words sound strange. He's from Egypt! Zipporah thought.

As Houssenek's sons were lifting their wounded brother, the stranger nudged them with the tip of his staff. "Now get out of here or I'll kill you," he said, in the same tone of voice, stumbling over the words.

Zipporah heard her sisters' cries of joy. She heard them coming closer, calling her name. But she was incapable of turning her head to them and replying. The stranger was looking at her. He was looking at her with eyes that seemed familiar. There was something about his expression, something about his mouth—a self-confidence perhaps. She saw his arms reaching out to her to take her waist and lift her, and she recognized them even though they were not covered with gold.

For the first time in many moons, her dream, the dream that had so troubled her, came alive again in her.

WITH the shepherds gone, there was a moment of awkwardness. Sefoba ran to take Zipporah in her arms and set about repairing her torn tunic, joining the pieces and trying to hold them together with her silver brooch.

"Are you all right?" she asked. "They didn't hurt you? Oh, may Horeb strike them dead!"

Zipporah did not reply. She could not take her eyes off the stranger with his white skin and burning eyes and large mouth. The one thing to distinguish him from the Egyptian in her dream was that he had the beginnings of a beard. It was reddish and sparse, leaving his cheeks visible, the kind of beard that looked as if it was often shaved, quite unlike the beards of the men of Midian.

He was looking at her, too, still clutching the staff tightly as if fearing he might have to fight again. It struck Zipporah that he must have seen black women before, because there was no surprise in his expression, but rather admiration. Nobody had ever looked at her so intently, and she found it unsettling.

Orma broke the tension. "Well, whoever you are, we owe you a lot!"

The stranger turned. It was as if he were seeing Orma for the first time. Zipporah saw his lips quiver and his smile grow wider. He finally released his grip on his staff and straightened his shoulders. His chest swelled. Faced with a beautiful woman, he was reacting like any other man.

"Who are you?" Orma asked, in a voice as sweet as her gaze.

He frowned, turned his eyes away from Orma, and looked toward the shimmering hills, the flock coming together again and climbing noisily back up the slope to the well. It was clear to Zipporah that the man was a lone wolf.

He raised his staff and pointed toward the sea. "I'm from there. Over there. From the other side of the sea." The words came out with difficulty, one by one, as if he were lifting stones.

Orma laughed, with a laugh that was both seductive and ironic. "From the sea? You crossed the sea?"

"Yes."

"You're from Egypt, then! That's easy to see."

He's a fugitive! Zipporah thought.

Sefoba put her hands together in a respectful greeting. "I thank you with all my heart, stranger! Without you, those shepherds would have taken my sister's honor. They might even have assaulted all three of us."

"And then they would have killed us," Orma said.

The stranger did not seem impressed. He glanced at Zipporah, who stood rigidly, like a statue. With a modest little gesture, he pointed to the coping of the trough, where he had left a gourd of fine hide that was quite flat. "Chance. I was looking for a well to fill my gourd."

"Are you traveling alone?" Orma asked. "With no escort and no flock? Drinking water wherever you can find it?"

The stranger immediately responded with a look of embarrassment.

"Orma!" Sefoba said, coming to his rescue. "Don't ask so many questions!"

Orma dismissed the reproach with her loveliest smile. She stepped away from him, went up to the well, and announced that the water was quite low. Zipporah was in no doubt that the purpose of all this movement was to make sure that the stranger kept watching her with fascination, like a bee unable to extricate itself from a fig that has burst open in the sun.

Orma was now casting the rope, at the end of which hung the little leather pouch that was used to bring up water for drinking.

"Zipporah!" she cried. "Come and have some water. Why aren't you saying anything? Are you sure you're all right?"

The stranger looked at Zipporah again, and she suddenly became aware of the pain in her thighs and belly where Houssenek's son had scratched them. She went to the well and took hold of the gourd that Orma had brought up.

"We are Jethro's daughters," she heard Sefoba say, behind her. "My name is Sefoba, that's Orma, and that's Zipporah. Our father is the sage and judge of the kings of Midian . . ."

The stranger nodded.

"Do you even know you are on the lands of the kings of Midian?" Orma asked, curling her lips.

Sefoba nearly protested, but the stranger did not seem to notice the irony in Orma's voice.

"No, I don't know. Midian? I don't know your language well. I learned it in Egypt. A little . . ."

Orma was about to say something more, but he raised his hand. It wasn't a shepherd's hand, any more than it was a fisherman's hand, or the hand of a man who works the land or kneads clay to make bricks. It was a hand that could hold weapons but also make the simple gestures of those accustomed to power: give orders, call for silence and attention.

"My name is Moses," he said. "In Egypt, that means 'pulled from the waters.'"

He laughed, with a laugh that made him seem curiously older. He glanced briefly at Zipporah, as if hoping she would finally speak, noted her waist, her slender thighs beneath her tunic, her firm breasts, but did not dare look at the luminous black pupils that stared at him. He pointed to the sheep.

"The animals are thirsty. I'll help you."

◆

SURPRISED, they watched him in silence, sure that the man was a prince. A fugitive prince.

Everything about him indicated a mighty lord: his clumsiness as well as his strength, the fineness of his hands as well as the quality of his belt. It was obvious he was not used to drawing water from a shadoof. He caught the cedar pole too high, then slid too close to the pivot. When the goatskins came up, dripping with water and as heavy as a dead mule, he had to hang on the pole with all his weight to maintain balance and turn it so that it was above the trough, where the sheep were waiting, bleating impatiently. So much pointless effort! Beneath the folds of the loincloth, his thighs swelled, powerful and hard; the muscles of his shoulders and lower back rippled, and his skin glistened with sweat.

Despite his lack of skill, or because of it, he persevered, and ended up watering the animals alone, without Zipporah and her sisters doing the slightest thing to help him. When he finished, he took his weight too quickly from the cedar pole and it went slack, with a dull vibration that made his shoulders shake, and caused him to almost lose his balance. Orma gave a throaty little laugh. Zipporah had the presence of mind to catch the empty gourd as it slapped the air. When she turned, she saw Orma's slender hand resting on the hoist, quite close to the stranger's hand.

"The sheep have enough water for the moment. Many thanks for your help. But it's obvious that in your country you aren't used to working a shadoof."

Moses let go of the beam. "That's true," was all he said. He rubbed his hands together to get some life back into them, went round to the other side of the well, picked up his own goatskin, and dipped it in the water.

"There is a feast in our father's enclosure tonight," Orma said. "He's receiving the son of the king of Sheba, who's coming to ask his counsel. He would certainly be pleased to have the opportunity to thank you for saving us from the shepherds. Come and share our meal."

"Oh yes!" Sefoba cried. "What a good idea! Of course Father must thank you. I'm sure he'll be delighted to meet you."

"Our beer and wine are the best in Midian, I can assure you." Orma's laugh was like a flight of birds. The Egyptian raised his eyes and looked at her in silence.

"You have nothing to fear," Sefoba insisted. "Nobody is gentler than our father Jethro."

"I say thank you, but I say no," he said.

"Yes, you must!" Orma cried. "I'm sure you have no place to sleep, perhaps not even a tent?"

Moses laughed. The hair on the back of his neck glistened. She wanted to pass her fingers over his cheek to take away the rough bristle of his beard. He pointed to the sea again with his staff. "Don't need tent. Over there, no tent. No need."

He slipped the strap of his gourd over his shoulder, turned his back on them, and started to walk away, his staff held out in front of him.

"Wait!" Orma cried, momentarily surprised. "Stranger! Moses! You can't leave like that!"

He turned to look at them, as if not certain he had quite understood, or as if there were some kind of threat in Orma's protest. But then he smiled again, a happy smile that revealed his white, regular teeth. "It is I who say thank you. For the water. You are beautiful. All three. Three daughters of the sage!"

When she heard him say, "All three," Zipporah regained her composure and raised her arm in farewell.

"SO!" Orma cried to Zipporah, pouting with disappointment. "Is that how you thank him? He saves you and you don't say a word?" She looked back along the path, where Moses was walking fast in the ocher dust, until he was swallowed up in the shadows. "You could have called him back—said something! You aren't usually lost for words!"

Zipporah still did not answer. Sefoba sighed and took her by the arm. "How handsome he is! He's a prince."

"A prince of Egypt," Orma said, approvingly. "Did you notice his hands?" She turned to Zipporah. "Well? Did Houssenek's son cut your tongue out?"

"No."

"At last! Why didn't you say anything to him?"

"You were speaking enough for both of us," Zipporah said, her voice quite hoarse.

Sefoba laughed.

Orma gave a grudging smile and even adjusted Zipporah's brooch in order to hold the strips of her torn tunic together. "And his clothes! Did you see his belt?"

"Yes."

"His loincloth is worn and dirty because he has nobody to take care of him. But I've never seen anything like his belt."

"That's true," Sefoba admitted. "No woman of Midian can weave such fine linen or dye it so well."

They tried to see Moses through the gray foliage of the olive trees, but by now he was out of sight.

Sefoba frowned. "Perhaps he isn't a prince."

"He is, I'm sure of it," Orma said.

"Perhaps. But, prince or not, what is he doing here?"

"Well . . . ," Orma began.

"He's a fugitive," Zipporah said, in a neutral voice. "He's in hiding."

Her sisters looked at her, intrigued, but, as Zipporah said nothing more, they were clearly unconvinced.

"Do you know something you aren't telling us?" Orma asked, suddenly suspicious. "Perhaps he's on a journey."

"An Egyptian, a prince, if that is what he is, doesn't travel alone to the land of Midian. No servants, nobody to carry his chests or water jars, no woman with him, no tent."

"Perhaps he's with a caravan."

"Yes? Then where is it? No caravan leader has come to pay Father his respects recently. No, he's in hiding."

"In hiding from what?" Sefoba asked.

"I don't know."

"A man like him is afraid of nothing!" Orma said, angrily.

"I think he's in hiding," Zipporah said. "I don't know if he's afraid."

"Are you already forgetting how easily he broke the bones of Houssenek's son? Without him . . ." Orma made a threatening little gesture with her chin.

Zipporah did not reply. At the foot of the slope leading to the well, there was nothing to be seen now but the gold-and-white earth, where the path disappeared among the silvery olive trees and the mass of dark, chaotic rocks on the cliffs overlooking the glittering blue sea.

"Zipporah's right," Sefoba said, thoughtfully. "He's a fugitive. Why else would he have refused to come and pay his respects to Father tonight?"

Orma shrugged and turned away. Sefoba and Zipporah followed her, and all three went back to the sheep and took turns in lifting the pole to fill the trough one last time. Each time they did so, they raised half as much water as the Egyptian had done, but with much less effort. They went about their task in silence, thinking of him: his strangeness, his beauty, his strength, his hands on the hoist, his smile—and the way he suddenly lowered his eyes and gave them a sidelong look.

It was as if these thoughts were like a gulf between them. Even Sefoba, who was married, could not help thinking about the man as any woman might.

Zipporah was at the point of confessing: "I dreamed about this Moses more than a moon ago. He's already saved my life once before! He took me in his arms and carried me off from the seabed when I was about to drown."

But who would have understood? It was only a dream.

On the other side of the trough, Orma was gathering the sheep with sharp little cries, hurrying them needlessly. It was clear from her determined expression and burning eyes that she intended to conquer the Egyptian. She had beauty, and she had white skin: There was no reason not to succeed. What she said on the way back came as no surprise:

"We're going to tell Father what happened at the well. He's sure to want to see the Egyptian. When he sends for him, the stranger won't be able to refuse. He'll be obliged to come to the domain."

"No!" Zipporah's tone was so peremptory that her startled sisters stopped in their tracks, letting the sheep carry on alone. "We mustn't say anything," she went on, less abruptly.

"Why not?" Sefoba asked, softly.

"Father will want to punish Houssenek's sons. There's no point."

Orma burst out laughing. "I should think there is! They ought to be beaten, whipped, left to fry in the sun without water!"

"They deserve a lesson, that's for sure," Sefoba agreed.

"They've had their lesson," Zipporah insisted. "The eldest may already be dead. They wanted to show off how strong they are, and they met someone stronger than them. What's the point of making them angrier and letting their cries and their plans for revenge poison our pastures?"

"There goes Zipporah thinking she's our father again!" Orma sniggered. She threw her veil back over her shoulder and set off again, swinging her hips. "I don't care about Houssenek and his sons. It's the Egyptian who interests me. I'm going to tell Father about him as soon as we get home!"

"Are you that stupid?" Zipporah's voice snapped in the hot air.

Sefoba looked at her, startled by her tone.

Zipporah strode up to Orma. "The stranger said no! You heard him as well as I did, didn't you? Don't his words mean anything to you? Can't you respect his wishes?"

"His wishes?" Orma repeated, glancing at Sefoba for help. "What do you know of his wishes? He was embarrassed, that's all. He doesn't speak our language well."

"He speaks it well enough to say yes or no. He knows the difference."

"You didn't even thank him. Not a word!"

"What of it?"

"That wasn't good. Because of you, we owe him—"

"I know perfectly well what I owe him. I was the one Houssenek's son attacked, don't forget."

"Father must thank him."

"He will do so when he must. I promise you."

"He . . . Oh, Sefoba, say something!"

"What can I say?" Sefoba sighed. "Zipporah's right: He said no!"

"His eyes told me the opposite. I know better than you two what a man's eyes say."

"Orma, listen to me!"

"There's no point. I've heard you. And I say this: I'll speak to Father, because nobody can stop me, not even you."

Zipporah gripped Orma's wrists and squeezed them hard, forcing her to look her in the face. "Yes, the man saved my honor. He may even have saved my life. I know as well as you do what I owe him. But I also know that he doesn't want anyone making a fuss over him. He can't speak our language well; he's afraid of the words he speaks. He wants to stay in the shadows. Didn't you see the way he rushed off just now? There's only one way to thank him for his help, and that's to respect his wishes and leave him alone. Can't you understand that?"

As always when Zipporah lost her temper, she started to sound like Jethro. Orma pursed her lips and lowered her eyes.

"Why don't we just give him time to change his mind?" Zipporah went on, more calmly now, as if speaking to a stubborn child. "Orma, please give him time! He won't forget your beauty. What man could?"

The flattery made Orma curl her lips. "What do you know? You always think you know everything, but what do you know?"

Sefoba approached and put her arms around her sister's waist. "Come on, now, let's not quarrel! Your prince won't fly away. We'll see tomorrow."

Orma pushed her hands away. "You always think Zipporah's right."

"In any case," Sefoba insisted, "what would you do with the stranger tonight? You're going to be very busy. Remember, Reba will be there."

"Oh, him . . ."

"'Oh, him'! Yes, him. He's just crossed the desert and he's thirsty for your beauty."

"I'm already bored with him."

"We'll see."

The Gold Bracelets

Jethro's domain resembled a small fortress. It was an enclosure a thousand cubits long containing some twenty flat-roofed houses of clay bricks, the backs of which formed the outer wall. There was only one opening, a heavy acacia door with bronze fittings that was kept open from dawn to dusk so that approaching travelers could be seen from a distance.

The doors and windows of the houses, painted blue, yellow, and red, looked out on a courtyard of beaten earth, where the servants would bustle about among the camels, mules, and asses on which Jethro's visitors had arrived, depending on their wealth and rank. Whether men of power or of lowly status, they came from far and wide, from throughout the five kingdoms that comprised Midian, to ask counsel and justice of the sage Jethro. He would receive them on a platform that had been erected at the end of the courtyard, just in front of his room, beneath a vast canopy of sycamore beams over which the foliage of a precious vine had been placed to provide shade.

In honor of young Reba, the platform had been covered with magnificent purple rugs, brought at great cost from Canaan. Cushions embroidered in gold had been placed around enormous brass-covered olive-wood platters, piled high with grilled mutton stuffed with aubergines, marrows, and little leeks and decorated with terebinth flowers. The jars were full of wine and beer, and bronze bowls studded with azurites overflowed with fruit.

Musicians and dancers in multicolored tunics were waiting impatiently on a nearby platform, which had been erected for the occasion. The intermittent crash of cymbals and jingling of little bells increased tenfold the excitement already prevailing in the house.

So far, the evening had gone as Sefoba had predicted. But Zipporah remained on the alert. Orma might well prove incapable of holding her tongue. Fortunately, the presence of the king of Sheba's son and the opulence with which he was surrounded captured all her attention.

Reba arrived on a white she-camel, followed by a troop of servants. On the ground, they unrolled a magnificent Damascus carpet purchased off a caravan from Akkad, and there he sat down before Jethro. After the customary greetings and the thanks to Horeb for the journey, which had passed without incident, he presented the old sage with a gift: cages full of pigeons and doves. Then a cedar chest, inlaid with bronze, was placed before Orma and opened, to reveal a fabulous length of fabric. The handmaids unfolded it. As they did so, it floated in the air like smoke, displaying all the colors of the universe. The fabric was passed from hand to hand, everyone getting a chance to feel how extraordinarily fine it was. At last, it reached Zipporah, who weighed its almost imperceptible touch on her palm.

"Is it from Egypt?" Orma asked at that moment.

Zipporah held her breath. Reba, pleased with the reactions to his gift, paused to drink some cool wine. No, he replied, in fact this marvel had been woven somewhere far to the east—not by women, so they said, but by men.

Egypt was forgotten. The lump in Zipporah's throat vanished.

Reba's gift was so dazzling, had cost so much—perhaps an entire herd of beautiful white she-camels?—and had required so much effort to be brought here and spread at Orma's feet that for once Orma's resolve seemed shaken. She did what her father and sisters had so long been hoping she would: She came and knelt on the carpet before Reba.

Her hands crossed over her chest, which was rising and falling in excitement, she bowed. "Welcome to my father's house, Reba. I am glad you have come. You are a man after my own heart. May Horeb watch over your destiny and keep his wrath from you."

Reba's face was radiant. Jethro, most unusually, blushed with emotion. Zipporah looked at Sefoba, who winked in return. Was this evening to be blessed among all others? Tomorrow, at last, Reba could ask for the hand of the most beautiful of Jethro's daughters without fearing ridicule.

But, much to the anxiety of his hosts, when the feast began Reba paid little attention to Orma, seeming far more excited by the music and his conversation with Jethro. Everyone wondered if he was merely playing a game or was still being cautious.

As the jars of beer emptied, the feast became noisier and merrier. The naphtha torches were sputtering when Sefoba began to dance in front of the women, who, like her, had been waiting long moons for their husbands to return. It was a signal. Orma gestured to a group of young handmaids, who now came and danced before Reba. Jethro stopped talking and watched, with a smile on his face.

When Reba's attention was sufficiently captured by the dancers, Orma appeared in their midst.

In the light of the torches everyone could see that she was no longer wearing her tunic, but had wrapped herself in the magnificent length of fabric Reba had given her. Held together with brooches, it covered her from the top of her torso to her feet, leaving only her shoulders, neck, and arms bare. It both clung to her body and surrounded her with a moving aura. As she began to dance, the necklaces and bracelets on her gorgeous skin jangled in time to the music.

Jethro raised his hand, as if he were about to reprimand Orma and order her to withdraw. But then he put his hand back on his knee and turned away with a somewhat exaggerated casualness, a wicked gleam in his eyes. Like the others, he had seen Reba's mouth open—and stay open.

Zipporah had been waiting impatiently for this moment. Nobody was paying her any heed. A shadow in the shadows, she moved away from the circle around the dance.

She crept into the lean-to that was used as a kitchen. Apart from two little girls sleeping next to a basket of figs, the handmaids had deserted it to join in the celebrations. Zipporah unearthed one of the saddlebags used for carrying provisions on the backs of asses and mules. It was a large sack of thickly woven unbleached linen, with two pockets. In the darkness, occasionally lit by the flames from the ovens, she filled it with all the food she could find: cooked meats, cornmeal, loaves of barley bread, watermelons, many dates, figs, almonds, medlars—as much as the packsaddle could take and her shoulders could carry.

Bending under the weight, she left the kitchen and went and hid the saddlebag near the door to the domain, which had, as usual, been closed for the night.

She crouched, and rested for a moment. From the courtyard came the trilling of the flutes, the rolling of the drums, and the tinkling of the dancers' ankle bells. From time to time, laughter pierced the air. Clearly, nobody cared that she had gone. Zipporah plunged farther into the darkness, creeping as far as Jethro's storeroom. Carefully, she pulled out the heavy bar blocking the door. Groping her way, she found a jar of beer, carried it out, and hid it next to the sack.

By the time she returned, Orma had stopped dancing, and now sat on a pile of cushions facing Reba, leaning forward, listening to the words he was whispering to her. A few steps away, two old nurses were sleeping in each other's arms, having long given up their supervision.

Sefoba had disappeared. Much to the delight of Reba's men, only the youngest of the handmaids, taking advantage of what was left of the celebration and the stamina of the musicians, were still dancing tirelessly. Jethro's noble head was nodding, clearly weighted down with the effects of alcohol. Zipporah slipped her arm under her father's shoulders, kissed his cheek to wake him a little, and helped him to his feet. "It's time for bed, Father. Lean on me."

"My little girl!" Jethro murmured in gratitude.

He let himself be led to his bed. As Zipporah was pulling the blanket over his chest, he caught her by the hand.

"It's not the wine," he muttered.

"Not the wine?" Zipporah repeated, not understanding.

"No, no . . ."

"I think it is. In fact, I think you had a lot of wine . . ."

"No, no!" He waved his hand and grimaced. "Are they still talking?"

This time, Zipporah had no difficulty in understanding. "Reba seems to have become a bottomless well of words! And, for once, Orma doesn't seem to be tiring of it."

Jethro closed his eyes and began to laugh softly, his old face as relaxed as a child's. "So much effort to make a silly, beautiful girl marry a rich, powerful, handsome man!"

Zipporah laughed, too. "But he isn't silly! That fabric from the East was a brilliant ploy! This time, my little sister isn't finding it so easy to resist. How could she? Has anyone ever seen such splendor?"

Jethro muttered some inaudible words and groped for her hand. "May Horeb hear you, my child."

Zipporah bent down to kiss his forehead.

When she got to her feet, he abruptly sat up. "Zipporah . . ."

"Father?"

"The hour will come when you, too, will learn what awaits you in the future! I know it. I know it. With my reason and my heart. You will be happy, daughter, I promise you."

Zipporah's lips trembled. Jethro collapsed back on his cushions and began to snore. Zipporah stroked his brow. "Perhaps," she murmured.

As she crossed the courtyard, thoughts and images danced in her head, more wildly than the young handmaids. She still had to endure the torture of waiting.

Thinking of what would happen when Orma returned in the night, how she would talk endlessly about what Reba had whispered to her, Zipporah decided not to sleep in the room they shared. She removed one of her blankets and went and lay down on the straw next to the saddlebag.

The music seemed to go on forever. She looked up at the blinding stars, searching with difficulty for those areas of total darkness where, it was said, Horeb might be watching.

SHE was up before dawn. She crept silently to the pen and untethered a mule.

Some young boys, from among both Jethro's and Reba's servants, were sleeping on top of straw baskets not far from the animals. They, too, had been at the celebration, and were snoring peacefully. The mule snorted when Zipporah slipped the saddle-bag over its back, but even that did not wake them. She attached the jar of beer with a leather strap. Carefully closing the door behind her, she set off without hesitation on the road to the sea.

When Moses, at the well of Irmna, had pointed to the sea-shore and stated that he did not need a tent, Zipporah had guessed the place where he had taken refuge. Wind and time—and men, too—had hollowed a large number of caves in the cliffs overlooking the beach. The caves were occasionally used by fish-ermen, who would rest in them before setting out to sea. Zippo-rah herself, when she was only a child, had hidden there after a reprimand from Jethro. She had no doubt it was where she would find the stranger.

But once she reached the escarpment overlooking the sea, she realized that it would be less easy than she had foreseen. The cliff stretched farther than the eye could see and, in places, the caves could be numbered in their dozens. Besides, from where she was standing, they were not easy to locate, and she could not venture with the mule on the narrow paths that led down the side of the cliff.

Tying the animal to a bush, she set off at a run along the first path she found, then along a second one a little farther on. What had seemed to her so easy proved to be almost impossible.

The sun was quickly rising. The shadows were retreating. Zip-porah began to have doubts. She thought about her father and Orma. She had supposed she would be back by midmorning, without anyone having noticed her absence, since, after the night's feasting, everyone would be getting up late. Now time was pass-ing rapidly. Should she turn back?

She should. She knew it. But to have come this far for nothing!

She suddenly remembered another path, wider and less steep, which the fishermen used to carry wood down to the shore for building boats. The mule would be able to pass, and, once she got down to the beach, she would have a view of all the cave entrances. Moses might see her, too . . .

That was what she called him now, to herself: Moses!

Since she had left Jethro's house, she no longer thought of him as the stranger. He was Moses.

What she was doing was madness. She had never behaved this way before—it was quite unlike her. It was as if she were no longer responsible for her own actions, as if something were impelling her onward.

She hurried on, nervously lashing the mule's back with the rope. Then she abruptly came to a standstill.

Down below, about ten cubits from the shore, up to his waist in the water, a man was standing.

He was only a silhouette, too far away for her to make out his face. But she could see his hair glinting in the sun.

After a long hesitation, he cast a small net. From the way he swung his shoulders and arms, she was certain: It was Moses.

He was fishing. He pulled in the net, folded it carefully, hung it over his arm, and waited, perfectly motionless, then cast it again, with a quick, broad gesture.

Zipporah saw a fish flashing silver in the dark net. Moses emerged from the water and threw his catch onto the shingle, where the waves could not reach it. The beach, at this point, was a narrow strip of pink and ocher shingle set against the vivid blue of the sea, which glowed like a huge jewel.

The heat was becoming ever-more intense and stifling. Zipporah had to take deep breaths. An image from her dream came into her mind: the moment when the boat had moved away from the shore, and she had felt the cool sea spray on her brow and cheeks.

For a moment, it seemed to her that the happiest thing in

the world would be to be down there, by Moses' side, while he turned in the water, seeking another spot from which to fish.

Apparently, Moses was perfectly capable of feeding himself. The food she had brought with her would not be as indispensable as she had thought.

Wouldn't he mock her?

During the night, Zipporah had chosen the words she wanted to say to him. Now, she had lost any desire to speak.

She had to take the food to whichever cave he had chosen and leave before he got back with his catch. He would guess. Or, more likely, think it was Orma's doing. Well, that couldn't be helped.

◇

CARRYING the jar of beer on her shoulder, she reached a point halfway down the cliff, where the path widened to form a sizable terrace under a rocky overhang, in front of the dark, gaping mouth of a cave. She had found it.

Against one wall of the cave stood a stone oven; against the other, a number of old mats with fringed edges that served as a bed, covered with a big blue-and-white canvas sack and a tunic. The location was perfect, protected both from the sun and from the gusts of wind that brought sand and dust from the mountain.

Zipporah approached the oven. Under a broad flat stone, the white embers smoldered, giving off a peppery odor of terebinth.

Moses not only knew how to fish, but also how to make a fire. And he had settled in a cave where it was quite possible to live for a long period of time.

She imagined him—a prince, a man accustomed to luxury— eating and sleeping on this pallet! He wasn't a prince here, only a fugitive. If proof were still needed, this pallet was it.

Why, then, was he fleeing? What fault could a lord of Egypt have committed to have to live so roughly?

Zipporah was about to put the jar down on the terrace when she hesitated, and decided that it was better to put it inside the cave, where it was cool. She crossed the threshold, and was surprised not only by the darkness of the cave, but by how long and narrow it was. The bronze-tipped staff with which Moses had fought the shepherds was there, leaning against the wall. His big gourd was there, too. She placed the jar beside it, like a gift.

Down below, Moses was still fishing, with the same slow, measured gestures. Not for a moment did he raise his eyes toward the cliff. She ran back up the path. The sun was burning her brow and mouth.

By the time she began her descent again, bent beneath the weight of the saddlebag, Moses was no longer casting his net. He was opening and cleaning his catch, walking back and forth between the sea and the shingle, washing and gutting the fish.

Breathing hard and sweating with the effort, Zipporah carried the saddlebag down as quickly as she could.

When she reached the cave, she could not help stealing another glance at the beach. It was then that she became aware of a vast shimmer on the sea, much more intense than any of the others, like a wind spreading light as far as the shore.

For a brief moment, Moses seemed suspended there, as if the sky and the earth were uniting beneath his feet. The beach, the water, the air had disappeared, leaving only a dazzle of light in which his calves and arms and hips and torso floated.

Zipporah stood rooted to the spot, both fascinated and terrified, heedless of the heavy burden she still carried, totally overwhelmed by an unknown sensation that spread through every particle of her thoughts and emotions and made her flesh and muscles quiver.

The shimmer stopped.

Once again the sea was a soft, transparent blue, pricked with needles of light. Moses gathered together the fish he had caught, forcing a cane stalk through their cheeks.

At last, Zipporah dropped the saddlebag at her feet. She doubted what she had just seen. Perhaps she had simply been blinded by the effort and the heat.

But she knew it was more than that. The sensation was still there, in the dryness of her mouth and the way her skin quivered.

She could not take her eyes off Moses. He placed the fish in a water-filled hollow in the rocks and covered them with a few stones. Then he walked out again into the water, and dived in. He swam with ease away from the shore, and put his head below the surface.

Looking down on him like a bird, Zipporah watched his body in the transparent sea. Waves sparkling like eyes glided over his back, and over his buttocks and thighs, which were white where the loincloth had protected them from the sun.

She suddenly felt extremely dizzy. There was a tightness in her stomach and chest, a heaviness in her back and shoulders. Her knees started to give way, and she pressed her hands on her thighs to steady herself. She should have turned away. A step or two back would have been enough. Lowering her eyes would have been enough. But she couldn't. Her dizziness had nothing to do with the void beyond the cliff.

She had never watched a man like this. And it was not only because he was naked.

Moses' head finally emerged from the water. He shook the water from his hair, passed his hand over his face, turned onto his back, and swam slowly in a wide circle, surrounded by glittering reflections, until he reached the beach.

What she could not see—his eyes, his mouth, the water

streaming over his temples—Zipporah tried to imagine. She was suddenly filled with a desire to go into the sea and swim to him, to see the creases around his eyes, to touch his shoulders. There was a painful feeling in her body. Her skin was as sensitive as if she had been rubbed with nettles. She was afraid.

Finally overcoming her fascination, she turned away.

For a few seconds, she bent double, as if she had been flattened by a blow from a stick. She waited with her mouth wide open, her eyes tightly shut, until she had regained her breath. The pounding of her heart made a deafening noise.

She cursed herself, called herself mad, straightened up again with a kind of rage.

Taking the saddlebag in both hands, she pulled it as much as carried it to the mouth of the cave. All she had to do was leave it there, in the shade, then run away quickly.

The thought of finding herself face-to-face with Moses filled her with terror. He would be sure to see the jar and the sack full of food. He would guess. He would understand. He would think: the girls from the well. Or perhaps he would think of her, the black girl. The girl the shepherds had wanted to violate. The girl for whom he had fought.

Perhaps he wouldn't think any of those things. They would soon see.

Unlike Orma, she would be patient. The prince of Egypt would be hiding here for a long time yet; there was no longer any doubt about that.

Zipporah pulled the sack over the uneven ground to the mouth of the cave. There, she stopped, taken aback by the darkness. The coolness of the cave froze the sweat on her brow and neck. She bumped into the wall with her shoulder, moaned with pain, and almost fell. Her heel hit something hard, which overturned with a dull thud.

She crouched and felt the ground around her with her finger-tips. Her heart was again beating fast, and her throat was dry with the sense that she was committing a sin.

"Horeb! Horeb!" she murmured. "Don't abandon me!"

Her fingers touched something wooden and angular. It was a long, narrow casket. She pulled it to her. In the light coming from the mouth of the cave, she made out the blue and ocher paint on its sides. On the lid, there were columns of small figures, silhouettes of birds and plants, simple lines and strokes, all meticulously drawn.

Egyptian writing!

She knew something of it from Jethro. Once, he had traced a few figures for her in the sand; on another occasion, he had written them in octopus ink on a sheet of crushed cane. Those designs she had found quite clumsy, but these were light and pure and of total simplicity.

She remembered the noise the casket had made after she overturned it. It was not empty. The fear that Moses would return again took hold of her. She listened, ready to run if need be. All she could hear was the surf against the cliff. She still had time to put everything back in its place.

She got down on all fours and groped about her feverishly, grazing her knees on the sharp edges of the rock. She saw something glinting in the darkness, a long, cylindrical object, then another one, identical, beside it. They were heavy. They were . . . Zipporah cried out in surprise. She could not believe her eyes. She stood up and went to the cave mouth to see better.

Gold! Two thick bracelets of polished gold, at least as big as her own forearms! On each of them, carved in relief, a snake. Between the coils of the snake, signs, strange crosses, tiny silhouettes, half men, half beasts.

A stone rolled somewhere, and echoed against the cliff.

Moses was coming up.

Zipporah thought of the golden arms of the man who had embraced her at the bottom of the sea.

She quickly put the bracelets back in their place, then rushed out of the cave, her mind racing.

The beach and the sea were empty. Moses was up here, some fifteen paces from her, his catch swinging from the reed he had placed negligently over his shoulder. When he saw her, he stopped in surprise, perhaps even fear.

She hesitated. He was still some distance away; she could run up to the top of the cliff. She told herself again that he would see the food and understand. He raised his hand to protect his eyes from the sun and see her better.

She was ashamed at wanting to flee. Wasn't she always telling her sisters that you had to learn to confront your own destiny? But, in truth, she did not really have a choice. Her feet refused to move.

He smiled. He took his hand away from his brow in a little gesture of greeting and approached.

IN the days, weeks, and years that followed, Zipporah was often to remember that moment, a moment she was sure was neither as brief nor as supernatural as it had seemed to her at the time.

Moses was here, in front of her, and she was mortified with fear, terrified that once again, as on the previous day, she would be incapable of uttering a single word. She looked at Moses' lips as if she might be able to find her own words there. Instead, she realized that when she had seen him at the well of Irmna, she had not really noticed the way his mouth stood out from his sparse beard, the lobes of his ears, or the irregularity of his eyelids, one of which was lower than the other. His nose and his high cheekbones, she remembered. And, of course, she still said nothing.

He had overcome his surprise and was looking at her with a candid expression, his eyebrows slightly raised, waiting for her to explain why she was here.

She had forgotten the casket and the gold bracelets, but the thought of the dizziness that had overcome her as she had watched him swimming made her chest tight again, like a threat. It was unthinkable that such emotion would not be visible on her face.

That must be what Moses was seeing. It was an image Zipporah did not like. The image of a woman dazzled by the presence of a man, by the sight of his body. An image he must know well, which probably had no great interest for him. How many women had already displayed the same open-mouthed amazement? Egyptian beauties, queens, handmaids . . . She was furious with herself.

But however much she might want it, she had no other image of herself to show.

Moses seemed to approve her silence. He nodded slightly and went and put his catch down by the stove. He lifted the stone covering the fire, removed the cane from the cheeks of the fish, broke it into several pieces of equal length, which he arranged on the stones of the oven, and placed the fish on them. He bent down to stoke the embers a little, and they began to smoke gently.

Although Zipporah was relieved, she was also offended that he should attend to his fish while she was here. But Moses soon stood up and smiled at her.

"They'll cook very slowly," he said. "I'll be able to keep them for a long time."

Moses was talking about the fish, but the look he gave Zipporah quivered like a harp whose strings were about to break.

She straightened, trying to hold her head high, and, when she spoke, she spoke slowly, to make sure that he understood. "I was afraid you didn't have enough food; that's why I came. You don't have a flock. Nor anyone to . . . But you know how to fish . . . I didn't think about your bed. You need a cloth and some new matting . . . I didn't think of it . . . The truth is, I didn't only come about the food. I wanted to thank you . . . For yesterday. I owe you . . ."

She stopped, searching for words to describe what she owed him.

Moses was following her gestures and the way her curly hair spread over her shoulders like black feathers. He glanced at the sack and the jar, then quickly looked again at Zipporah's lips in order to be sure of what she was saying.

He was waiting for her to finish her sentence, but she left it unfinished.

They heard the surf and breathed the scent of the terebinth embers, now mixed with the smell of the fish. With a perfectly natural movement, Moses approached Zipporah. They were on the border between the sun and the shade, two cubits from the void.

She took a deep breath, and, as she did so, she could smell Moses. He smelled of sea salt. She saw him fold his arms, as Jethro sometimes did. This time, she thought of the gold bracelets and her dream.

"I'm pleased," Moses said, in that accent of his, that slow, hesitant way of speaking, nodding his head along with the words. "I hear your voice. Yesterday, you said nothing. Not a word. I thought: What's happening? Can't she speak? Is she a stranger here?"

She laughed. "Did you think that because my skin is black?" she asked, very quickly, as if she had been waiting a long time to ask the question.

"No. Only because you said nothing."

She believed him.

"You said nothing. But you listened. You understood where I was. There are many caves here. If not . . ."

If not, Zipporah thought, I would have walked the length of the beach until the sun went down to find you. She did not have to say it.

"There is something you should know," Moses went on. "I am not an Egyptian. I may look like one, but I'm not. I'm a Hebrew."

"A Hebrew?"

"Yes. A son of Abraham and Joseph."

Again, she felt a tightness in her chest, remembering the casket and the bracelets. He stole them! she thought. That's why he's a fugitive. He's a thief! Her blood pounded in her temples.

"Like my father," she replied, mechanically. "My father Jethro, the sage of the kings of Midian, is also a son of Abraham."

If he was wondering how a son of Abraham could have a daughter with black skin, he did not show it. "In Egypt," he said, "the Hebrews are not kings, or the sages of kings. They are slaves."

"You don't look like a slave."

He hesitated, turned his eyes from her, and said something curious: "I'm not from Egypt anymore, either."

Both fell silent again. Moses' words could mean so many different things, Zipporah found it impossible to make sense of them in her mind. Perhaps he wasn't a thief? Perhaps he wasn't a prince, either? Perhaps he was simply the man in her dream?

The thought terrified her. As he watched her, she took a step away from him. "I must go back," she said.

He nodded, pointed to the interior of the cave, and thanked her.

"You will always be welcome in my father's house," she said, still trying to read his face. "He will be very pleased to see you."

She turned away from him and walked back out into the heat of the cliff. "Wait," Moses called. "You can't leave without a drink."

Without waiting for a reply, he went to the mouth of the cave and picked up his gourd. He came back, took the wooden stopper from the neck of the gourd, and held it out to her. "It's still cool."

Zipporah was quite used to drinking from a gourd, but she felt incapable of even lifting it, so Moses lifted it for her. The water squirted out, spattering her chin and her cheek. She laughed. Moses laughed, too, and lowered the gourd.

Zipporah did not know how to seduce a man, even though she had watched Orma. She did not know what love was, even though she had watched Sefoba. But what she felt now, rising within her, was both love and the desire to seduce. She defended herself against both.

"I'm wasting your water," she said.

Moses raised his right hand, put his fingers on Zipporah's cheek, and gently wiped away the cool water from her dark skin. Then his fingers slid down to the hollow of her chin, brushing against her lips as they did so. Zipporah gripped his wrist.

How long did they stay like that?

Probably no longer than it takes for a swallow to pass overhead, but long enough for Zipporah to feel Moses' caress, for that was what it was, all through her body, as if he were enveloping her, lifting her, as the man in her dream had done. Long enough for her to lose consciousness of what was really happening.

Then she opened her eyes again and saw the same desire on Moses' face. She saw the gestures he was about to make; she even thought of the bed awaiting them, so close. She still had the strength to smile, let go of Moses' wrist, and run out into the furnace of the day

THE sun had long since passed its zenith by the time Zipporah got back to Jethro's domain. Silence reigned, and not only because of the afternoon heat. Reba's tents, servants, and she-camels were gone.

She pushed the mule back into the pen. The men took care to look away, while the handmaids threw her worried glances and ran into the shade of the house. Clearly, her absence had not gone unnoticed.

She had been dreaming of her cool room and the jug of water she would pour over her body before she changed her tunic, since the one she was wearing was by now sticky with sweat. But, afraid she would find Orma in her room, she headed for the big room used by all the women. She had almost reached it, and could already hear the cries of the children playing there, when her name rang out. Sefoba was crossing the courtyard to meet her, a distraught expression on her face. She threw herself into her arms, and hugged her tight, her chest heaving.

"Where were you? Where were you?"

Zipporah had no time to reply. Without pausing for breath, Sefoba told her that everyone had feared for her safety, thinking of Houssenek's sons and all the horrors those savages were capable of as revenge for the punishment inflicted on them the day before by the stranger—may the wrath of Horeb be assuaged!

"Oh, my Zipporah, if only you knew! I imagined you in their hands, I couldn't help it, I saw them doing to you what they couldn't do yesterday!"

Zipporah smiled, stroked her sister's brow and neck, kissed her damp cheeks, and, without telling a lie, assured her that nothing terrible had happened to her and there was no need to get into a state.

Sefoba did not have the time to question her further, because just then a mocking laugh rang out behind her.

"Of course not! Of course nothing terrible happened! Don't worry, Zipporah, Sefoba was the only one here who imagined any such thing!"

Orma, looking all the more beautiful in her rage, took Zipporah by the arm and pulled her away from Sefoba. The poison of jealousy was clearly visible on her face.

"Where you were, you weren't in any danger, were you? Certainly not from the vengeance of Houssenek's sons!"

There was no doubt that she had guessed where Zipporah had been. Orma might be silly, but only about certain things.

Zipporah remained calm. "Has Reba already left?" she asked.

Disconcerted, Orma screwed up her eyes, as if sensing a trick. But all she could see was the dazzling light of the courtyard. She waved her hands in the air. "Who cares about Reba?"

"She gave him back the fabric this morning," Sefoba sighed.

"You gave him back the fabric?" Zipporah said, genuinely surprised.

"The fabric! That's all you can think about. Do I have to marry for a piece of fabric?"

"You seemed very proud to wear it last night."

"Oh, I admit it suited me! It looked good, and it was fine for dancing in, so I put it on and danced. What of it? That was nighttime. In the torchlight, it looked beautiful. This morning, in the light of day, I realized I didn't like it any more. I didn't like it at all. I gave it back to Reba, and that was it. Of course, if you'd been here, you'd have stopped me."

Orma was smiling, proud of how provocative she was being. Sefoba dried her tears with the back of her wrist and grimaced.

"Reba was so humiliated," she said, "that he took his knife out and cut that wonderful fabric up into little pieces. Then he called for his she-camels and left without a word of farewell to Father. Poor Father was already ill from drinking too much last night. You can imagine what he thought about it all. Of course, you weren't there . . ." She broke off, and smiled to soften the effect of her words. "I picked up the pieces of the fabric. They're under my bed."

"I don't care a fig for Reba," Orma muttered, clearly feeling the argument slipping away from her. "Let's not talk about Reba. Besides, all this is your fault, Zipporah."

"My fault?"

"Don't make that face. You found out where the Egyptian is hiding, didn't you?"

Zipporah's hesitation was an admission.

"I was sure of it," Orma said, triumphantly. "So that's where you've been!"

"Is that true? Did you go and see him?" Sefoba's surprise, with its hint of reproach, upset Zipporah more than all of Orma's nagging.

"Yes," she admitted at last.

Orma, who until now had perhaps not been so sure of what she was alleging, seemed to find this confirmation hard to swallow.

"You found him?" Sefoba said, wide-eyed and openmouthed. "You saw him?"

"I saw him."

"Of course!" Orma said. "What a hypocrite you are, Zipporah! Yesterday you told us to say nothing to Father, to leave the Egyptian alone. Oh, the poor man, we must let him keep his secrets! But today you didn't even wait until daylight to run after him!"

"I took him something to eat and drink, that's all."

"Oh! How kind of you!"

"I thanked him for what he did yesterday."

Orma laughed, with a laugh that made Zipporah blush. "Where is he?"

"He is where he is."

"Oh, all right," Orma hissed, scornfully. "Don't tell me anything, there's no point! Father also wants to thank the stranger. He's been waiting for you to come back to find out where he is."

"What did you tell him?"

"The truth. I'm not like you. I don't put on airs to hide the truth."

JETHRO was lying on his bed, where Zipporah had left him the previous night. A few extra cushions had been arranged around him. It was very dark in the room, and his white hair shone like a block of limestone. His eyes were still shut, and his hands were crossed high on his chest. With rapid fingers, a young handmaid was massaging his stomach through the thin linen of his tunic, while another, so old that her face was nothing but a mass of lines, stood near the doorway, preparing an infusion.

Occasionally, a little murmur would escape Jethro's lips, although it was hard to say whether it was an expression of suffering or relief. The young handmaid would relax the pressure of her hands and peer into her master's face, but all it revealed was the extreme pallor of an old man whose insides were a mess.

Neither handmaid interrupted her work when Zipporah appeared. She stood waiting in the doorway, watching, with some repulsion, as a brown liquid oozed from a distended cloth held by the older handmaid. When the old woman finally made way for Zipporah, Jethro became aware of her movements through his closed eyelids. He opened his eyes wide, and his lips quivered in a smile of contentment. "Daughter, you're finally back."

"Good day, Father."

"Let him drink his infusion first," the old handmaid interrupted. "You can speak afterward. The infusion mustn't be allowed to rest, or it'll lose its effect."

She pushed her young companion aside unceremoniously and placed the wooden bowl in Jethro's hands with an authoritative gesture. He sat up, grumbling, and barely looked at the mixture before gulping it all down. Looking straight ahead, he held out the empty bowl, with a scornful "Bah!"

The old woman clucked sternly. "What did you think? That Horeb would make your innards young again in a flash?" She gathered her things together in a basket. "It'll be better in a moment," she went on, in a tone it would have been impossible to contradict, "and tonight you'll feel fine. But next time, ask me before you drink something you don't know."

Jethro said nothing in reply. He lightly touched the young handmaid's thigh with his wrinkled fingers. "You can go, too, my dear. Your hands are blessed by Horeb."

The two women went out into the dazzling light of the courtyard. Jethro's eyelids closed again like rumpled curtains. He groped along the side of the bed until he found Zipporah's hand and clasped it firmly.

"Reba gave me an Eastern concoction. A kind of tar. You heat it on the embers and breathe in the smoke. Apparently, if you go about it the right way, it causes all kinds of images in your mind, and everything seems different—tastes, smells, objects. Perhaps I'm too old, or it wasn't properly prepared . . ." He laughed into his silky white beard, and his laugh immediately turned into a reluctant sigh, accompanied by a grimace. "I know perfectly well what I feel. It's as if I've drunk all the jars of wine and beer in the house and Horeb is punishing me by patting me amicably on the head with rocks from his mountain."

"Do you want some water? More cushions?"

"No, nothing. Your presence is enough." He opened his eyes again, and his pupils gleamed in the darkness. "Reba's a good boy, worthy of the duties awaiting him. He's curious about the world, and he has a sense of justice. He knows the difference between truth and illusion. I felt ashamed when he left this morning. For the first time in a very long time, I, Jethro, was ashamed. Of myself and my daughters!"

"Father! I had no intention of—"

He squeezed Zipporah's hand tighter. "Not so loud. Words also become stones if you throw them too hard."

"Please don't think I could have prevented Orma from giving the fabric back to Reba. Right now, there's nobody she hates more than me."

Jethro groaned, although whether it was a result of the pain in his body or Zipporah's words was unclear. "The stranger," he sighed. "Is it true there's a stranger among us? A stranger who rescued you from the hands of Houssenek's sons?"

"Yes."

"Yesterday?"

"Yes, at the well of Irmna."

"And you said nothing to me about it."

"We were safe. And Reba was here last night. I would have told you today."

Jethro's chest shook with laughter. "After your long walk?"

The old woman had told the truth. The infusion was already starting to take effect. Color was returning to the old sage's cheeks and his voice was not only regaining its clarity but was capable of mockery. Zipporah set her lips and said nothing. She did not feel guilty, but hurt. Realizing this, Jethro patted her hand.

"According to Orma, the stranger is a prince of Egypt. What is a prince of Egypt doing in the land of Midian?"

"He may be a prince, but he isn't Egyptian."

"Oh?"

He waited for her to continue. She paused for a moment. Here, in front of Jethro, the memory of Moses' fingers on her face filled her with embarrassment. "He told me this morning."

"That's good news. So Orma's talking nonsense."

"I took him some food and beer."

"Why doesn't he come here, so that I can thank him for what he did for my daughters?"

"I don't know."

Jethro gave her a sharp look.

"I don't know," she repeated, and hesitated. On the way home, she had decided to confide in her father, to tell him everything. She had never in her life tried to conceal anything from him. Yet now she could not bring herself to say anything. The words she had planned to use, all the things she had wanted to confess, including her fears—none of it crossed her lips. There was only one thing she felt able to reveal: "The reason I didn't say where I was going this morning was to stop Orma from going with me."

Jethro groaned, and cautiously shook his head. "My daughters!"

"Orma is Orma. I'm not like her."

"As far as pride is concerned, anyone would think you had the same father and mother!"

Zipporah shrugged her shoulders, sending a ripple down through her wide tunic.

"What is he, then, your stranger, if he isn't Egyptian?" Jethro insisted.

"A Hebrew."

"Oh!"

"That's what he says."

Surprise jolted Jethro out of his stupor. "A son of Abraham?" he asked.

"He says, 'Of Abraham and Joseph.'"

Jethro nodded. "Of Abraham and Joseph, of course. A Hebrew of Egypt." For a moment, he stared up into the darkness at the beams and palm leaves above his bed, where flies were buzzing. Then he leaned down, picked up a goblet of water left by the hand-maid, and sipped at it. "That may be. Those who trade with Phar-aoh say that in Egypt the Hebrews are slaves. If this Moses is a slave from Egypt, Orma is even sillier than I thought to take him for a prince."

"No," Zipporah said gently. "I don't think he's a slave."

"Oh?"

"Sefoba and I also took him for a prince. He has the bearing. He doesn't fight like a slave, either."

"You talked to him. What did he say?" Jethro's gaze now was calm but forceful.

"He said: 'I'm not from Egypt anymore.'"

"And then?"

"That's all."

"Just one sentence. You went to see him and he only spoke one sentence?"

Zipporah laughed, but the laugh sounded false. "He isn't at ease with words. With our language."

"A Hebrew?"

"So it seems."

"But you're at ease with yours," Jethro said with a smile.

Not with him, Zipporah thought. Not with Moses.

"Orma says you forbade her to tell me about him."

"You can't forbid Orma anything," Zipporah sighed.

Jethro waited.

"If you saw him . . . His manners . . . Orma and Sefoba said

to him straight away: 'Come and see our father!' He refused. He
didn't even hesitate. I immediately thought: He's a fugitive. He
wants to stay in the shadows. He's a man in hiding. And I owe it
to him to respect his wishes and not force him to talk about
things he'd prefer to keep quiet about."

Jethro looked at her for a moment and nodded, more in admiration than with irony. "You did the right thing. But I'm your
father, and he's on my land . . . I'm curious. I want you to send
him two boys, with a camel and a sheep. The sheep is for milk
and the camel so that he can come and see me. He's to be told
that I would go and see him myself to express my gratitude, but
I'm too old and frail. He's also to be told that he would do me
the greatest of honors if he came and sat down with me under
the canopy."

Zipporah sat in silence, her eyes lowered, her fingers fidget-
ing with the folds of her tunic.

"Well? Aren't I polite enough for a prince of Egypt? Have I
forgotten something?"

"What if he still refuses?"

"Let's wait until he does."

"I'm sure he's done nothing wrong."

"You're making me even more curious."

"Orma will want to go with the boys."

Jethro wagged his finger, a merry gleam in his eyes. "Oh no!
Not you, not Orma. I said two boys, and two boys it will be."

Orma's Anger

The stranger Moses did not come back with the young shepherds.

"He said thank you for the animals. He asked to be shown how to get milk from a sheep, that was all."

Jethro looked pensive, but made no comment.

Two days passed, and there was no sign of a prince of Egypt coming along the road from the west on a camel. The hours went by with a slowness such as Zipporah had never known. The more time passed, the more anxious she became. She had to admit it: The fear never left her. Fear of Moses coming and fear of him not coming, it was all the same. Fear of the memory of their last moment in the cave.

Sleep became difficult. She had to endure Orma's sighs as she tossed and turned on her bed. "Zipporah, are you asleep?" Orma would whisper from time to time, half sitting up.

Zipporah would not move.

"I know you're not asleep. You're thinking of him."

Zipporah still would not move.

"Me, too," Orma would moan. "I'm also thinking of him. You're stupid to pretend."

Zipporah would wait until her silence wearied her sister. But when Orma had finally dozed off, she was left with her own confused, half-conscious thoughts, and beneath her closed lids she would see again all the moments she had already shared with Moses, both in dream and in reality.

On the second morning, she lost patience. She rose at dawn and rushed to the door of the domain to look along the west road. It was still as pale as milk—and empty. Zipporah waited for the rocks and bushes to regain their dusty colors, then for shadows to form. But the road remained empty.

Wearily, gritting her teeth against the desire she had to jump on the back of a mule and trot to Moses' cave, she went back to the women's room. Faces turned to her, all bearing the same question: "Isn't the Egyptian coming?"

When Orma arrived, she sensed something. "What's happening?"

There was a silence, then a voice replied: "Zipporah went to wait for him at dawn at the door of the courtyard. And still he didn't come!"

Chuckles and stifled laughs broke out here and there. Orma's face, previously taut with anger, now assumed a mocking expression, which merely enhanced her beauty. Zipporah left the room, her back arched in defiance. She promised herself not to show any more signs of impatience.

On the evening of the third day, when the sky was aflame but still no man or camel had appeared, Orma went and asked Jethro for permission to go herself to see Moses the next day.

"To do what?" Jethro asked, feigning surprise.

"To get him to come, as you asked!"

"No, I didn't ask any such thing! I invited him to sit beside me, which would have given me pleasure and done me honor. But if he doesn't want to, I'll respect his refusal as much as his acceptance. He can keep the camel and sheep I sent him, and then I won't feel as if I'm indebted to him."

This answer was somewhat disconcerting for Orma, but did not convince her. "You're wrong, Father," she said, knitting her lovely brows. "He won't come. And I know why."

"Oh?"

"He's a prince of Egypt."

"So it would seem."

"A man accustomed to being shown a lot of respect."

"You mean a camel and a sheep are not enough to express my gratitude?"

"No, I mean that sending two boys to tell him you want to see him isn't enough to overcome his wounded pride."

"Is his pride wounded?"

"If it weren't, he would have come by now."

"Do you think so?"

"He fights for us, your daughters, and saves us. One against four. He could have been killed. And then he runs away! It makes no sense, Father. Have we ever seen a stranger refuse to sit with you? Something has been said or done that has displeased him."

"By whom?"

"Zipporah. You know the way she speaks sometimes. As if she were you! Or else she says nothing when she ought to speak. Did you know that when we were at the well, she didn't utter a word, not even thank you?"

"She went to see him to apologize. She took him fruit and beer. The only thing she didn't do was pass on my invitation."

"But was she able to forget her pride and be less stiff in the way she spoke to him?"

"She had no reason to be stiff toward him. Didn't you ask her what they said to each other?"

Orma laughed scornfully. "You don't ask Zipporah such things! All I know is what I saw. When she came back, she looked like someone who has something to hide."

Jethro sighed. "Whereas if you'd gone to the cave, I suppose things would have been different?"

"He'd be here by now." There was no getting away from it: Orma's smile, at that moment, was irresistible.

Jethro pulled at invisible knots in his beard, surprised at how perceptive Orma was being, for once. He thought of curbing her enthusiasm by telling her that this prince of Egypt was merely a Hebrew, perhaps even a runaway slave. But he said nothing, fearing the scene his daughter might make if she heard this. He himself, in truth, was beginning to feel annoyed at being kept waiting so long. Orma was right: Had they ever seen a stranger refuse to sit with him? Why did the man not come? What made him so extraordinary? It might be quite normal for Orma to think about nothing else than seducing a stranger, but the same could not be said of Zipporah, the most sensible of all of them. At least until now!

"No," he said, abruptly. "You won't go. Jethro welcomes any- one who wants to enter his house in friendship. But that's all. Conceited as your prince of Egypt may be, I've done what I had to do, and that's enough."

SEVERAL more days passed. Twilight followed twilight.

The endless waiting should have worn down Jethro's daughters, but the opposite happened. Impatience spread to all the women of the household, like an illness. The few men—husbands, brothers, and uncles—who had not left with the flocks started to wonder if they would ever see this stranger who occupied so much of the women's chatter.

None of them any longer went to work, whether within the domain or outside, or even took a nap beneath the terebinths or tamarisks without turning their eyes automatically toward the west road. But there was nothing to be seen there but the changing blue sky, a flight of curlews or cormorants, or, sometimes, a runaway ass.

Finally, it happened.

One afternoon, when the heat was like a furnace, without anyone having seen him come, Moses was there, at the door of the domain.

There was a shout, from a young girl or a child. Openmouthed with astonishment, everyone emerged hurriedly from the shade and ran to the door. Yes, there he was.

Nobody dared say a word.

He was not wearing a tunic, only a pleated loincloth, held in at the waist by the magnificent belt that had so impressed Jethro's daughters at the well of Irmna. On his head was a hat with purple stripes. Although he was naked above the waist, and his chest was hairless, he did not seem to mind the sun. His beard, although now as thick as a Midianite's, did not conceal the beauty of his mouth. There was a sharpness in his eyes that was hard to describe, at once shy and powerful.

The women understood immediately why Zipporah and Orma had not been the same since their encounter with the stranger, while the men were somewhat irritated by his stiffness.

With an accent that gave his words a new sonority, he asked if this was really the house of Jethro, the sage of the kings of Midian. Before anyone could reply, he saw Zipporah among the faces looking up at him, and smiled at her.

He struck the camel's neck with his long, bronze-tipped staff.

With the composure of a beast that trusts the man it is carrying, the animal stretched its neck, bent its forelegs, and let Moses down. Now that he was standing before them, everyone became aware that he was taller than the men of Midian, even though his feet were bare.

Orma's voice rang out. "Moses! Moses!"

The silence was broken, and everyone joined in the welcome.

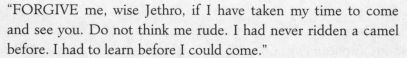

"FORGIVE me, wise Jethro, if I have taken my time to come and see you. Do not think me rude. I had never ridden a camel before. I had to learn before I could come."

He spoke all the sentences without taking a breath. It was obvious that he had been repeating them over and over to himself. Jethro, who was about to eat a fig, stopped, openmouthed. "You had to learn . . . to ride a camel?"

Moses bowed solemnly. "I had to. You gave me an animal in order to come here."

There was general laughter, but Jethro remained silent.

They were in the shade of the canopy, comfortably reclining on cushions, pitchers of beer and bowls of fruit within arm's reach. Sefoba, Orma, and Zipporah stood nervously behind Jethro, holding baskets filled with cakes. At a distance, in the baking sun, the handmaids and the children formed a large circle. They were laughing so much they had to wipe their eyes, but they did not miss a scrap of what was being said.

Jethro raised his hand to silence them, and threatened to send them all back to their chores if they did not show the stranger more respect.

Moses smiled modestly. "They're right to laugh. Here, it's stupid not to know how to ride a camel."

"Now you know—and you learned quickly," Jethro replied, with genuine admiration.

Moses dipped his lips in the goblet of beer, receiving the compliment with as much humility as he had accepted the laughter. Jethro's curiosity about the stranger was, if anything, even greater than before.

"But perhaps you can ride a horse? They say there are many horses in Egypt."

The question seemed to embarrass Moses. "There are horses." He fell silent. Jethro waited.

"Pharaoh has them. And they're used in war."

"Does Pharaoh ride a horse?"

"No, he stands."

"He stands?"

"In a chariot pulled by four horses. The generals and the great warriors who accompany him ride horses. The others walk. Or run when they have to. There are boats, too. On the great River Iterou. Yes. Many boats. Sometimes, also, horses."

With each sentence, Moses' voice became more muted, as if he were less and less sure of his ability to express what he wanted to say. His accent obscured the meaning of the words, making him seem less confident and forcing him to say both too much and not enough.

The children and the younger handmaids were unable to hold back their laughter, or their harsh judgment of the stranger. He was even more unfamiliar with the language of this side of the Red Sea than he was with sheep and camels! He was certainly different, and there was something seductive about that, but it would have been better if he had remained silent.

Jethro tried to ignore these shortcomings. Not only did courtesy demand it, but he was eager to learn everything he could about how people lived far from this desert where he held sway. As he was about to ask another question, the swishing of material made him look up. Zipporah was kneeling between Moses and him.

Without having been asked, she filled their goblets, even though they were not yet empty. As she held out Jethro's goblet, she gave him such a firm look that he could not mistake her silent command: "Stop asking all these questions. You can see they're embarrassing him. Just thank him—that's what he came for!"

Jethro had no time to ponder what to do next. Pushing Zipporah aside, Orma now also knelt before Moses and presented him with a basket of honey cakes—as well as herself in all her splendor.

They all heard the most beautiful of Jethro's daughters declare, with unaccustomed humility, how happy she was to be able to offer these gifts, which in all honesty were paltry indeed, considering what Moses had done for her and her sisters and the luxury to which a lord of Egypt must be accustomed.

Jethro saw Zipporah clench her fists with anger, and Moses' expression change to one of embarrassment. For a moment, he feared that a terrible quarrel might be about to break out between his daughters. But then, quite unexpectedly, Moses got to his feet, gripping his staff. A strange silence fell on the courtyard. Orma retreated, one hand raised in front of her beautiful face. The women put their arms around the children's shoulders.

Moses bowed, as if about to take his leave. "You're wrong, daughter of Jethro," he said, his voice quite clear now. "You're wrong."

Taken aback, Orma laughed inanely.

"Don't laugh! You don't know what you're saying!" Moses' voice was harsh, like pebbles being rubbed together. Orma looked around her in alarm, seeking help, but everyone was watching Moses, anxious not to miss a single word emerging from his mouth. "I'm not a lord of Egypt, daughter of Jethro. You think I'm from Egypt and a prince, but I'm not."

Was it his accent, or was he really angry? It was impossible to say. Orma got to her feet, her cheeks flushed and her lips quivering. She took a step back and found herself, without intending it, beside Zipporah. Moses' golden eyes swept over the two of them and Jethro, and then he turned to face the people standing in the courtyard and opened his arms, although not very wide. His voice was no longer at all menacing.

"It's the truth. I'm not an Egyptian from Egypt. I'm a Hebrew, the son of a slave, a son of Abraham and Joseph."

Jethro had already stood up, his tunic moving around his thin body. He caught Moses by the elbow, seized his hands, and forced him to sit down again. "Yes, I know, I know! Sit down, please, Moses. I know. Zipporah told me."

Orma looked at Zipporah in astonishment, but Zipporah ignored her. Moses and their father sat down again on the cushions. Jethro patted Moses' knee with tender familiarity.

"What you say is good news for me, Moses, and makes me all the happier to welcome you. We Midianites are the sons of Abraham and his second wife, Keturah."

"Oh?"

"I want you to think of this as your own home, and to stay for as long as you wish. I owe you everything my daughters owe you."

"All I did was fight. The shepherds weren't strong."

"But you didn't know that before you put them to flight! As of today, Moses' name and Jethro's name are joined in friendship."

"You are good. But you don't know the reason that led me to the land of Midian." Moses smiled sadly, apparently determined to continue being humble, even though it was no longer necessary.

Jethro launched into a long, vigorous tirade. "No, I don't know it, any more than I know the manner in which you came here. You will tell me if you like. I love to hear men's stories. But, for what I have to say to you, that doesn't matter. You are alone here. You have no companion, no flock, not even a tent to shelter you from the heat of the day and the cold of the night. You have, it seems, no handmaids with you, no wife, nobody who knows how to bake your bread, brew your beer, or weave your garments. Let me welcome you to my domain as if you were one of my people. It is the least I can do, considering what you did. My daughters and I thank Horeb for your arrival. Choose twenty sheep to start your flock and take the canvas you need to erect a tent in the shade of one of the great trees beyond these walls. I insist. It will make me very happy. As you have no doubt noticed, and for a reason I will explain to you later, for the moment I have almost nothing but women around me—daughters, nieces, or handmaids. Among them, you will find hands to take care of you. And I daresay I shall have someone to talk to in the evenings."

Zipporah expected to see a smile of relief on Moses' face. Instead, she saw his whole body grow terribly rigid.

"I came to Midian because I killed a man," he said.

A murmur went through the courtyard. The laughter and high spirits abruptly ceased. Zipporah felt the breath go out of her chest. On either side of her, Sefoba and Orma gripped her wrists, as if holding on to the branch of a tree to stop themselves falling. The only person who remained impassive, without even a glint of surprise in his eyes, was Jethro.

Moses placed his staff across his knees, and took a deep breath. "I killed a man. Not a shepherd, but one of Pharaoh's lords. A highly placed architect and overseer. I am wearing noble garments; they are not mine. I stole them in order to flee. This staff, too, I stole from Pharaoh's court. That is what you must know before you welcome me among you."

"If you killed a man," Jethro said, in a voice of unruffled calm and tenderness, "you must have had a reason. Do you want to tell us about it?"

◇

MOSES was not the kind of man to take a long time telling his story. In any case, his lack of fluency in the language of Midian forced him to skimp on the details. But to everyone, including the children—those who had been standing in the courtyard had drawn closer—his story was all the more terrible for that. They filled his silences with their imagination, seeing in their own minds the incredible, teeming world beyond the Red Sea. Names with strange consonants—Thinis, Waset, Djeser-Djeserou, Amon, Osiris—that they had heard mentioned from time to time by passing traders assumed a new reality as Moses spoke.

They saw as if with their own eyes the splendor of the cities, the roads and the temples, the fabulous palaces, the huge stone sculptures of animals asserting the power of men who were no longer entirely men. Having established this background, Moses turned next, in his staccato phrases, to the *nekhakha,* Pharaoh's whip. A whip he held tight against his chest in the hundreds of statues of him found everywhere in the country, in temples, and on tombs. A whip that cracked incessantly, raining blows on the thousands of Hebrew slaves. For it was with their blood, their screams, and their deaths that extraordinary buildings were erected in honor of the living god, the Life of Life, that ever-reborn power that reigned over the vast land of the Great River.

"Where the slaves work, anyone who tries to protest dies," Moses said. "On a building site, the death of a Hebrew counts for less than a broken plank."

From dawn to night, insults, cries, accidents, and humiliation were the slaves' constant diet. As punishment, the weakest were set to making bricks, stamping on mud weighted with straw until they could no longer lift their feet.

"Anyone no longer able to stamp is beaten until he falls in the mud and chokes. Then the overseer beats him again because he's stopped stamping. If his companions try to help him, they, too, are beaten."

Here, in the heat of Midian, everyone heard the cracking of Pharaoh's whip. Even the flies seemed to have stopped buzzing.

"Anyone no longer able to pull the sledges carrying the stones is beaten," Moses resumed, his voice increasingly heavy. "Anyone who is thirsty, anyone who makes a mistake, anyone who tries to bandage his wound: All are beaten. Young and old, men and women."

At times, Moses would fall silent, and his eyes would wander over the baskets of fruit placed before him. They respected his silence, trying to see what he himself was seeing with his inner eye: the long chains of men attached with ropes; the thousands of arms beating the stone, cutting it, polishing it, lifting it; the endless days spent extracting rocks from the cliffs, transporting them from one end of a vast land to the other, and finally piling them high in dizzying constructions.

"It wasn't always thus," Moses murmured, shaking his head. "But today, Pharaoh's whip is greedier for their blood than the mosquitoes."

He looked around, and his eyes met first Jethro's, then Zipporah's. There was no pain on his face, nor any real anger, either, but rather incomprehension.

"I stood next to a man who felt pleasure in the suffering of the slaves, even pride in inflicting as much harm on them as he could. His name was Mem P'ta. To be anywhere near him made you feel dirty. I was so ashamed. Ashamed of what he was doing and ashamed of not stopping him. One morning, it just happened. I hadn't planned it. Mem P'ta went off alone to the river, and I followed him. I waited in the reeds while he did his business. It wasn't difficult. I was so relieved at the thought that he'd never again raise his whip! I really wanted to kill him!" Moses gave a half smile. "Then I was afraid they would discover his body too quickly if the river swept it away, so I pulled him over to a strip of sand and buried him. I think that's where I was seen."

Again, he fell silent. It was not difficult to imagine what he left unsaid.

He rolled his staff between his hands and looked at the faces around him without lingering on any single one. Curiously, he seemed more at ease, more sure of himself than he had before. He shrugged his shoulders with a certain lightness.

"I killed the Egyptian, and it was a mistake. It didn't lessen the suffering of a single Hebrew. All it did was increase Pharaoh's wrath toward his slaves. To strike Pharaoh's architects or overseers is to strike Pharaoh. And who would dare to take on Pharaoh?"

Jethro did not know if that was meant as a real question. He remained silent, not moving a muscle. Moses' weary smile grew wider, although the look in his eyes was still serious.

"I stole garments, and a boat that carried me here. Until your daughters said to me, 'You are in the land of Midian, on the property of Jethro, the sage of the kings of Midian,' I had no idea where I was."

Jethro nodded. "You are in the land of Midian, on the property of Jethro. Nothing you've told us has made me want to take back anything I've said. I stand by my word: This is your home. If such is your wish, and a modest life suits you, tomorrow you will pitch your tent and choose the first animals for your flock."

THE sky had turned a heavier blue. The constant plume of clouds and smoke that wreathed the summit of Horeb's mountain was tinged with an almost liquid pink. It had been a long time since Moses, sitting upright on his camel, had ridden off into the west.

As soon as he had left, everyone had started speaking at once, but it was Orma's voice that had stood out from the rest. Fearing that her own emotions would be drowned out by it, Zippporah had kept her distance. She had only to close her eyes to see the muscles rippling on the stranger's back as the camel swayed from side to side. In the same way, she was able to relive each moment of their encounter. Everything was inside her: Moses' voice, his expressions, his moments of embarrassment, and, ultimately, all he had left unsaid.

"What a strange man!" her father said, as she and her sisters were setting the evening meal before him. "Is it only because he doesn't know our language well that he seems such a mass of contradictions? Have you noticed how he answers questions without really answering them? I'm certain he knows how to ride a horse and that he was once at Pharaoh's side. A man like that ought to be more confident. His eyes glow with pride, but he's humble. I can't believe he was a slave. Yet he holds those slaves in greater esteem than himself. Yes, what a strange person this Moses is! He seems to be one thing, but he's also its opposite. He's caught between light and darkness. I like him."

His words were enough to inflame Orma, like fire touching dry grass. "He killed a man and you like him!"

"Yes, he killed a man. But you heard his reasons."

"How do you know he isn't lying?"

"It's true, father," Sefoba pitched in, anxiety written on her brow. "Moses has qualities . . . But so much hesitation! How do we know he doesn't say one thing and also its opposite in order to cover a lie?" She glanced at Zipporah, whose face was thoughtful but impassive.

"A man who killed another man can easily lie," Orma asserted.

"I'm pleased we're helping him," Sefoba said. "But is it necessary for him to pitch his tent so close to us?"

Jethro smiled and shook his head. "A man who has killed another man can lie to conceal his sin. But a man who confesses his murder without anyone asking him—why would he lie? His confession proves he has a strong sense of justice that won't allow him to lie."

"He lies in his appearance at least," Orma replied, implacably. "As you say yourself, Father: He pretends to be something he is not."

"No, that's not what our father is saying," Zipporah intervened, unable to conceal her irritation. "Moses is honest. He simply has the manners of a stranger. And it is not for us to judge what he did in Egypt."

"Oh you!" Orma said, indignantly. "Naturally you take his side. Especially if it means saying the opposite of what I'm saying."

"Orma, my daughter—"

"You, too, Father! You, too! You knew he was neither Egyptian nor a prince. And you let me make a fool of myself. Kneeling and . . . and saying all those stupid things in front of everybody!"

The tears Orma had long been holding in at last gushed from her beautiful eyes. Her mouth quivered, her temples throbbed, and her face was infinitely more animated than usual. Jethro looked at her with a great deal of tenderness. Carried away by her own resentment, the shame of her tears adding to the shame she already felt, Orma began to ape Moses' severe manner. "Don't laugh! You mustn't say such things! I'm not a lord of Egypt, daughter of Jethro." The imitation was so accurate that Jethro, forgetting his tender feelings, could not help laughing, any more than could Sefoba and Zipporah.

Orma's anger exploded. "Go on!" she cried, pointing her finger at her father and Zipporah. "Laugh! Make fun of me! That's what you like to do, isn't it? Everything is grist to your mill!"

She was beside herself with rage, shouting at the top of her voice, as furious as she could be. Handmaids appeared in the doorways. The whole courtyard vibrated with Orma's words.

"You don't love me! I know, Father, you think I'm silly. For you, only Zipporah counts! And it doesn't surprise me you like the stranger. He's deceitful; he plays at being a slave. They should understand each other! His skin may be different, but he'll end up just like this woman you've forced us to accept as a sister, but who's never been my sister!"

Sefoba gasped. Orma ran to the other end of the courtyard and vanished into the women's room. There was a stunned silence.

Jethro sighed with emotion. "Daughter, daughter!"

Sefoba slipped her hand into Zipporah's. "She doesn't really mean what she says."

Zipporah nodded, her eyes a little too bright in the twilight.

"She doesn't mean it," Sefoba repeated. "She's disappointed. She lost a prince today."

Jethro shook his head sadly. "Yes, she means it. At least a little. And she may be right about one thing. I don't love her enough."

Sefoba and Zipporah lowered their eyes in embarrassment.

Jethro touched his eldest daughter's shoulder. "Go to her. She needs cuddling. It wasn't only a prince she lost today, but some of her own vanity."

AFTER Sefoba had gone, Zipporah and Jethro remained silent for a long time. Orma's terrible words brought them closer, but also intimidated them. They both realized that there was real pain beneath her rage, and they felt more guilty than offended. They were truly, deeply, father and daughter, with a joy and a strength that went beyond ties of blood or color of skin. Who could possibly understand? Nobody in the land of Midian, not even Sefoba.

The summit of Horeb's mountain had turned gray. The evening breeze was blowing in little gusts, carrying with it the scents of the garden and the cries of the children trying to avoid their bedtime. The handmaids lit the lamps. The moths immediately began their persistent dance.

Zipporah had forgotten Orma's outburst. She was thinking of the gold bracelets she had discovered in Moses' cave. She had not yet mentioned them to Jethro, but could not bring herself to do it, even now, united as they were in the heat of the evening. What she had seen in the cave was a secret that belonged only to Moses, a secret she must not reveal.

"Of course he didn't tell us everything!" Jethro said in a low voice, as if he had been following her thoughts. "He spoke of Pharaoh's slaves like a man whose eyes have only just seen the truth, not like someone who was born into that suffering and has known it all his life."

"He isn't lying, though."

"No, no, he isn't lying."

"He's a Hebrew, not an Egyptian."

Jethro's voice became pensive again. "He's a son of Abraham, I do believe that. But the Hebrews of Egypt apparently know nothing about us, the people of Midian."

"Moses doesn't know," Zipporah corrected. "Just as he doesn't know our language."

Jethro smiled. "You're right."

"You didn't ask him who his god is. Usually, Father, it's the first question you ask strangers."

"There was no point. He has no god. Neither the gods of Egypt, nor the God of the Hebrews. That's why he doesn't know what he must do with his life."

Zipporah did not ask Jethro how he could be so sure of what he was saying. By now, darkness had fallen. Children and hand-maids glided past the walls like shadows. Jethro chased away a moth that was about to fly into his beard.

"When he said he'd killed a man," Zipporah said, "you didn't seem surprised."

"There was no reason to be. What else would force a man to cross the sea without knowing where he's going and with no other company than his own fear?"

So Jethro, too, had sensed Moses' fear. Zipporah was glad that it did not make him mistrustful. She thought of the expression on Moses' face as he had got back on his camel. He had said nothing to her, had not bidden her farewell, had not said that he would see her tomorrow. He had simply looked at her with that mixture of determination and awkwardness that was so characteristic of him at all times. A look that said: "Don't get me wrong. You know the kind of man I am."

"Almost a moon ago, I had a dream," she murmured suddenly, as if the words had come out by themselves, against her will. "A dream that terrified me and attracted me at the same time. I asked Horeb to help me understand it, but he remained silent. I didn't dare tell you about it. I was like Orma—afraid of being ridiculous and losing my dignity."

Zipporah told him her dream, and how she had struggled to make sense of it. Did it mean that she had to take a boat back across the sea and go to live in the land of Cush? Losing everything she had, everything Jethro had given her, especially a father's love? That was something she could not imagine.

"But we know what awaits me here. Sefoba has found a husband, as have our elder sisters. Soon, Orma will accept Reba, or someone else. It will all be over. You will have no more daughters to marry off. No man in Midian, not even a shepherd, will come to your domain to ask for my hand. I will give you no grandchild."

She had uttered these words as lightly as she could, but they seemed to drop from her mouth like stones.

Jethro let the silence take away the stench of sadness. "Nobody knows for certain what dreams tell us. They come to us at night and there is something dark about them. But they can also be as blinding as the brightest sunlight. The wise men say, 'Live your dream in sleep, but do not let your life become a sleep.'"

Zipporah, too, waited a moment before speaking again. "Do you think he will come and pitch his tent here tomorrow?" There was no need to say Moses' name.

"I'm sure he will," Jethro replied. He paused to reflect. "We must be patient. He bears a heavy burden. He cannot relieve himself of it so soon."

"May Horeb come to his aid."

"What makes Horeb all-powerful is that he doesn't do what we expect him to do. He surprises us, and, through these surprises, he corrects us, encourages us, and shows us the path to follow. Let him surprise you. Have patience. There are many days before you."

The Handmaid

What Jethro said came true.

The next day, Moses arrived early, riding on his camel, with the mule and the sheep on a lead behind him, his few possessions in the saddlebag Zipporah had taken him. He pitched his tent beneath the big sycamore that marked the beginning of the road to Epha. It was a good choice, far enough from Jethro's domain to preserve the solitude that Moses liked, and near enough not to give the impression that he was keeping his distance.

Moses had quickly learned to ride a camel. With the same ease, he learned to live in a tent and to tend a flock of sheep. In less than a moon, he was able to gather the animals himself, pen them in, and distinguish those that needed to be taken care of. He was shown how to make the tools needed for cutting flints so that they were as sharp as blades of precious metal. He was taught how to cut and sew leather, how to make comfortable saddles, how to dry meat, how to recognize from a distance the cool, shady spots where scorpions and snakes might be lurking.

Day by day, his presence and his manners became more natural. He even abandoned the habit of walking barefoot on the burning stones and started wearing sandals like everyone else.

Imperceptibly, Jethro's household, too, began to change.

At first, the attraction of a new face and the strangeness of his accent made him congenial company for the young handmaids. Moses did not hesitate to laugh at himself, to mock his own clumsiness, and they could laugh with him. But what, above all, made the days quite different from what they had been before his arrival was everything he told them about Egypt.

The children of the household, starting with small groups of the older ones, then the younger ones, got into the habit of joining him outside his tent at twilight. They would ask a thousand questions and Moses would answer them, never tiring, his voice increasingly confident. He would tell them, in both words and gestures, how the quarrymen cut the blocks of stone out of the mountain, and how they were transported on the Great River. How, sometimes, the needles of rock were so huge that it took more than a hundred boats and thousands of men to get them from the mountains to the esplanades of the temples, ten days' journey away.

In the sand he traced the outlines of the cities and the palaces. He drew gardens, and sometimes flowers that did not even have a name in the language of Midian.

The children's eyes grew large at the scale of the marvels they heard about. Their nights were filled with fabulous dreams, their thoughts now no longer of the slaves or Pharaoh's whip, but only of those incredible cities, those paradise gardens, those stone animals drawn from the heart of the mountains, animals so enormous that a single one of their claws was taller than a man.

Soon, the children were joined by the young handmaids. Once twilight had come, Jethro's domain would be filled, as if by magic, with a new kind of silence, until the sky above Horeb's mountain was swallowed up in the darkness.

For a whole moon, applying to himself the same counsel of patience he had given Zipporah, Jethro had been careful to avoid sharing his meal too often with Moses. It was just as well, since, whenever he did so, they sat for the most part in gloomy silence, Moses seemingly weighed down with the burden of respect and gratitude, Jethro with the burden of caution.

It was quite otherwise when Moses sat outside his tent with the children and the handmaids, and it did not take long for the pleasure he dispensed on these occasions to reach Jethro's ears. One evening, he asked for his meal to be taken to Moses' tent, along with a great jar of honey wine.

As soon as he was seated, he drowned Moses' predictable embarrassment in wine, served in olive-wood goblets. He asked the children to come closer, practically pushing them into Moses' arms. Although he did not let it show, he was surprised to discover the ease with words that Moses had acquired. His accent was no longer a hindrance to understanding, but gave the language of Midian a new flavor, a new seductiveness. Jethro listened with the same astonishment as the children to Moses' account of how the priests of Egypt transformed the bodies of the dead kings and princes into sculptures of flesh, emptied of their entrails and ready to face eternity. He laughed as they did when Moses imitated the cries of the monkeys that were kept as pets by the Egyptians and much prized for their playfulness.

At dawn on the following day, when Zipporah brought him his morning meal of cakes and cold milk, Jethro seized her hand and squeezed it with unusual emotion. "I listened to Moses last night," he said, "and discovered a new man. He knows more than I do. He has seen more things in heaven and earth with his own eyes than I have. I'm sure now he was never one of Pharaoh's slaves. I'm even certain that until he fled the land of the River Iterou, he was happy and proud to be Pharaoh's subject."

Zipporah said nothing. Jethro paused for a moment, a wicked gleam in his eyes, and asked if Moses had told her anything about his past since he had pitched his tent here.

"No, of course not! Why should he? And besides, he's very busy with the children." There was a trace of bitterness in her voice. Jethro was still looking at her intently. To evade the questions she feared to hear, she added, with a genuine laugh: "If he continues to please everyone so much, people will start forgetting that Jethro is the master here. The whole household is at his beck and call. He just has to raise an eyebrow and all the handmaids come running!"

"The whole household, except your sister," Jethro grumbled, dipping his fingers in the bowl of cold water Zipporah was holding out to him.

It was true. Orma was the only one to keep her distance. Her anger had not abated since Moses' first visit. She never went near the tent beneath the sycamore. As soon as Moses' name was mentioned, her mouth tensed in a scornful grimace. Whenever he entered Jethro's domain, which rarely happened, she was careful not to look at him. And if ever their paths crossed outside, she immediately turned her head away.

Watching her, Sefoba and Zipporah laughed just as much as the handmaids, who would nudge each other with their elbows and wink. But, in Zipporah's case, the laughter was less an expression of gaiety than of her own dismay and sorrow. Now that Moses was here, so close to hand, and pampered by the household, it was she, suddenly, who felt a stranger, forgotten and ignored. In the two moons since Moses had pitched his tent, none of the things she had been hoping for deep in her heart had come to pass. Quite the contrary, in fact.

At first, fearful of appearing too impatient, perhaps even impudent, she had obeyed Jethro's words: "Have patience. There are many days before you." With all the willpower of which she was capable, she had resisted the burning desire to make any move that might have recalled their brief moment of intimacy in the cave. She had deliberately refrained from taking him his morning meal, had left to others the pleasure of initiating him into his new existence and receiving a grateful smile in return. The pleasure of being there, as if by magic, when he needed help.

She had succeeded so well that her contacts with Moses became rare and superficial. As things followed their course, Moses soon found himself busy with one task or another, and gave most of his attention to the handmaids or the children. The two of them hardly ever met. And whenever they did meet, instead of the joy she had imagined she would feel at seeing him so close and, perhaps, loving him, she felt only emptiness and disappointment. Moses paid her no greater heed than he did, indiscriminately, to everyone in the household.

She began to doubt that she had ever been overwhelmed by the sight of Moses fishing. To doubt that he had once touched her lips with his fingers. Even to doubt that the stranger was what he said and what he seemed.

She would go to sleep remembering Moses' body, naked in the sea, and the gold bracelets in the painted casket covered with writing. Did any of that really exist? Had she forgotten the difference between dreams and reality?

Her desire for a moment alone with Moses turned to pain: the pain of jealousy. It made her awkward and given to extremes. Never before had a man so occupied her thoughts. She felt frustrated and ashamed. She did not dare show it, let alone talk about it, even to Sefoba.

One morning, at last, she rose, determined to have done with her torments. It was time she became herself again. She had been patient too long.

The sun was just starting to touch the sycamore on the road to Epha when she came within sight of the tent. She stopped dead because, at that moment, the flap of the tent was raised and a handmaid appeared. Zipporah recognized her and whispered her name: "Murti!"

She was a pretty girl, not much younger than Orma, with a slender figure. She looked graceful as she leaned against the trunk of the sycamore.

It felt to Zipporah as though her blood were turning to sand. How stupid she had been not to think of it! She had seen the way the young handmaids looked at Moses. There was no shortage of attractive women around Jethro. What had happened was inevitable. There was no point in being angry with Moses.

Murti was on all fours outside the tent now. She seemed on the verge of collapse. But she immediately got up again and began running like a madwoman, her mouth wide open and her cheeks streaked with tears.

As she came closer, Zipporah stepped out into the middle of the path and caught her arm. Murti had been running so fast that both of them nearly lost their balance. "Murti! Murti! What's the matter? Where are you running?"

Murti was sobbing. Zipporah repeated her name softly. The handmaid's sobs grew more intense, and her chest heaved. Zipporah pulled Murti to her and put her arms around her. Beneath the sycamore, the flap of the tent did not move.

"Murti, what happened?"

The handmaid shook her head and pushed Zipporah's shoulders, trying to break free of her.

"No, don't run away!" Zipporah said, holding her back. "You can talk to me! I won't say anything. It'll be just between the two of us, you know."

Murti knew it, but she still needed time. She remained with

her head on Zipporah's shoulder, her body shaken with spasms, until she regained her breath. "You won't tell anybody?" she asked, in a barely audible voice.

"I promise before Horeb. I won't tell anybody."

Murti put her hands over her face. "I'd been wanting to do it for days. I couldn't help it. I thought about it as soon as I woke up."

It was not difficult for Zipporah to believe her and understand her. There was no doubting Murti's sincerity, no doubting her torments, or that she had been powerless to resist the force that had impelled her toward the stranger.

She had slipped into the tent while Moses was still asleep, and had woken him with her caresses, the caresses she had been giving him in dreams night after night. She had not doubted for a moment that he would welcome them with joy. But, when he opened his eyes, he had seemed more surprised than pleased. He had taken hold of Murti's hand. But she had persisted; she had taken off her tunic and placed Moses' palms on her bare skin.

What happened next was so terrible, Murti found it hard to talk about: the way Moses had looked at her, the tunic she fumbled to put back on, the noise of her tears, which filled her with shame.

Zipporah stroked her neck and shoulders. "What did he say?" she asked.

Murti shrugged.

"Did he throw you out of the tent without a word?" Zipporah insisted.

Murti sniffed, dried her cheeks, and broke away. She glanced anxiously at the tent. "I don't know; I wasn't listening. We mustn't stay here."

"Try to remember."

Without answering, Murti began walking quickly toward Jethro's domain. Zipporah followed her. She felt no anger toward her, only a kind of tender complicity, mixed with fear and sadness. And a curious sense of relief.

What would have happened if she herself had woken Moses?

As they were nearing the enclosure where the mules were kept, Zipporah stopped Murti. The handmaid was no longer crying. Her face had grown curiously ugly. Without waiting for Zipporah's question, she pointed to the west, which was still milky with dawn. "He told me I was beautiful," she said, in a voice swollen with rage, "and that I shouldn't be angry with him. But he couldn't. That's what he said: 'I can't!' Not because he wasn't a man, but because there was something stopping him. I tried to mock him. 'What?' I asked. 'What can stop a man taking a woman?'" She broke off, and gripped Zipporah's wrists. "Do you promise me you won't tell anybody? Even your sisters?"

"Have no fear," Zipporah assured her. "And he will say nothing, either. I know."

Murti sighed, a veil of incomprehension over her eyes. "I was struggling to get dressed again. I felt like scratching his face. He helped me to fasten my tunic by putting the brooch back in place on my shoulder. That was when he said: 'Memories. That's what stops a man from taking a woman.' I didn't even know what he was talking about!"

PART TWO

The Call of Yahweh

News from Egypt

Winter had come, and with it the rains that each year made the plains between Horeb's mountain and the sea green again. Moses now had his flock. It was a small flock, one of those reserved for younger sons as a means of teaching them about breeding and migration.

Jethro sent for Moses and told him that it was now time to leave for his first pasture.

"My son, Hobab, my sons-in-law, and my nephews have gone to Moab to sell our biggest animals. On the way back, they'll take advantage of the rains to put the lambs and calves out to pasture on the hills of Epha and Sheba, which are infinitely greener and better for the young animals than ours. That's the way the rulers of those territories pay me back for the counsel I give them and the offerings I make to Horeb in their names. Go to them. Tell them Jethro sent you." From his tunic, Jethro took a thick metal disk with a hole pierced in it, through which a length of thin woolen rope had been threaded. "Show them this, and they'll know you're telling the truth. They'll welcome you with open arms and teach you what you don't yet know."

Moses was so moved, his fingers shook as he touched the metal coin. "How will I find them? I don't know any of the roads in Midian."

Jethro could not help laughing merrily. "You're not alone any more, Moses! I'll send some handmaids and shepherds with you to show you the way."

Moses was about to put the medallion around his neck when he stopped. "You have long since paid your debt to me, Jethro. What I did for your daughters, you have paid me back a hundredfold. Why are you still so good to me?"

Jethro screwed up his eyes, and gave a sharp, ironic little growl. "I don't think I can answer that question yet, my boy." As Moses appeared disconcerted by this answer, Jethro laughed openly and covered his hand with his. "Go in peace, my boy. All you need to know is that I like you and that I'm weary of being surrounded by so many girls."

❖

OF course, all the children wanted to go with Moses. Jethro had to lose his temper and make a selection himself, much to the delight of those chosen. The little caravan, consisting of the flock, the mules, and the camels, set out under a sky full of low clouds. The sun did not appear all day. At twilight, the winter wind swept over Jethro's domain, bringing with it a kind of languor.

The next day, a fine rain began to fall, and the surface of the courtyard and the paths around the domain turned to mud.

"Come," Sefoba said to Zipporah. "Let's weave a woolen tunic for Moses. You can give it to him when he gets back."

Zipporah hesitated, claiming that she had other chores to attend to.

"Come on!" Sefoba teased. "Don't think you can hide anything from me!"

As Zipporah's lips set in stubborn pride, Sefoba pointed out astutely that now, in any case, was the time for weaving and that Zipporah had to join in. Besides, nothing could be more pleasant than to work like this, by the fire, while outside the palms swayed in the icy wind.

They set to work, and for several days nobody spoke the name Moses. On the other hand, there was much talk of the latest gift Reba had sent Orma: a belt made from stones, feathers, and pieces of silver.

"This time, Reba didn't take the risk of coming and giving it to her himself. But how constant he is! Has anyone ever seen such perseverance? And the belt is so beautiful!"

Like the fabric Orma had disdained, it came from somewhere far away in the East. Sefoba and the others chuckled, and discussed how long it would be now before Reba finally declared himself.

"Who knows?" Sefoba said. "The belt may also end up in little pieces under my bed, just like the fabric."

The women responded with giggles.

Later the same day, when they were alone, Sefoba suddenly cried, "I'm so happy for you!"

Zipporah stared at her in surprise.

"For a long time," Sefoba went on, a wicked gleam in her eyes, "I thought, like the rest of the women, that you would never find a husband. And now look!"

"Look at what?"

"The men of Midian are stupid. Too bad for them! It took a man from Egypt to come along and see the daughter of Cush for what she really is—a precious jewel!"

"What are you talking about?"

Sefoba's laugh now was more high-pitched. "Zipporah! Don't pretend, not with me. Or I'll think you don't love me anymore."

Zipporah lowered her eyes to her work.

"I have eyes in my head," Sefoba went on, enthusiastically. "Orma isn't the only one who can read a man's face. Or a woman's."

Zipporah's hands were shaking, and she gripped the weaving frame to steady them. "And what do you read in my face?"

"That you love Moses."

"Is it so obvious?"

Sefoba laughed. "As obvious as the nose on your face—even on you, my girl. On his, too, I promise you."

"No. You're making a mistake."

Sefoba protested with another laugh.

"You're making a mistake, Sefoba, because you love me."

"Am I making a mistake? Are you telling me you're not in love with him? Are you telling me you don't fall asleep every night thinking about him, that you don't wake up in the night hoping he's beside you in the darkness? Are you telling me it isn't true?"

"It was true, but it's not true anymore."

"What do you mean? May Horeb protect us! Are you going as mad as Orma?"

Zipporah tried to laugh, too. Instead, she could not stop the tears, long held in, from welling up in her eyes. Sefoba's laughter vanished like a flame that has been extinguished.

"What's the matter? Zipporah, my darling!" Sefoba knelt by her sister and lifted her face. "I wasn't mocking you. I've seen the two of you and . . . Not often, I admit, but I know what I see."

Zipporah pushed Sefoba's hands away, and wiped her eyes with her sleeve. "You're making a mistake."

"Perhaps I am. Explain it to me, then!"

"Leave it be. It doesn't matter."

"Come on, now!"

Zipporah hesitated. She had given her promise to Murti. But Sefoba was like a part of herself. "You must promise to say nothing. Not to Father, not to anybody!"

"I promise before Horeb," Sefoba said, raising her hands.

And so Zipporah told her all about her days and nights of torment since Moses had pitched his tent nearby, and how, one morning, she had found herself beneath the sycamore on the road to Epha just as Murti was fleeing from Moses' rejection.

"Poor Murti!" Sefoba said. "But what a stupid girl! You can do something like that to a shepherd, not to a man like Moses!" She touched Zipporah's face with her fingertips, wiped away the last tears, and sighed. "What a relief she didn't tell you it was because of Orma."

"Yes, it was," Zipporah admitted. "I was afraid Murti would say, 'Moses wants your sister, and nobody but her.'"

"He's much too intelligent for that," Sefoba chuckled. "Only Reba wants Orma and nobody but her."

"I was relieved at first. Then I realized what a fool I was. Of course he had a life before he came here. A wife, perhaps children. If not a wife, then a woman. Many women. They say Egyptian women are beautiful. And I'm sure he's just waiting for the moment when he can go back to Egypt. What am I to him? Jethro's black daughter."

Sefoba had been listening in silence, but now her anger burst out. "Listen to you! 'Not a wife, but a woman! Many women! They say Egyptian women are beautiful . . .' Why not goddesses with the heads of cats or birds? Or Pharaoh's own daughters, while we're about it? May Horeb and my father forgive me, but this is the first time you've been in love, and it's really making you stupid. Moses rejected a handmaid. So what? Moses thinks about his past! He has memories! Does that stop him from taking a woman into his bed? Don't make me laugh! I don't believe a word of it. I've also looked at him long and hard, this Moses of yours. I'm a married woman; perhaps that's what gives me a clearer view of things. All I've seen is a man like any other man. From head to foot, and even in the middle."

"Sefoba—"

"Let me speak! Moses is like any other man. Of course he thinks about his past. But he's here now, and his past is vanishing like water from a gourd in the desert! And soon, when his gourd is empty, Moses will be quite new, and he'll be looking for love, he'll want a woman, like any other man. Or rather, not like any other man, but like a lord. He certainly behaves like one, and he doesn't want to be caressed by just anybody when he wakes up. Not by a handmaid, that's for sure. Jethro's daughter, though, the finest, the most intelligent, her father's favorite, now that's another matter. . . . No! Don't protest! That's how it is! It's about time you faced the truth. You haven't seen the way Moses looks at you. You're in love, and that's worse than shedding blood every moon. You don't know day from night. But as Horeb is my witness, I tell you this: Moses hasn't just been taking an interest in the children since he came. He's been watching you—your skin, your breasts, your waist, your lovely buttocks. He's been hanging on your words and your silences, your knowledge and your pride. He has quite a lot of pride himself, so he has the full measure of yours! And he likes it all. When he sees you, I'd put my hand in the fire and swear that he isn't thinking about his memories then. Wait until he gets back, and you'll see for yourself."

But when, twenty days later, the caravan of Jethro's sons, sons-in-law, and nephews returned, Zipporah was unable to verify the accuracy of Sefoba's words, because Moses was not with them. One morning at dawn, a few days from home, he had disappeared.

IT was not until evening that Jethro, who had arrived back that day, dusty from the journey, after a visit to the palace of King Hour, whom he had advised not to launch a punitive expedition against some lords of Moab who had stolen a flock and killed three shepherds, absorbed the news. "Disappeared? Moses?"

Hobab nodded and drank a long draft of beer. Like his companions, Jethro's son seemed as thirsty as if he had crossed the desert without a gourd full of water within arm's reach.

"One morning I went to his tent," he said, handing his goblet to a handmaid. "I was thinking of going hunting with him. We'd seen a small herd of gazelles the previous days. But his tent was empty. We waited two whole days before we set off again. Everyone was impatient to get home."

He fell silent and watched with a smile as more beer was poured into the goblet.

Softened by his son's smile, Jethro waited for him to drink another long mouthful. Zipporah was biting her lips to hold back the cry of impatience rising in her throat.

It was already night, and she had had to champ at the bit all day. Several times, she had broken off from her work with tears in her eyes, barely able to breathe. Since learning of Moses' absence, she had been tormented by wild thoughts, like a knife twisting in her guts. The handmaids looked at her anxiously and spoke in low voices when she came near, as if she were a woman in mourning. Two or three times, Sefoba had put her arms around her trembling shoulders and hugged her, trying to find something to say to console her. She knew only too well that Zipporah would not be satisfied with the usual banal words. But they would not know more until Jethro started to ask questions, and so they had to wait, as if for deliverance. And Jethro, drunk with joy at seeing his beloved son again, seemed to have forgotten Moses.

They had been inseparable all day, sitting side by side under the canopy to receive the greetings of the members of the household and the caravan. Jethro kept asking the same questions of those returning from the long journey: How had the journey been? Whom had they met? How well had they traded? How had the women and children fared? Who had been born, who had died? Hobab called his companions one by one, and each time the greetings began over again.

Jethro and Hobab had the same thin face, the same incisive eyes. The long road from the land of Moab, the dust and fire of the desert, had furrowed deep lines in Hobab's face, making him look older than his years. They could easily have been confused with one another, were it not for their hair and beards—Jethro's thick and white, Hobab's short and black. Like Jethro, Hobab looked scrawny, but everyone in Midian knew he was capable of enduring long treks across the desert. Nobody had a better sense of direction amid the deadly valleys of sand and stone in Ecion or the Negev, or in the sunbaked folds of Horeb's mountain. Admittedly, he possessed neither Jethro's wisdom nor his sharp intelligence, but his father was very proud of him. "Hobab," he would say, "knows the strength of the desert and the power of Horeb's mountain. That's just as important as being wise."

Now, as he warmed his hands over the fire, Jethro frowned. "There must be a reason. A man doesn't just disappear without a reason. Especially that man."

A half smile on his lips, Hobab looked at his father, then glanced across at his sisters. Orma seemed the least concerned of the three, but it was obvious that her apparent indifference was assumed.

"A man unlike other men," Hobab said at last, still smiling. "And a man who seems to have you very worried, you and my sisters!"

"Speak for them, not for me!" Orma protested. "I've long had my own ideas about him—the Egyptian slave! I'm not surprised he vanished without as much as a thank you. He came to us out of the desert, like a mad dog. He would have stayed there if Zipporah and our father hadn't become besotted with him!"

Sefoba shook her head and sighed. Jethro, as if he had heard nothing, took a piece of meat from the platter of roast lamb before him and began chewing diligently.

Zipporah found it impossible to be so casual. "Did you give him a good welcome, you and your families?" she asked, with a throb in her voice.

"We gave him all the consideration he was due, seeing that he was recommended by Father."

"Did he tell you who he was?" Orma mocked.

Hobab paused to take another big gulp of beer. "Orma, beauty of the age," he replied, tenderly, "don't pull that face at me. I know as much about him as you do. I also know he thinks you're beautiful and that he's sorry he disappointed you by not being a prince of Egypt."

"He disappointed me? Just listen to that!"

Hobab ignored Orma's squealing. "I was with him in the desert, I hunted with him, I sat with him and the armorers in the evening," he went on. "He didn't need any prompting to tell us about Egypt and the reasons he fled. I liked the way he said straight out what he needed to say. I'm pleased you gave him your trust, Father. It isn't my usual way, but it didn't take me long to know that I wanted him to be my friend. The fact remains—he left without saying a word."

"Perhaps he didn't plan to be gone for very long," Zipporah suggested.

"I doubt it, sister."

"Why?"

"The day before yesterday, we were joined by a group of armorers returning from the quarries on the mountain. They said they'd seen a man on a camel riding away from the road to Yz-Alcyon."

"Going west," Jethro muttered.

"Yes, straight to where the sun sets. At first, the armorers thought it was a thief wanting to steal metal from their quarry. One of them turned back and followed him for almost half a day. Of course, we can't be sure it was Moses."

There was a silence, while everyone mulled over what had been said.

Hobab ate a little meat. "He's gone off the road to Yz-Alcyon," he said, in a pensive voice. "If he doesn't get lost, and if he doesn't fall off a cliff, he might be able to go round the mountain and get to the Sea of Reeds. It's a long journey, though, and not an easy one for a man on his own."

"He's going back to Egypt!" Zipporah and Sefoba cried at the same time.

"Yes," Jethro agreed. "Egypt, of course!"

"'Of course?'" Orma cut in. "Why 'of course'? If he killed a man, why go back to Egypt and face punishment?"

Jethro clicked his tongue. "Moses is on his way to Egypt. Right now, he could be on a boat in the middle of Pharaoh's sea."

"If he can handle his camel," Hobab said.

"You haven't answered my question," Orma squealed. "What's he going to do in Egypt?"

Hobab laughed. "See Pharaoh, perhaps?"

They all looked at each other. Zipporah suspected that beneath his mockery, her brother had another thought in mind. "You know something!" she said, angrily.

"Don't make those lioness eyes at me, sister," Hobab joked.

Jethro raised his hand to interrupt them. He nodded at Hobab. "Tell us."

It had happened the day before Moses disappeared. At the hour when the sun was about to reach its zenith, Hobab's caravan had met some Akkadian merchants returning from Egypt with a long column of about a hundred heavily laden camels and an equal number of other animals that were not yet fully grown. They were on their way back to the opulent cities on the banks of the Euphrates, which they had left a year earlier. The saddlebags on the camels' backs were full to overflowing with fabrics, graven stones, wood from the land of Cush, even cane boats such as were only made in the land of Pharaoh.

As was the custom, both caravans had halted and pitched their tents for the night. Then they had sat down to drink and exchange news. When the merchants discovered that the armorers were with them, they had been keen to buy weapons with long iron blades, and were disappointed to learn that everything had already been sold in the markets of Moab and Edom.

"I was as disappointed as they were," Hobab sighed. "I'd have liked to exchange the weapons for some of the young animals they were offering. Gray-haired she-camels from the delta of the Great River Iterou, far more beautiful than ours. When they saw how downhearted I looked, they promised me they'd pass this way one day and then we'd be able to do the business we couldn't do this time."

"But what of Moses?"

"Ah, yes, Moses . . . He'd been with us for nearly a moon. He sat down with us to drink milk with the merchants. He didn't say a word, didn't even seem particularly curious, but listened, even smiled whenever the merchants cracked a joke. When everyone had spoken, he asked if the merchants had any news of the sacred cities to the north of the Great River. 'Yes,' one man said, 'every day new walls of stone go up, palaces for the living and the dead, and the slaves are working harder than ever under the whip of the new Pharaoh. He's young, but he's more terrible than any

Pharaoh before him.' 'A young Pharaoh?' Moses asked in surprise. 'Are you sure Pharaoh is young?' 'The people in Egypt say
that the last flood of the Great River designated him. He's been
destroying the statues of the previous Pharaoh.' Hearing that,
Moses stiffened. He questioned the other man as if he'd forgotten us. 'Did you see that with your own eyes or is it just hearsay?'
'No, no,' the old merchant protested, 'I saw it with my own eyes!
I was in the city of the kings during the last great flood.' "

The merchant had explained how he had traveled along the
Great River Iterou as far as Waset, the city of the kings, to sell
the blue stones from the mountains of Aram that were so prized
by the princesses of Egypt for their jewels. When he got there,
he found out that he was unable to practice his trade before the
following season. Pharaoh had just succeeded his old wife, who
was also his aunt, and had herself been Pharaoh before him, and
strangers were not allowed inside the palaces.

"What are you saying?" Jethro exclaimed. "His wife was a
Pharaoh?"

"That was what the merchant said," Hobab said, amused.
"The new Pharaoh was first the nephew, then the husband, of the
old Pharaoh, who was a woman. He mentioned her name, but I
couldn't repeat it. Everything seems very complicated in Egypt."

"A woman?" Jethro repeated, his face a picture of curiosity.

"Yes," Hobab laughed. "But listen to this. Before she became
Pharaoh herself, this woman was the daughter of one Pharaoh
and the wife of another Pharaoh, who was her brother. May
Horeb laugh with us, Father! That's how the rulers are in the
land of the Great River Iterou."

"But what of Moses?"

"Well, none of this seemed to surprise him. What did surprise
him was when the merchant of Akkad said the people of Waset
hadn't seen any more of Pharaoh's former wife, that she'd been

confined in a palace of the dead but hadn't been given the tomb she was entitled to."

Moses had stood up, gripping his staff. He had looked pale, and his eyes were shining. He had asked the merchant if he knew the Egyptian language. When the other man said yes, he had questioned him in that language. His voice was harsher now, and he spoke more quickly. The merchant answered, sometimes at length, with the respect that men of trade display in their dealings with those in authority.

Hobab and his men, of course, could have taken offense at being prevented from following the conversation because it was in a language that made it impossible for them to understand. But they were discovering a new Moses, confident, authoritative, solemn—and emotional, too—and nobody had thought of protesting.

"When they stopped talking," Hobab said, "it was as if Moses had swallowed poison."

"And you have no idea what the merchant was saying?" Orma asked, no longer feigning indifference.

"As I said, he spoke the language of Egypt."

"Didn't you ask Moses what was upsetting him like that?" Sefoba asked.

"I didn't like to."

"And the merchant," Orma insisted. "You could have questioned the merchant afterward—"

"Hobab did the right thing," Jethro cut in. "Such curiosity would have been out of place."

"Moses isn't a man you ask questions," Zipporah said, stony-faced. "He's someone who says what he means. He showed us that."

Hobab threw her a sharp look, then smiled and nodded. "You're right, sister. Anyway, after remaining for a moment in thought, he stood up and apologized for speaking in a language we couldn't understand. 'I know I've been rude,' he said, 'but my knowledge of the language of Midian is still very poor, and I wanted to be sure I understood what I was hearing.' He bade us good night, and the next day at dawn, he was gone."

"Hmmm!" Jethro said. "It was only a pretext. Moses knows our language quite well by now."

"What does that mean?"

Hobab looked directly at Zipporah. "It means that whatever he wanted to hear from the merchant, he didn't want us to know about."

The She-Pharaoh's Son

The summit of Horeb's mountain had long since vanished, shrouded in the clouds that moved endlessly southward like ash. From time to time, Zipporah had to lift her veil to protect her face from the sand and dust rising off the road. She held tightly to the jar of beer balanced on her shoulder. The folds of her tunic flapped around her hips and thighs. She had to lean forward to resist the fury of the wind.

Coming over a crest of scrub-covered rock, she found herself below the village of the armorers.

Cradled in the hollow of a long fault that snaked from cliff to cliff at the foot of the mountain, the village was something like a vast, elongated circle in shape. Its walls of rough bricks and roofs of palm leaves covered with earth blended into the rocks and ravines around it. But the courtyard, five or six times as large as Jethro's, was alive with noise and activity, visible through the smoke of the fires and forges, the stench of which caught Zipporah by the throat. The smoke curled in the wind, as if rolled around an invisible finger, before dispersing into the turbulent clouds.

The perimeter wall, onto which all the houses backed, had only one door in it, a heavy wooden door coated with earth. The village was really a small fortress, closed to all except those the armorers wished to enter, anxious as they were to guard the secrets of making precious weapons from iron, which were much sought after by rulers from the Euphrates to the Iterou.

In between the gusts of wind that flattened the thornbushes, Zipporah heard the first blows. With a firm stride, she turned onto a path in which the recent rains had left gullies. Immediately, the grave, piercing sound of a ram's horn rang out, announcing her approach. She continued her descent, pushing her shawl back so that her face was clearly visible. When she reached the foot of the slope, she walked past the pen where the mules—powerful, long-haired beasts capable of carrying heavy loads of wood or ferrous earth from dawn to dusk—were kept.

The door in the perimeter wall opened, and two men came out, clutching long iron swords. The door closed behind them. Zipporah took a few steps forward.

"Zipporah! Daughter of Jethro!" the shorter and fatter of the two men cried, his toothless mouth open in a wide smile, revealing his pink tongue and gums. "Welcome to the armorers' village!"

"Greetings, Ewi-Tsour! May Horeb preserve your smile."

Ewi-Tsour stared shamelessly at the jar of beer on Zipporah's shoulder. "Zipporah! What a joy to get a visit from you! Especially as you never come empty-handed!" He laughed, and slapped his companion's shoulder. "Go on, then, relieve Zipporah of her burden!" Then he turned to the door. "Hey, you in there!" he cried. "Open the door. The daughter of Jethro the wise wishes to regale us with her father's beer."

A moment later, Zipporah was crossing the great courtyard. Wives and handmaids appeared in the doorways. Children came

running, recognizing her and calling her by name, jostling each
other to take her hand. She reached inside her tunic, took some
honey cakes from a canvas sack, and distributed them amid cries
of joy.

Ewi-Tsour shook his head. "You certainly know how to make
yourself loved!" he said, with pretended mockery, and chased the
children away.

"My father informs you that we have jars of honey for you."

"Your father is wise and good," Ewi-Tsour said approvingly,
screwing up his eyes. "But I don't suppose you came here just to
give us beer and honey?"

In a few words, Zipporah explained the reason for her visit.
Ewi-Tsour nodded and pointed toward the north end of the huge
courtyard. "Follow me," he said.

The furnaces stood in the eastern curve of the courtyard.
Like the silos used for storing grain and oil, each was covered in
a thick layer of red clay, but had an opening at the top, like the
neck of a jar, from which emerged coils of brown smoke and,
from time to time, explosions of sputtering flames, so bright as
to be almost transparent. All around, men were moving, pushing
hollowed canes through the holes at the base of the furnaces and
then breathing hard into them. In front of a larger hole, from
which a beak of charred pottery protruded, two men in leather
tunics were using long stalks with flat ends to guide a glowing
thread of molten iron into hollowed stones.

Twelve paces away, under a vast canopy, other armorers, also
dressed in leather, but with their black arms bare and glistening
with sweat, were beating with sledgehammers on shapeless ingots
that lay on burning embers as part of the annealing process. The
sound of the hammers was so loud that Zipporah felt as if it were
going through her chest. She was tempted to put her fingers in her
ears, but did not dare. The stench of burned earth was so strong
that the air was barely breathable. From time to time, sparks spat

from the furnaces, butterflies of fire that the wind dispersed in threatening arabesques into the gray sky.

Ewi-Tsour saw Zipporah's grimace. "You're out of luck," he shouted to make himself heard. "It's really stinking today! The boys are making coal in the well."

He pointed to a small group of young men bustling around a brick coping from which coils of thick brown smoke emerged.

Ewi-Tsour smiled, uncovering his pink gums, and led her to a half-open door. Beyond the door, men sat on the floor of a large room, polishing iron blades with sand and strips of ox hide still dripping with grease. They looked up when Zipporah entered. The greetings over, Ewi-Tsour turned to one of the men, still young, half of whose face had been consumed by fire. The skin on that side was taut, cracked in places and strewn with monstrous, hardened swellings, making what had once been lips, cheek, temple, eyelid, and ear quite unrecognizable. As the man had a beard that only grew on the intact part of his face, seeing him was like being confronted by a creature with two heads, one ordinary and the other like something from the underworld.

"Elchem," Ewi-Tsour said, "Jethro's daughter wants you to tell her where you saw the stranger from Egypt."

"You told Hobab, my brother," Zipporah said, making an effort to sustain the gaze of the man's one eye. "He thinks that when you saw Moses, he was heading for Egypt."

Elchem grunted in assent. Ewi-Tsour made a gesture to urge him on. With a slight tension of his upper body that seemed habitual to him, the man turned, so that only the more attractive side of his ruined face was visible. "Yes, I talked to Hobab," he said. His voice surprised Zipporah, being youthful and clear. "I followed the stranger. He was leading his camel away from the roads. I thought he was a thief. There are often thieves lurking around our quarries. But, in fact, he went right past the quarries. Your brother, Hobab, thought he was going north, hoping to cross the desert to the land of the Great Flood. It can be done, if you're very brave. But he must have given up, because I saw him again the day before yesterday, on the road to Yz-Alcyon."

"You saw him?"

Elchem nodded, half opening his mouth in what must once have been a beautiful smile. "He was a thousand paces from me. He wasn't on his camel, but walking next to it. He must have tired the animal out."

"That's a long way from here," Zipporah could not help murmuring.

The man stared at her insistently with his single eye. "The sky was gray, there was a lot of wind, and I have only one eye. But, as everyone will tell you, it's the good one. It was him, you can take my word for it, daughter of Jethro. Ask them." He indicated his companions, who grunted their assent.

"Have no fear," Ewi-Tsour said. "Elchem's words are as solid as the metal we make."

"He was bare-chested, like an Egyptian!" Elchem went on. "None of us would go around like that. Especially not in this cold weather."

"I believe you, Elchem. I'm just surprised. So he's back on my father's land?"

"No, he wasn't going in the direction of Jethro's domain. He was heading straight for the sea. For the great cliffs."

A big smile appeared on Zipporah's face. "Yes, of course! You're right!" She gave a joyful little laugh and, in a gesture that impressed the rough armorers and made them lower their eyes, bowed, seized Elchem's hands, and lifted them to her brow. "May Horeb give you rest from his wrath, Elchem!"

SHE heard Moses' voice.

A low murmur, like a hum.

She came to a halt on the path, a few paces from the terrace outside the cave.

She had to catch her breath before she could allow Moses to see her.

She took a few steps back, until she touched the cliff. Below, on the beach, the sea, alternately flashing green and gray with spindrift, made a regular crunching sound as it washed over the shingle.

Afraid of being dizzy, she closed her eyes and placed her palms flat against the rock. The wind was blowing, hard and relentless, sometimes bringing her Moses' voice loud and clear, sometimes obscuring it. She realized that he was not speaking the language of Midian. The sounds he was making were long ones, both urgent and gentle. Moses' voice was suddenly very close. She opened her eyes.

He was there, three or four cubits from her, advancing toward the edge of the terrace and the void beyond, his eyes closed, his forearms—adorned with the heavy gold bracelets—held out in front of him, his palms open. She almost screamed in terror at the thought of seeing him topple over into the void.

He stopped a few steps from the edge and stood there in a curious posture, with his chest thrown out and his back arched. His eyes still closed, he resumed his droning, in a throatier, more ardent voice, as if trying with all his might to project his prayer beyond the sea.

He's speaking the language of Egypt! she thought. He's praying to the gods of Egypt!

He had not yet become aware of her presence. She felt ashamed to be watching him like this. But she was too fascinated to leave. Fascinated by his face, by the newfound clarity of his features. She had never seen Moses' face like this. He had shaved! Clumsily, though—there were small cuts on his cheeks and chin.

For the first time in her life, she saw a man without a beard. Moses' face looked unexpectedly and attractively youthful and vulnerable. And so shameless! She lowered her eyes, thinking with some embarrassment of how soft those hairless cheeks, which exposed chin and neck, would feel if she touched them with her fingertips.

Moses suddenly crossed his arms over his chest. The bracelets made a jangling noise and flashed in the sun. His voice became lower, almost inaudible, until it ceased altogether.

Silence enveloped them, broken only by the wind and the surf.

Not daring to look at him again, Zipporah moved away from the rock. Trying to avoid dislodging any stones, she began to climb up the path.

"Zipporah!" Moses' voice echoed behind her in the cold wind. The voice she knew, the voice he always used when he spoke the language of Midian. "Come back, don't go!"

Pulling her shawl tight over her chest, she turned. Seen head-on, his bare face was even more unsettling. His nose seemed stronger, his jaws broader, his eyes darker. He reached out a gold-circled arm. The memory of the man in her dream came back to her, sending a shiver of fear and desire through her whole body.

"I'm very happy to see you," Moses said, more gently, taking a step toward her.

She struggled to sustain his gaze, incapable of the slightest movement.

"Oh," Moses said, laughing and touching his cheeks, "it's my face that surprises you! It's an Egyptian custom. To address Amon, you need to be clean shaven."

He laughed more openly, which gave Zipporah the courage to look at him and smile. She stammered an excuse for disturbing him while he was praying. With a gesture, he indicated that it was of no importance. "So, you knew where to find me," he said. He did not seem surprised. On the contrary, he appeared quite happy, and his eyes shone.

"We were afraid you'd left for Egypt."

"Your brother must be angry. It was not very polite of me."

"No, no, he isn't angry!" Zipporah heard herself protesting in a voice that was too loud and too sharp. "Nor is my father, nor me . . ."

She was afraid. Afraid he wouldn't find her beautiful enough, afraid her skin was too black for him, afraid of her own Cushite face. Moses had become a stranger again, an unknown man, with bare cheeks and a prince's bracelets.

"The whole household has been hoping you would return," she said, the words half swallowed in her throat.

Twilight was approaching. On the horizon, a cloudless strip of sky was turning red. Reflections shimmered on the sea like thick pools of blood.

"It's true," Moses said. "I wanted to leave for Egypt, but I had no idea of the route. The camel your father gave me had more brains than me. I led him into a quicksand. He managed to get out, but then refused to go any farther north. I listened to what he was telling me, and we came back here. The truth is, I have no desire to go to the land of the great Maat! No desire at all!" He made an unexpectedly violent and angry gesture, and turned away to look at the reddening horizon. He shook his head. "No, there's nothing for me there," he said, as if talking to himself.

"Why come back to this cave and not to my father's domain?" Zipporah asked.

He glanced at her coolly, but did not reply immediately. "Come, don't stay on the path. There's water in my gourd if you feel thirsty."

The gold glittered on his arm as he pointed to the cave. Only now did he seem to become aware of the bracelets on his arms. He took them off.

"I had to speak to Amon, the god of Pharaoh and my mother," he explained. "It was easier to do that here. In your father's house, it might have offended Jethro and the altar of Horeb, where he makes his offerings."

He reached the far end of the terrace. His sack and staff were there, and so was the painted casket. He opened it and put the gold bracelets inside. He was no longer hiding anything from her, Zipporah thought, but the thought did nothing to calm either the fear or the desire that were warring in her blood. The light was quickly fading. The horizon was aflame, like the armorers' fires. Soon, it would be dark. There was still time for her to get back. She knew the way well enough, even in the dark. To stay here, with Moses, would be a significant step, and the thought of it made her tremble. But modesty and shame made her tremble even more. She lowered her eyes, turned her hands over, and looked at her palms, as if they contained an answer.

Guessing her thoughts, Moses came closer. "It's late to be getting back to your father's house," he said, "but I'm sure you know the way, even at night. I could go with you."

She looked up again. They stood there in silence, intimidated, aware that every moment they remained without moving, without speaking, contained a promise.

Moses was the first to open his mouth. "Stay with me," he whispered. "I want you to know who I really am."

"Why?"

Zipporah saw the blood beating under the bare skin of his neck. It was still not too late—if she could find the strength—to turn away and go back up the path to the top of the cliff. She thought one last time of her sisters and Jethro. Especially Jethro. She wished he were here, to give her encouragement.

"Because you are the one who could understand," Moses said, and his voice sounded as it had when he was praying to Pharaoh's god.

His gaze was difficult to sustain, and Zipporah lowered her eyes. There was another silence, heavier than before.

She broke the spell. "It's getting cold," she said, somewhat curtly, stepping to one side. "We have to light a fire and get the wood ready before night comes."

"THE Akkadian merchant I met with your brother, Hobab, told me my mother was dead," Moses began. "The woman I always called 'my mother,' although she wasn't really. I didn't come out of her womb. I never saw my real mother's face. I don't even know her name."

The flames were high, and whirled in the wind that beat brutally against the cliff. Beyond the shifting reflections on the walls of the cave, the darkness was total. There were no stars in the sky. The night seemed empty of life. It was as though they were the last man and the last woman left alive in the world, both protected and lost in this halo of quivering light suspended between earth and sky. The murmur of the surf faded on the sea. Moses spoke calmly, hesitating only when a word escaped him or some especially emotional memory made his voice throb. Wrapped in a thick blanket impregnated with the smell of sand and camels, Zippora listened. From time to time, she would stoke the embers, adding a dead branch to the dancing flames.

Some years earlier, the name of the Pharaoh who ruled over the land of the River Iterou was Thutmose-Aakheperkare. He was considered one of the wisest and most powerful of the Divine Sons and Protectors of Maat. Thanks to his alliance with Amon, the greatest of the gods, the floods of the River Iterou had never failed to bring abundant harvests. He was a great warrior, who conquered lands to the north and the south, and regained the strength and wealth that had been lost due to the weakness of his fathers and forefathers. Making full use of the Hebrew slaves, he enlarged palaces and temples, extracting whole cities from the sand and the mountains.

Until the day it became clear that the descendants of Abraham and Joseph were becoming ever-more numerous, multiplying in proportion to their ever-increasing burden. Pharaoh had to listen constantly to his counselors' fears: "What will happen when the Hebrews are equal in number to the people of the River Iterou? What will happen if they become aware of their own strength? If war comes, they'll side with our enemies! If we're wise, we'll destroy the seeds of revolt before they bear fruit. Let us exhaust them in work! Let us stop them from multiplying!"

So it was that Thutmose-Aakheperkare decided that all the firstborn sons of the Hebrews should have their throats cut at birth.

How to describe the cries, the tears, the weeping of women already big with child? Many hid, or lied to save their sons. Others invented all kinds of subterfuges to avoid their being put to death. Among them was the woman who bore Moses.

"Who she was, where she lived, how I was found—even today I don't know any of those things. What I do know is that the woman I called my mother did not give birth to me."

Here, Moses paused for a long time. Her face burning, Zipporah did not move.

"The woman I knew as my mother was the beloved daughter of Thutmose-Aakheperkare," Moses resumed, in a colder voice. "Hatshepsut. Mother Hatshepsut, I called her. As far back as I can remember, hers was the name and face that calmed my tantrums and nurtured my childish pleasures. The face of a gentle and wise sovereign."

As soon as his beloved daughter was born, Thutmose-Aakheperkare had wanted to make her a queen, but the priests opposed the idea. So, after much maneuvering, Pharaoh had given her a husband: his own son from another wife. A weak man who would succeed him and become Thutmose II.

"That way, my mother was able to rule the country in secret without attracting the wrath of the priests. But she knew her frail husband couldn't give her a son. I suppose that was why she went against her father's orders and took a Hebrew baby to her breast and pretended that he had come from her womb through the will of Isis and Nephthys—which made me the son of Pharaoh."

So, Zipporah thought, clasping her hands together to stop them shaking, Moses was indeed what Orma had first thought him to be. A prince. Nor could there any longer be any doubt that he was the man in her dream, a man like no other.

"Mother Hatshepsut was as tender to me as a mother could be. I can still feel the touch of her lips on my brow and the memory of her scent in my throat. Where I came from, only she and one of her handmaids knew. It was easy enough to convince her husband, whom she despised, that I was his son. But to lie to Pharaoh, her father, before he died and climbed into Amon's boat was more difficult. . . . I was given the name Moses. Nothing was too splendid for me! I was taught everything that one 'appointed by Amon' had to know: written words, the order of the stars, time and the seasons. I was taught to love and be loved. I was taught to fight, to command, and to despise everything that was not the will of the rulers and gods of the River Iterou."

Moses looked at Zipporah, but she averted her eyes. He waited a little, as if drawing his memories from the wind and the surf.

"I lived and thought not only like the son of Hatshepsut and Pharaoh, but also like a man of the Great River. Occasionally, when I went to admire some new column or temple, I would see slaves. To be honest, I didn't think of them as men and women. They were Hebrews, and they were slaves. It took hatred and intrigue to open my eyes and lead me to the truth."

Thutmose II had died young. Moses, now a man, felt no sorrow at his death. He looked with indifference at his corpse on Amon's boat. But, as soon as the stones of the tomb were sealed, the palaces and temples came alive with plots. Hatshepsut, radiantly beautiful and confident, as nobody had been since her father, of the help and support of the priests of Amon, advanced, under the sun, in male garb, clasping to her chest the scepters of Osiris, the whip, and the gold crook, and the tiara of the kings of Upper and Lower Egypt was placed on her golden wig. The priests of Osiris muttered, but bent their heads and their knees.

The abundant harvests that followed earned her the trust and gratitude of the people, which merely increased the anger of the nobles, who hated the fact that she was a woman. In the hope of pacifying them, she married her own nephew, a young man the same age as Moses, promising that when the time came, he would become Thutmose III. But what should have been a guarantee of peace became a further source of hatred.

"How could it have been otherwise? Thutmose is strong and handsome, loved by the priests and feared by the soldiers. We are the same age. We played the same games and were taught by the same masters. We fought together and prayed to Amon together. Suddenly we both found ourselves in my mother's room, I as her son and he as her husband! It was all too obvious which of the two of us she loved! The corridors of the palace were buzzing with rumor and suspicion! Thutmose was told that he would never become the Divine Son and Protector of Maat, because my mother, Hatshepsut, was trying to maneuver so that I would be the one designated by Amon. Of course, he believed it. Who wouldn't have believed it?"

It was known that Thutmose II had been weak. Doubts were cast on Moses' paternity. An investigation was launched. The handmaids were questioned—presumably under torture—about how Hatshepsut had spent her nights and what men might have shared her bed. No lover was discovered—but an even greater secret came to light.

One day, Thutmose summoned Moses to the great hall of his palace. They had often eaten there together, enjoying the dancers and magicians. That day the room, with its high columns, was empty but for the throne of Thutmose. Armed guards stood behind every door. On his brow, Hatshepsut's young husband bore a gold serpent, the royal insignia of Ka. His eyes sparkled with joy and venom.

Moses stepped forward, sustaining his gaze.

"Come no farther, Moses!" Thutmose commanded, in his high-pitched voice. "I know who you are."

"Who I am?" Moses asked, genuinely surprised. "What do you mean, brother?"

"I'm not your brother!" Thutmose screamed. "Never say that word again!"

"What do you mean, Thutmose? Why are you so angry?"

"Be quiet and listen. The priests have consulted Hemet, Khnum, and Thoth. They've also questioned one of your mother's handmaids . . ." He laughed sardonically. "Your 'mother Hatshepsut,' my devoted wife, Divine Daughter of Amon, queen of Upper and Lower Egypt! This is the conclusion they've come to. You're a nobody, Moses."

Moses realized at that moment that those who had been plotting against Hatshepsut had finally found the weapon they had been looking for. He waited for Thutmose to stop laughing. "I have never claimed to be what you are, Thutmose," he declared calmly.

"Quiet! Keep your mouth shut, you heap of dung!" Thut-mose's cheeks were scarlet, and he was gripping the arms of his throne so tightly that his knuckles were white. "Slave! Slave, and son of a slave! You're a Hebrew, a son of the multitude, a blemish on my palace! That's what you are, Moses. Hatshepsut never gave birth to you. You're a lie, a Hebrew firstborn who has no right to live!"

Moses was stunned. When he tried to ask questions, Thut-mose screamed more insults and called the guards. That night, Moses was thrown into the prisoners' pit.

"After a few days," Moses said, gently taking wood from Zipporah and putting it on the fire, "they took me out and led me to a building site to the south of the Great River Iterou, where they put me to work among the slaves—my own people, although I couldn't even understand their language! It was there that I killed Mem P'ta, the architect and overseer. I had to flee without seeing my mother, Hatshepsut, again. I had no idea what had happened to her until we met the merchant from Akkad and he told us the news. 'In the land of the River Iterou, Pharaoh is again a man! The name Thutmose the Third is divine. The name Hatshepsut has been banished. The stones on which it is written have been broken, her statues have been overturned, and her temples destroyed. When she died, she was given no boat to take her to Amon.'"

Zipporah shivered. Moses had fallen silent after these last words. She was surprised to hear him sobbing. He had got to his feet, and was standing with his face half in shadow. He turned his back to her, walked nervously to the edge of the cliff, and faced the night and the wind.

"I grew up and was loved," he cried, "but knew nothing of the slaves who built the palaces where I slept. I thought I was someone I wasn't. I'm a nobody! Thutmose is right. But my people . . . Oh, my people! How can they live as they do? How can they bear it?"

Zipporah stood up. The cover fell from her shoulders, but she was hardly aware of the cold. Moses turned to face her. In the light of the flames, tears glistened on his cheeks and in his rage-filled eyes. He opened his arms as if he were about to shout some more, but, at that moment, there came a loud rumbling sound, like a roll of drums, not from the sea, it seemed, but from the depths of the cave. It was a dense, fierce, powerful sound, and, when it came a second time, they both cried out in fright. Then it stopped.

"Horeb!" Zipporah whispered, in a strangled voice.

It returned, like a lament from deep within the cliff. This time, it seemed that the rocks themselves trembled in response.

"What is it?" Moses asked, in a toneless voice.

"Horeb," Zipporah repeated, in a more soothing tone. "Horeb is speaking. Horeb is angry."

With a grimace, Moses turned to the darkness, then again to Zipporah. She had crossed her hands below her chest, with her palms open, and closed her eyes. Neither said anything. They listened to the silence.

There was no sound now but the noise of the wind and the surf.

They kept listening, but now, in the darkness, where Horeb's anger had sounded, they were aware only of a vast emptiness. The rumbling did not return.

Zipporah relaxed. "Tonight," she said, smiling, "his rage was a small one. Perhaps he heard you and was answering you. Perhaps your rage is his."

Moses looked at her suspiciously. Was she mocking him? "No! Horeb is not my god. I have no god. Who is the God of the Hebrews? I don't know him."

"I saw you praying for the woman who was your mother," Zipporah countered, gently.

Moses shrugged, and the tension went from his face. "I wasn't praying to Amon. I was praying to her."

She did not know what to say in reply. Now she felt the cold of the wind through her tunic. Moses did not seem to mind. She thought of how warm she would feel if he took her in his arms. But, when he took a few steps toward her, she instinctively retreated.

He stopped still. "Now you know who I am. I haven't hidden anything from you. My soul is as naked as my face."

She kept retreating, until her back hit the rock. "What about me?" she said. "Do you know who I am?"

"Jethro's daughter."

She laughed, and held out her arms and hands, their color blending into the darkness. "With skin like this? Do you really think so?"

Before she could react, he imprisoned her fingers and drew her to him. "You are Zipporah the Cushite, the woman Moses saved from the hands of the shepherds at the well of Irmna. You are the woman who always knows where to find me, the woman who brought me food without knowing who I was."

◇

THEY were standing flat against the wall, breathing in short gulps, their faces distorted by the flickering flames. In spite of the sharp edges of rock digging into her buttocks and shoulders, Zipporah was aware of nothing but Moses' body pressed against hers. What was happening now was something she had wanted with as much fear and as much passion as others might put into wanting to live and die happy. She thought of pushing him away, but that would have been to lie to herself.

"You know who I am!" she heard him say again. "Oh Zippo-rah, don't look at me as if I were a prince of Egypt! Don't be like your sister! I have nothing! I'm a Hebrew with no god and no family. Your father gave me my first camel and my first flock. You are rich in every way, and I am nothing but the reflection I see in your eyes. You are the woman who desires my kiss, and I thirst for you."

Moses' fierce breath was like a wind stoking the fire of her lips. The heat of his body protected her so well from the wind and the vast night outside! He was right. That was what she was, and only that: the woman who desired his kiss. He was right, too, that she could not help thinking of him as a prince, a powerful man, a Pharaoh's son, and of how different they were, how white he was and how black she was—black, and even weaker than the Hebrews themselves.

Moses touched her lips lightly with his fingers, as he had done once before, in this very cave, the day she had been overwhelmed by the sight of him. She wanted to say: "No, Moses! We can't, it's a sin! I've never been touched by a man!"

She could feel his member pressed against her belly, and its hardness took the words out of her mouth. She could hold back no longer. Urgently, she gripped Moses' neck, pulled his face to hers, and opened her lips to let him draw her moan from her. . . . If Horeb had rumbled at that moment, she would not have heard him.

◆

THEY were rolling on the blanket. The flames were less bright now, but they could still see each other.

"I see you, I see you!" Moses was saying. "Your skin is no longer as black as the night."

She was kissing him as if their kisses could wipe away the tears forming in her eyes.

Moses removed the brooches to loosen her tunic, kissed the hollow of her shoulders, and placed his bare cheek on the tender curve of her breasts. She pushed him away, stunned, already hungry for the skin she could feel beneath her Cushite fingers. She closed her eyes.

Moses undressed her completely, heedless of the icy wind. He, too, closed his eyes now. "I see you with my fingers!" he said.

He caressed her hips and belly and thighs as if sculpting the darkness. Zipporah felt and saw Moses' slender fingers, his princely white hands giving shape to his desire.

He leaned over her. "I see you with my lips," he said. "You are my light."

She saw his luminous brow, his lips kissing the hollow between her breasts, searching for the nipples as if drinking some mysterious intoxicating draft, parting her thighs and drawing his pleasure there like water from a well.

She gave her whole body to him, gripping his shoulders, putting her hands together on the small of his back, crying out to catch her breath. There was a pain that lasted an instant, and then he was inside her. Fire spread through her chest, fire that did not come from the flames. She was shaking like a little girl. Dizziness ran down her spine and whirled around the increasingly fine, sharp, tender mixture of pain and pleasure that opened her chest to Moses' mouth as he bent over her, swayed over her, and whispered words she neither heard nor understood. She gripped his thighs and buttocks as she had gripped the man who had saved her from drowning at the bottom of the sea, bringing her back from dream to day. At that moment, in a moan the wind carried away, they at last breathed in unison.

COMING together and moving apart, exhausted but not sated, they barely slept that night. When dawn came, the wind was still blowing, and Horeb's mountain was still disgorging turbulent clouds like smoke from a forge, but, between the clouds, the sky was getting bluer.

Zipporah was the first to rise. She bustled about, washing herself in the cave with water from the gourd, out of sight of Moses. Soon she was the same woman she had been when she arrived the night before.

Below, on the beach, the surf also seemed the same, although the sea was more transparent. In the light of day, the hollow formed by the terrace and the cave seemed as tiny as a nest. They themselves were merely a man and a woman lost in the immensity.

Moses had crept up behind her. Now he put his arms around her waist. He was still naked. "I'm going to see Jethro," he said, his mouth close to her ear. "I'm going to speak to him and ask him to grant me his most precious daughter."

Zipporah did not move, did not reply. She did not stroke the arms that embraced her, nor did she lean against the body that had left the imprint of its desire on every pore of her skin. She kept her eyes fixed on the horizon. Somewhere out there was the shore of Egypt, although she could not see it. She remained motionless and silent—so much so that Moses took his arms away and stepped to one side to get a better look at her, anxiety written on his brow.

"What were you saying to your god yesterday?" she asked.

Moses looked even more disappointed. Without taking her eyes off the sea, Zipporah held out her hand, lightly brushed Moses' chest, stroked his stomach, slid her fingertips over his member, then took his hand in hers and squeezed it.

"Yesterday," she said, very gently, "you were praying for your mother. I'd like to know the words you cast on the sea."

"I'm not sure I could say them in the language of Midian."

"Oh yes, you can."

He hesitated. She gave his hand an impatient little shake. His body close against hers, Moses turned his eyes toward the unseen shore of Egypt.

"*I am a perfect Mummy,*
"*I am a Mummy living in the truth,*
"*I am pure, I am pure,*
"*Here are my hands, here on my palms is my mother's heart,*
"*It is pure, it is pure.*
"*Let this heart be weighed in the balance of Truth,*
"*I am a Mummy nourished by truth, I have not known the*
    hardness of the heart, I have given cool water to whoever
    was thirsty, wheat to whoever needed it, linen to
    whoever walked naked.
"*Oh forms of Eternity, cover with your wings the egg of a sweet*
    mother."

Zipporah's eye's filled with tears. Without letting go of her hand, Moses moved closer to her so that their bodies touched. "It isn't that I worship Amon, or any of the other gods of Egypt. I no longer belong to them, and their heaven is no longer for me. This prayer is spoken as the boat takes the dead person toward the heaven of rebirth. My mother Hatshepsut was very faithful to Amon."

A limpid tear ran down Zipporah's cheek, perfectly transparent against her dark skin in the daylight. She waited until there was no longer a knot in her throat. "My mother died on that sea as she led me to the arms of Jethro," she whispered.

Moses looked at her, waiting for her to say more, ready to listen.

"You were right to want to return to Egypt," she said. "Your place is there."

He could not have been more astonished if she had hit him. He let go of her hand and stepped back. "What are you saying?" He suddenly appeared much more naked.

She did not reply, merely smiled patiently.

"My place is here, Zipporah, with you and your father. What is there for me in Egypt?"

"When you killed that overseer, you began your battle against Pharaoh," she said, in a clear voice, the voice her sister Orma disliked so much. "You have to continue."

Moses stared at her, uncomprehending, pain spreading over his features. "Are you chasing me away? After last night? I told you, I'm going with you to see Jethro. This very morning, on the camel he gave me. I'll talk to him. I'm going to pitch my tent again beneath the sycamore on the road to Epha . . ."

She shook her head.

Moses held his arm out in the direction of Jethro's domain. "'Jethro,' I'll say to him, 'give me your daughter Zipporah as a wife! She is the seed of my future life. I will be your son and will give you back a hundredfold all you gave me—'"

"Moses—"

"I'll build up my flock. I'll go to every pasture in Midian. I'll sell the animals next winter. We'll have several tents. You will be Zipporah, the wife of Moses, a respected woman. Nobody will ever again mutter about the Cushite. Nobody will ever again dare raise his hand to you!" He could have spoken until he was breathless.

She pressed both her hands against his chest. "Moses! Moses! Don't lie! You know who you are now. You are not a nobody, as your false brother in Egypt claims. You are a Hebrew. A son of Abraham and Joseph."

"Why should that matter to you?" he cried. "You yourself aren't a Hebrew!"

She saw terror in his golden eyes. How could so much fear have been instilled in a man like him? She dug her nails into

Moses' chest and pushed her hips against his. "Last night," she breathed, "when you were screaming into the wind, you weren't weeping for your mother. You were crying out in anger against the suffering of the slaves. That was what Horeb heard."

"I don't know what you're talking about! Horeb isn't my god; he doesn't know me."

"Don't blaspheme! You know nothing about Horeb. He is wrathful and he is just. And you were born among the slaves, even though you acquired the knowledge and strength of Pharaoh. Why else did you kill the overseer?"

Moses pushed her away. "Nonsense!" he cried. "You know nothing of the power of Pharaoh. You know nothing of the cruelty of Thutmose! It's impossible to fight Amon's designated one!"

"I know you must put on your gold bracelets and go among those who are your people. You must hold back the whip that strikes them."

"I killed a man because I was angry, and I ran away like a little boy! That's the truth. There is no other. No man can hold back Pharaoh's whip. You don't know what you're talking about!"

She let him shout and said nothing. Her silence increased his rage.

"What do you take me for? I told you, I'm not a prince. I thought you were more sensible than your sister. Don't you want to see the man I am?" Moses' cries echoed against the cliff.

Zipporah seized his wrists. "I know the man you are! I saw you in a dream before I even met you. I know who you are and who you can become. Your future is not here, among the pastures of Midian."

Moses' anger suddenly faded, and he laughed long and loud and mockingly. He shook his head, then raised Zipporah's hands to his lips and kissed them. "If your father Jethro didn't place such trust in you, I'd think the woman I want as my wife is not only a Cushite but also a little mad."

Zipporah pulled away abruptly, her eyes as dark as her skin. "If you don't believe me, there's no point in going back to see my father."

"Zipporah, how can you be so sure of my future?"

"I repeat. I saw you in a dream. You are one of those who save life when it's in danger of being swallowed up."

Moses shook his head, an ironic smile still on his lips. "Tell me about your dream."

"There's no point. You wouldn't understand." She walked past him and set off up the cliff path.

Moses put his hand on her stomach to stop her. "Don't push me away! Tell me the dream. Let me go to your father."

She pushed his arm away, gently, and could not stop herself stroking his cheek, where the beard was starting to grow back. "First, you must understand who you are."

"I know who I am! I'm nobody anymore. Those who flee Pharaoh lose even their shadows!"

"So I, too, am nobody anymore. My skin is the color of shadows and, although you've possessed me, we will never be husband and wife. Shadows don't marry."

The Wrath of Horeb

"**I**s that what you told him? Really? That you're not going to marry him?"

There was incredulity in Sefoba's voice—as there was, too, in Jethro's gaze, along with a touch of reproach, which the old sage tried to soften.

When she had returned, Zipporah had seen everyone looking up at the clouds massing around the summit of Horeb's mountain. She had gone straight to her father and told him the truth about Moses, how he had been Pharaoh's son and had then been banished as a Hebrew thanks to his false brother's hatred and jealousy.

"His anger against Pharaoh's injustice is greater than he thinks," she had added. "Just thinking about the sufferings inflicted on the slaves makes him scream with rage. And, when he screamed, Horeb rumbled with him. But he knows nothing of Horeb, and he's afraid."

Her sisters had come running to hear her, and Jethro had not ordered them away.

"Did you sleep there?" Orma had asked. "In the cave? Next to him?"

Zipporah had looked directly at Jethro. "He wanted me," she had replied, her voice as strong as ever, "and I was happy to let him take me."

They were all speechless with astonishment.

"Moses is like any other man," she went on. "I know that. I see it on his face and sense it when I'm close to him. But he himself doesn't yet know his own strength. All he thinks about is his past in Pharaoh's house. He is blind to the future."

Jethro looked steadily at his daughter. Zipporah knew him well enough to sense the mixture of embarrassment, joy, disapproval, and even hope in his gaze. She was ready to listen to his judgment, perhaps even to obey it. But he did not have time to utter a word. Orma was already on her feet, her lips white.

"Listen to her! Just listen to her! How dare she talk like that? She who has just cast a blemish on us. Father, how can you let her say such horrid things? She offered herself to the Egyptian, and you say nothing."

Now Sefoba, too, stood up, tears in her eyes. For once, she could not understand Zipporah, and thought Orma's anger justified. Jethro was not even looking at them. He seemed suddenly made of stone, his mouth hidden by his beard, his eyelids closed and smooth as ivory.

Orma took this silence as a weakness. "I was the first!" she shouted angrily. "I was the first, I told you, I knew he was a prince. Here, under the canopy, Father, I told you, you heard me, I said he was lying when he claimed to be a slave. As soon as he appeared at the well of Irmna, I knew! And Zipporah and you humiliated me by believing his lie!"

In the courtyard, the handmaids turned to listen, but did not dare approach. They were more worried than curious, and even somewhat scared by Orma's strident voice, as though the wrath of Horeb had descended to earth in a mass of black clouds.

Zipporah stood up. Her hands were shaking, and her throat was dry. Orma's hatred was a living thing, a wild beast. She felt it clinging to her face and chest, tearing at her body, wiping out the memory of Moses' caresses. And she, too, was beginning to feel hatred. She made as if to respond, but Orma screamed even louder than before:

"Quiet! Every word you say is a blemish on this household. You are a blemish on all of us! That's why Horeb is angry!"

"Silence!" Jethro's solemn voice rang out. He had raised his arms, with a strength that belied his frail body. "Silence, stupid girl!" he thundered. "Shut your mouth before it spews out any more hate!"

Orma swayed, as though Jethro had slapped her. In the stunned silence that followed, she let out a strange moan, clearly a prelude to a flood of tears.

Sefoba bit her lips, not daring to go to her aid. She threw an anguished look at Zipporah, who had covered her mouth with her hands. Never before had the two sisters seen Jethro's face like this: his eyes and cheeks hollow with rage, the skin at his temples so taut as to be transparent and as pale as the bones beneath.

"Stop this foolish whining," he said, pointing imperiously at Orma. "Don't use Horeb's name to me! Don't speak of his wrath. You know nothing about it," he thundered on, pointing now at the mountain.

All eyes in the courtyard turned to the threatening summit, which had been jarring their nerves since dawn.

Orma moaned again. Her knees gave way, and she collapsed on the cushions. Neither Sefoba not Zipporah dared touch her. Nobody in the courtyard even risked batting an eyelid.

Jethro stood over his huddled daughter, towering above her, frightening now for all his thinness. "You are the child of my loins, but you are my shame. You have nothing in you but envy and spite! I can't stand your jabbering anymore."

Although her shoulders heaved with sobs, Orma was not ready to admit defeat. Moving with the agility of a young lioness, she clutched her father's knees and kissed them passionately. "Don't be unjust, Father, please don't be unjust!"

With a grimace, Jethro seized her shoulder and pushed her away. Orma only clung to him even tighter. "Stop this nonsense," Jethro growled.

"Zipporah fornicates with the Egyptian without being married to him and I'm the one in the wrong? Is that your justice, Father?"

"My justice is something you can't understand."

Orma let out a sharp cry, and let go of Jethro as if a snake had bitten her, an insane laugh distorting what remained of her beauty. "The only reason Zipporah opened her thighs to Moses was to take him from me! I was the first to recognize him for what he was. And I was the one he chose! I saw in his eyes!"

"No," Zipporah cried. "No, you're lying!"

She was about to do something violent, perhaps, when a crack rent the air. The summit of Horeb's mountain was like a thousand mouths of fire spitting white and yellow clouds into the endless sky, where they were twisted by an unseen hand. Screams echoed through the courtyard as the rumbling increased in volume and intensity.

"Horeb! Horeb!"

Sefoba rushed into Zipporah's arms, while Orma clutched Jethro's legs. He looked up at the fearsome convulsions of the mountain and calmly put his arm around her shoulders. The ground shook. Another rumble echoed across the desert. Blackness poured from the mouth of the mountain, a blackness flecked with incandescent jets of flame.

"Horeb's fire! Horeb's fire!"

Some clung together, joining their tears and their terror. Others ran like insects or fell to their knees. The animals squealed and pushed over the cane fences around their pens. Red slime glistened in the blackness that now covered the mountain. A gray light was spreading over Midian, draining it of both color and shadow.

Sefoba was trembling and crying. "Horeb's fire!" she, too, muttered. "Horeb's fire!"

Jethro held out his free arm and pulled her to him tenderly. "Horeb's wrath," he corrected, in a soft, calm voice.

Zipporah looked at him.

He nodded. "He awaits our offerings."

Zipporah could hear no fear in his voice, no anxiety, but rather a curious kind of satisfaction.

◈

ALL day, Horeb continued to rumble. Jets of soot rolled down over the slopes of the mountain toward the sea. Fires sprang up, and here and there bushes burst into flame. The stinking air grew thick with the dust of ashes, which not only extinguished the flames but also choked young birds in their nests. Fortunately, just before the close of day, a violent wind rose in the east, and the clouds being disgorged from the mountain were blown away toward Egypt, sparing Midian further damage from fire.

In the west, the sun was hidden, and a strange shadow spread over the land that was neither night nor twilight. The slime flowing down from the top of the mountain had come to a standstill and had turned to mud; from its disordered folds, smoke rose, and small explosions occasionally glittered, like some monster batting its thousand eyelids as it reluctantly fell asleep. Above, the mouth of the mountain was still incandescent, still wide open to the turbulent sky.

Moses reached Jethro's domain soon after the wind had risen, his beardless cheeks gray with dust, one hand gripping his staff, the other clinging to his camel's ashen fur. He had almost lost his way in the unbreathable fog. His eyes were still wide with terror.

Hobab, who was repairing the ravaged fences with the help of Sefoba's husband, Sicheved, greeted him effusively. "Horeb be praised! We were worried about you."

They gave him water to wash himself, and wine, dates, and cakes dipped in oil to take the taste of ashes from his mouth.

"You've come just in time," Hobab said, once Moses had eaten his fill. "A lot of our animals took fright and ran away. We must find them before they get lost and die of thirst because of all this ash. Come with us; you won't be in the way. The others are with my father, helping him with his offerings and prayers to Horeb."

Until nightfall, they searched for the mules and sheep. Whenever they caught an exhausted, trembling animal, they quickly hobbled it and immediately began their search again. By the time it was too dark to continue, they had gone too far to return to Jethro's domain. Sicheved had been wise enough to put a saddlebag on his camel with canvas and posts to make a tent. They settled down to spend the night, sharing the gourd and dates Hobab had brought. The mountain had stopped rumbling, but its mouth still glowed red in the darkness, stoked by the wind. Hobab and Sicheved stood with their palms open, and offered up a prayer to Horeb. Moses listened, his body turned away, his head tilted. A sharp, distant rumble seemed to answer them. More strongly than at any other time that day, Moses had the strange feeling that the mountain was alive, like a wild animal. Neither Hobab nor Sicheved flinched. Their calm impressed him. This had been a day when the whole world had seemed about to explode, and yet they went about their work without showing any fear. It was not until later, as they sat outside the tent, slowly chewing a few dates, that he asked the question he had held back until then:

"Why aren't you afraid? The mountain is still rumbling, the fire might spread and destroy everything."

"That doesn't seem to be the will of Horeb," Hobab replied. "The wind has risen and is taking the ash out to sea. It won't harm the pastures or the wells. And the mountain has stopped spitting fire."

In the darkness, Sicheved indicated the sky in the east. "Look, the stars are shining over Moab and Canaan. That's a good sign. Whenever Horeb is angry but the sky is still clear in the east, then his rage passes and we're spared."

Moses was astonished. Did it happen often, then? Sicheved and Hobab outdid each other in eloquence, describing Horeb's most terrible rages, which had sometimes come close to destroying Midian.

"The only rages I've known have been gentle ones," Sicheved said in conclusion. "They say it's thanks to Jethro and the justice he's brought to the kingdoms of Midian. Horeb is quite lenient with us."

Hobab agreed with a proud growl.

"But why do Jethro and all of you sacrifice to Horeb and not to the god of Abraham?" Moses asked. "Jethro claims that you're Hebrews, and even sons of the sons of Abraham."

Hobab gave a little laugh. "You should ask him that. He's the sage."

There was a long silence, broken suddenly by Sicheved's snoring. He had fallen asleep before he had even had time to get inside the tent.

"Tomorrow," Hobab said in a low voice, as they lay down side by side, "we'll go back, and you can speak to my father about Zipporah." Moses immediately sat up, but Hobab placed a hand on his shoulder. "Have no fear, I'm on your side. I'm happy with your choice. I love Zipporah. Like everyone else, I used to think she would never find a husband. Nothing could please me more than to have you as my brother. I know you'll make her happy. Even if she isn't always the easiest of women."

Moses sighed and shook his head. "Think again, Hobab! Zipporah doesn't want me. When I told her I'd go to your father and ask for her hand, she said no. And now I don't know what to do. I'm at fault with her, your father, and all of you. But she's the only woman I want."

Hobab laughed. "Be patient. Zipporah loves to do things in her own way. You mustn't let these doubts make you sad. All she wants is you. My father, too. It's rare for Zipporah and him to disagree, and she always obeys him in the end."

Moses sighed again, not totally convinced.

"Speak to my father tomorrow," Hobab insisted. "He will command. He seems the most amiable of men, but once he's made his mind up, it stays made up. He's certainly made his mind up about Orma!" Hobab gave an amused, affectionate chuckle. "He's told the handmaids to calm her down with a lot of kindness and a lot of cakes and sweet drinks. But then I'll have the job of escorting her to Reba, the son of the king of Sheba, the man she should have married moons ago. Feel sorry for me, Moses! I'm the one who'll have to listen to her whining day and night. She'll talk about you, you can be sure of that. She'll talk until she's breathless. But I tell you this. You won't have Jethro's most beautiful daughter in your bed, and you'll be very lucky. May Horeb forgive Reba much in

advance! Nor will you have the gentlest of Jethro's daughters —
she's already married, and her husband is right here, snoring away.
The one who's left is the wisest and the liveliest. You'll see! You'll
be kept so busy you won't have time to bother with anyone else."

Moses could not help joining in his laughter.

◈

THE wind from the east did not subside, and the mountain rumbled less frequently. The sun finally broke through the clouds,
which were less thick now, creating a strange half-light, as if the
sky in the west were dirty and bloodstained.

Tirelessly, Jethro had performed sacrifice after sacrifice. By his
request, Zipporah had stayed by his side, assisting him in offering
barley and wine, grinding the flour, baking the cakes according to
the rites, opening the fruit, refilling the pitchers of oil. She only left
when he slit the throats of the year's lambs and calves and cut
open the chests of twenty doves.

Not for a moment did she stop thinking about Moses. She
knew that Hobab had welcomed him and had gone with him and
Sefoba's husband to search for the escaped animals. She was full
of gratitude toward her elder brother. It was his own discreet way
of showing everyone his trust and affection for Pharaoh's son.

She knew Moses had returned, and had again pitched his tent
beneath the sycamore. She feared that she would not be able to
resist the desire to go to him. She was told how Orma had shamed
Hobab as the two of them were setting off to see Reba. As they
passed Moses' tent, a tearful Orma had begged him loudly to follow her. Moses had looked at her without a word, made a gesture
of reassurance, and gone back into his tent. But then he left again
with Sicheved to visit the wells and make sure that the ash had not
got inside them.

Finally, on the third morning—the mountain having stopped rumbling the previous day—Sefoba joined Zipporah as she and the handmaids were washing the clothes that had been allowed to get dirty to conserve water during those difficult days.

Pink-cheeked and smiling radiantly, Sefoba knelt beside Zipporah, and placed on a basket the tunic they had woven together for Moses. "You look exhausted. You should get some rest. I'll take your place."

Zipporah returned her gaze. "To judge by the rings under your eyes, you don't seem much fresher than I do."

Sefoba chuckled. "Sicheved came back last night, after dark. He was hungry and thirsty and very grumpy! Men! Horeb rumbles and spits, but we don't look after them enough! I had to spend all night reassuring him of my love."

They burst out laughing. Before their laughter had subsided, Sefoba took Zipporah's hand and placed it on the tunic. "Moses is back," she whispered. "He's with Father now. Rest now, make yourself beautiful, and, when they call you, go to him with this tunic."

Zipporah stiffened.

"Come on!" Sefoba murmured gently. "Forget what you told us. Horeb's wrath has come and gone. Calm down. We're all going to be happy!"

JETHRO greeted Moses as best he could, given that his domain was still in disarray. He sat him down beside him beneath the canopy, and asked the handmaids to bring pitchers of beer, goblets, and something to eat. They ate and drank, watching the white clouds around the summit of the mountain rising straight into the sky, where the wind continued to push them westward.

Jethro's face looked tired and drawn, but there was a sly gleam in his eyes. Pharaoh would soon see his sky grow dark, and perhaps he would not have such rich harvests. Had Moses seen such things when he lived in the land of the Great River Iterou?

Moses evaded the question, preferring to say all he had to say on the subject of Zipporah. But, after three sentences, the words he had long prepared failed him. "You see!" he sighed, angry and ashamed. "I thought I'd made some progress in the language of Midian. But as soon as I have something important to say, all that comes out of my mouth is noise."

"Let me speak, then," Jethro said, shaking his head and laughing. "I, too, have something to ask you." He looked Moses straight in the eyes, his own eyes shining so brightly that it was as if they were still smarting from the smoke of his offerings to Horeb. "I know what is in your heart. Zipporah told me everything. She has also told me about the life you led in Pharaoh's house."

Moses tried to interrupt, but Jethro silenced him with a gesture.

"Let me tell you this. Nothing I have learned surprises me or displeases me. There are things a father prefers not to know, which I shall simply forget. Zipporah is the jewel of my heart. That's the way it is, and, as Orma so cruelly remarked, it has made me an unjust father. You have only seen three of my daughters here. I have four others who live with their husbands, in the kingdoms of Midian. They'll all tell you I love them dearly, that I give them everything they deserve to have. But Zipporah is special."

He sighed, drank a long draft of beer, and again looked up at the top of the mountain. He nodded his head slightly and his mouth quivered in an inaudible murmur. Moses wondered if he was praying, or if he was slightly drunk. But then the old man looked straight at him, with the eyes of a man who has seen much in his life, and Moses was surprised to discover that they were moist with emotion.

"I remember that day as if it were yesterday—the day the boat brought them to our shore, her mother and her. Horeb wanted me to be there. I rarely went to the seashore, but, that day, Hobab, who was still only a little boy, wanted to fish. From the top of the cliff, we saw a boat lying overturned on the shingle and, in the middle of the beach, what looked like a heap of black seaweed. The Cushite mother, exhausted as she was, had taken the child on her back and, with the strength of a lioness, had crawled across the shingle to get away from the waves. She died before she could utter a word, but with her eyes she told me everything she needed to say. Her daughter was not much bigger than my hand. She was bawling with hunger and thirst . . .

"It was the saddest day of my life, and the most beautiful. My beloved wife had been dead for many long years. And now Horeb was providing me with the opportunity to give life! Alas, there was a price to be paid. The woman who had given birth out of her own womb had to perish . . .

"I held the baby against my chest. Swallows were circling overhead. I said, 'Your name will be Zipporah—Little Bird.'"

Jethro paused for a moment, as if the silence might reduce the power of his memories.

"In her way, Zipporah became flesh of my flesh. I brought her up like my own daughters, just as if she had been the fruit of my loins. I gave her everything I could—food, jewelry, trust, and knowledge! Knowledge above all. Even when she was a child, she was wiser and more perceptive than her sisters—and even Hobab. Apart from Orma, everyone felt for her what I myself felt. Nobody was jealous. Alas, Zipporah's skin is black. The men of Midian are men of Midian. Their prejudices blind them more than the sun. How could they recognize her worth?"

"Jethro!" Moses interrupted, picking up his stick, which he had placed across his knees, and shaking it. "Jethro! When I saved your daughters from the hands of the shepherds, I hadn't even noticed Zipporah, hadn't seen whether she was beautiful or ugly, hadn't seen what color her skin or her eyes were. But the moment I saw her, may your god strike me dead if I lie, my one hope was to have her become the woman I spend my days and nights with. It's like a spell cast by one of Pharaoh's court magicians. Whenever she looks at me, I feel confident. When she's by my side, not even the iciest of winds gives me gooseflesh. As soon as she's far from me, I feel cold and weak. My sleep is filled with nightmares, so I spend my nights with my eyes open, thinking about her. It isn't me you have to convince, Jethro, it's her. It's Zipporah who doesn't want me. Ask her, you'll see."

Jethro laughed, curling his thick beard with his thin fingers. "Listening to you, my boy, I take note of two things: that you are now much more fluent in our language than you think, but that you still know nothing at all about women. Anyone would think you had never met any women in Pharaoh's house."

Moses lowered his eyes.

Jethro stopped laughing and called a handmaid. "Ask my daughter Zipporah to join us."

Moses became agitated, opening and closing his mouth like a fish out of water, which made Jethro burst out laughing again.

"Trust what my eyes tell me, my boy. My daughter Zipporah looks at you as she has never looked at any other man. Her one desire is to be your wife. She'll tell you so herself."

❖

"IF you're talking about what I want," Zipporah replied curtly when Jethro asked her the question, "you're right, Father. I have no other desire than to be Moses' wife. It's even a necessity, if I don't want to remain a *naditre*, a fallow woman, as they say in Midian, and bring shame on you."

"Good!" Jethro cried, slapping his thigh. "Your wedding feast will be soon, then."

"No!"

"Oh?"

"For the moment, it cannot be." Zipporah's face was as hard as her words.

"Oh . . . ," Jethro repeated, although he did not seem too upset. "Sit down, I beg you, and give me your reasons."

Without looking at Moses, who was nervously rolling his staff between his hands, Zipporah knelt on a cushion and sighed. "What's the point of explaining to you what you already know, Father?"

"Does Moses also know your reasons?"

"Moses knows. But he thinks he is a shadow. He cannot walk in the footsteps of what he has been, but neither does he want to embrace his destiny. What good would a Cushite be to him? And what good would one more shadow be to a Cushite? What a burden!"

Twice already, Moses had tightened his grip on his staff, as though he were about to stand up and leave. He had hoped for Jethro's support, but the old sage seemed to take a wicked pleasure in his daughter's replies. Hobab had been wrong: Jethro was not going to come to a decision and force Zipporah to his will. He merely rolled a few hairs of his beard around his fingers and observed, "You're really hard, daughter."

"She isn't hard, Jethro, she just isn't thinking straight!" Moses cried. "'Go to Pharaoh,' she says, 'and tell him that what he's doing to the Hebrew slaves is unjust!' Jethro! Jethro! If I show myself to Pharaoh, he'll kill me! I won't have time to open my mouth. The slaves themselves don't fight Pharaoh, even though there are thousands of them. They just submit to their punishment. Who am I to help them? Why should I succeed where all of them fail?"

"Because you're you, Moses!" Zipporah cried. "Not only the son of a slave woman, but also the son of the queen of Egypt."

Moses waved his staff as if he wanted to break it in two, and roared almost as loudly as Horeb. "Jethro! Jethro, tell your daughter she's wrong! Thutmose refused Amon's boat to the woman who was my mother. He's had all her statues torn down. Why should he listen to me? What would the Hebrews gain from my making him even angrier?"

"There is truth and wisdom in what you say," Jethro admitted.

"Of course!" Moses exclaimed in relief.

Zipporah remained impassive.

Jethro was silent for a while. "What do you think of that, daughter?" he asked her at last, tilting his head.

Zipporah turned to face Moses. She seemed as determined as ever, but there was a touch of tenderness in her look now. "There are always many reasons not to do what we fear. Often they seem like wise reasons. But anything bred by fear is always evil. Lift your eyes to the summit of the mountain, Moses, and see in which direction Horeb is sending the clouds of his wrath."

"Horeb isn't my god!" Moses said, irritably.

"That's true," Jethro said, having nodded his head at each of Zipporah's sentences. "Horeb isn't your god. He's our god, the god of the sons of Abraham and those who suffer Pharaoh's whip."

Moses flushed and lowered his head.

Zipporah took his hand. "Moses, I had a dream, and for moons I searched for its meaning. When you arrived, I finally understood it. Horeb rumbled to greet your arrival among us. He is speaking to you."

"Is that so?" Moses mocked. "Who am I listening to now? Jethro's wise daughter or a superstitious old housewife?"

Zipporah rose to her full height, her lips quivering. "Listen to this, then: As long as I live, no man other than you will touch me or be my husband. But you will only be Jethro's son-in-law the day you set off on the road to Egypt."

"You know very well it cannot be!" he cried.

Jethro quickly took both of them by the hand. "Hush now, hush . . . Why assert today what may prove false tomorrow? Life is made of time, and so is love."

The Firstborn

J ethro had told them to take their time, and it was a
strange time that now began. For more than a year,
Zipporah and Moses alternated between quarrels
and lulls.

At first, they carefully avoided each other for days on end.
Then, one night when the moon was full, the earth shook again.
Jethro's household was in a panic. Everyone rushed out into the
darkness, eyes and ears alert. There was rumbling, but it was weak,
almost gentle. The summit of the mountain was surrounded by a
huge halo of pinkish light. Everyone feared that the times of wrath
had returned, and the men remained watchful. Moses was also
standing outside his tent, beneath the sycamore. He did not see
Zipporah until she was quite close.

Neither said a word, but stood there with their faces lifted
toward the mountain.

"Listen!" Zipporah said at last, in a low voice. "Listen! Horeb
is speaking to you."

Moses laughed deep in his throat and turned to her. They

were both trembling with desire. Moses stroked the line of Zip-porah's lips. "It's your mouth that's speaking to me. That's what I want to hear. Its silence consumes my nights."

Moses moved his fingers down from her lips to her neck, then to the hollow of her throat. Zipporah seized his wrist as if to push him away, but all she could do was cling to him and receive his kiss like the breath of life.

Before long, their caresses impelled them inside the tent, bodies entwined, heedless of anything that was not their love.

In the morning, when Sefoba, who guessed that Moses and Zipporah had been overcome with passion, reproached her, Zipporah answered with a laugh that it was perhaps that very passion that had appeased Horeb. Moses had, in fact, awoken at dawn and, finding himself alone in the tent, had rushed out, calling Zipporah's name, scattering the birds out of the sycamore, to find that the sky was a limpid blue as far as the eye could see. A few wisps of smoke hovered over the summit of the mountain. Horeb had stopped rumbling. Never had Midian seemed more peaceful.

Before nightfall, Moses went to see Jethro and asked him the question he had asked Hobab on the day the ash had fallen: "Why do you sacrifice to Horeb rather than the God of Abraham, if you are his sons?"

Jethro nodded, paused a moment for reflection, and replied with another question: "What do you know of the God of Abraham and Noah?"

"Only what I heard from the Hebrews in Egypt—that he had abandoned them."

Jethro sighed. "He abandoned us because we were no longer worthy of his trust. A long time ago, a very long time ago, he offered his covenant to Abraham. 'Go,' he told him, 'I will make you a great nation, I will uphold my covenant between me and you and your children and all their children. . . .' Abraham obeyed and gave birth to sons and nations. There was a time when everywhere, from horizon to horizon, men and women were protected by the God of Abraham, whom they called the Everlasting. But generations passed and men became men and gave rise to as much hate and wickedness as there are nations, sons, and brothers. In return for his covenant, they offered the God of Abraham only sand. So the Everlasting withdrew, full of wrath. That is all we have left of him now. This wrath that rumbles over our heads, this wrath we call Horeb."

Jethro paused, closed his eyes, raised his hands, palms open, then clapped them together and nodded vigorously.

"That is the truth, my boy. All we have left of our ancestors' great covenant with the Everlasting, who brought them out of nothingness, is darkness and wrath. With every day that passes, Horeb's wrath feeds on our sins. He demands justice and righteousness. He watches us, impatiently. He knows our past, but he also knows the future that awaits us. He sees that we are advancing into darkness. In his impatience, he rumbles to shake us out of our torpor. But all he obtains in return is fear, even though what he wants is a little courage and dignity!"

Jethro had become so impassioned that Moses felt afraid as he listened to him. In the words of the sage of Midian he heard an echo of Zipporah's words. Moses could no longer be in any doubt that father and daughter thought as one.

◇

AT the end of spring, Zipporah announced that she was with child. Jethro was the only one to take the news in his stride. The others, including Sefoba and Hobab, all urged her to accept Moses as a husband in order not to bring a child into the world alone.

"Alone?" Zipporah would reply. "My mother was much more alone than I when she put me in the boat that brought us to Midian. I have all of you. I have my father Jethro."

"Moses has been entrusted with a great task," she would continue when they objected. "Who knows if he'll be able to fulfill it? It is a heavy task, a terrible one. But my promise remains: The day he sets out for Egypt, I will be his wife."

They would respond with grimaces and assertions that Moses would never have the courage.

"You mustn't think he's a coward!" she would retort. "The only reason he refuses to return to Egypt is that he doesn't yet know who he is. Perhaps he'll finally know when he sees his child."

Meanwhile, Moses fretted and fumed. Despite the desire that set his body aflame, he did not dare approach Zipporah for fear of her reproaches. He was told that she was in good health, and that her belly was starting to swell. Then he would hear of things she had said about him that sent him flying into a rage, and he would set off with his flock and be away for days on end. But he would always end up missing Zipporah. He would come back and lurk near Jethro's domain in the hope of seeing her, then, once he had, would retreat to his tent, tense with desire, his beloved's new silhouette imprinted on his brain: still standing straight and tall, but with a round belly. He would spend all night thinking about the face he had glimpsed, her skin bronze in the evening sun, her almond eyes, the delicacy of her nostrils. He would clench his fists and moan like a caged beast, desperate for her heavy breasts and the curve of her back.

Whenever Hobab and Sicheved, with whom he often shared his meals, plied him with questions, he would reply: "I'm becoming skillful as a shepherd. Is there anything wrong in that? Do the women of Midian despise shepherds? What more could a mother expect for her child than a good shepherd to watch over them?"

They would laugh and joke about what women, wives, and

mothers wanted and didn't want. Sicheved would mock Sefoba, who was always waking him in the middle of the night to make sure he was still devoted to her.

But these moments of gaiety did not last long, and Moses would soon resume his grim mood. "There is no man alive," he would mutter darkly, "who could rise up against Pharaoh and defeat him. Of course I could take the road to the west with my beautiful Cushite wife. We'd be captured before we even reached the banks of the River Iterou. Much good that would do the Hebrews! Is that my great destiny—to lead my wife into the lions' den?"

One dawn, at the end of his tether, before anyone had risen, he went and knelt by the side of Zipporah's bed. She woke up and saw him. His beard had grown again, and was now thicker than ever and cut in the Midianite fashion. He looked quite different now from the man who had possessed her in the cave.

She smiled and, without a word, took his hand and placed it on her soft, taut skin, beneath which life throbbed. Moses savored the caresses he had so long awaited. It was a moment of pure joy. But the caresses ceased, and they looked at each other in embarrassment.

Zipporah smiled again. "Whenever you want to see my belly," she whispered, "there's no need to roam the pastures with your flock. Just come to me."

Moses blushed. "But we are in sin. I don't even dare share a meal with your father. He's always saying that nobody acts justly these days, nobody behaves the way his ancestors did . . ."

Zipporah could not help laughing. "Oh, if you're talking about sins like that, Jethro's ancestors committed lots of them. Even worse ones!"

She told him the story of how Abraham had persuaded Pharaoh that Sarah was his sister.

"He, too, was afraid of Pharaoh. And Pharaoh was so attracted to Sarah that he didn't want any other woman, even though he had spent only one night with her."

"And what did he do when he learned the truth?"

"He expelled Abraham and Sarah from Egypt, cursing them for his lost happiness. But Abraham was never punished by his God for that sin, even though it's one of the worst anyone can commit."

Moses was so astonished that he asked Zipporah to tell him everything she knew about Abraham. And so it was that they often came together early in the morning or at twilight, before and after the daily chores. Moses would stroke Zipporah's belly while she told him what Jethro had taught her about the Hebrews. Moses could hardly believe what he heard. Sometimes, he doubted Zipporah's words, thinking she was either embellishing the stories or making them darker to provoke him, and he would run to Jethro.

"Is it true," he would ask, "that Noah and his household were the only people left alive on earth? Really the only ones? Is that possible?"

Jethro would laugh and nod his head. "Listen to my daughter!" he would reply. "Listen to my daughter!"

But Moses would return with other questions. "Zipporah says that Lot had sons from his daughters? Is that true?"

Or else it was Abraham's anger at his father, Terah, that he found hard to accept. Or the jealousy of Joseph's brothers. The fact that Joseph, after being sold to Potiphar, had become almost a brother to Pharaoh and had saved the country from famine, was what shook him most.

To each of his questions, Jethro would laugh and give the same reply: "Listen to my daughter! Listen to my daughter!"

Zipporah was pleased that Moses was so interested in these stories. To her father, though, she would express her impatience. "He listens, but does nothing. His child is about to be born, and he still hasn't decided to be what he must be."

"You must be patient," Jethro would say to calm her. "He's

listening and learning. Time is doing its work in his head as it is in your womb."

One day, Zipporah broke off in the middle of her story. Her eyes were wide, her body shook, and she was having difficulty breathing. At the very moment she cried out in pain, Moses leaped to his feet. Zipporah regained her breath and mustered enough strength to smile, seeing him looking so pale and lost.

"Call Sefoba. Call the handmaids!"

Soon, the old woman who acted as a midwife was growling orders in the courtyard. Sefoba and the handmaids held Zipporah over the bricks of labor until the sun was more than halfway across the sky.

Moses, Hobab, Sicheved, and a few others took their places around Jethro and were served beer and wine. They could hear Zipporah's moans through the walls. Moses' brow glistened with sweat. With each cry, he swallowed a mouthful of wine. By the time Zipporah's cries were joined by a baby's, he was in a drunken sleep and did not hear anything.

THE boy was resting, tiny and pink, between Zipporah's breasts. He had her broad face, but Moses' skin.

"That's good," Zipporah said, in a husky voice. "The more he resembles Moses, the better."

She fell asleep without difficulty. In the morning, Jethro came to see her. He seized her hands, his eyes bright with joy.

"It is you," she said to him, "who will choose the name of my son and will cut his foreskin according to the tradition of Midian."

"The name is easy," Jethro replied, lifting the child. "We'll call him Gershom—'the Stranger.'"

When Moses learned that his son would have to lose a piece

of his tiny member on Horeb's altar, he protested. "Do you want to kill him when he's just opened his eyes? Do you want to make him impotent?"

"They did it to me when I was born," Jethro replied, without taking offense. "As you can see, I'm still alive and I've had seven girls and a boy."

Moses was not appeased. Jethro explained that the God of Abraham had demanded that his covenant be inscribed in the skin of all his sons. "We still do it here in Midian, because it's the last link we have with our ancestors."

"That doesn't apply to my son! I'm not from Midian—Zipporah even less so."

He went to see Zipporah. "It isn't possible," he told her. "You can't do that to my son."

"Who are you to speak in the name of your son?" Zipporah replied, angrily. "Do you think that just because you took your pleasure between my thighs, you can decide his fate? Until you are my husband, my father Jethro will be a father to the child of my womb."

Moses felt so ashamed that for a hundred days he stayed away from Jethro's domain and did not see Gershom again.

With tears in his eyes, he watched the circumcision from a distance and heard Jethro cry the name of his firstborn before the altar of Horeb: *Stranger! Stranger!*

Each time he echoed the voice of the sage of the kings of Midian, repeating Gershom's name as if hugging his son to his chest.

The Bride of Blood

Zipporah learned how to be a mother. Gershom filled her nights with cries and tears she soon calmed, and her days with adorable grimaces that gradually turned into smiles. She learned to fasten her tunic in such a way as to carry her child with her at all times, to guess when he was hungry or thirsty simply through the touch of his skin, to think of him every moment of the day, to share his joys and fears. The women were always with her, giving her endless advice, sometimes mildly reproaching her.

All this female hustle and bustle kept Moses at a distance. Zipporah never asked for him to be allowed to approach her or their child. For several moons, they seemed to completely ignore each other. Sefoba, just once, remarked, with a touch of sharpness in her voice, that Gershom's name suited him all too well.

"Stranger! He's certainly a stranger to his father! It's almost as if he'd been born through the good graces of one of Horeb's angels."

The handmaids chuckled. Her eyes blacker than her skin,

Zipporah silenced them. After that, Sefoba had to do all her grumbling at night to her husband. Sicheved would advise her to be as patient as Jethro and her sister.

"They know what they're doing. Moses is the best of men. Things will change, you'll see. Even Hobab makes a joke of it. 'According to Moses,' he says, 'there's no man alive who can rise up against Pharaoh. What he doesn't know is that there's also no man alive who can go against the will of my father and Zipporah!'"

But if any found fault with the unusual conditions in which Gershom was being raised, they did so far from the ears of Jethro and his daughter.

Winter came. It was once again time to trade. Moses set off with the other men to Edom, Moab, and Canaan. Ewi-Tsour, the head of the armorers, joined the caravan, his carts so heavily laden with bone-handled knives, curved daggers, and long hammers that each cart required four mules to pull it.

When their return was announced, Zipporah climbed onto a silo to see the dust raised by their caravan in the distance. Like all the wives in the household, she hurried to make herself beautiful. She put on a bright yellow tunic, embroidered with a red-and-blue woolen design in the shape of a bird's wings. She adorned herself with necklaces and bracelets and, for once, used kohl to make her eyes sparkle. Sefoba, herself splendid beneath her long veil, brought her a piece of amber. Zipporah rubbed her wrist with it, breathed in its heavy, spicy odor, and put it away in a linen pouch.

"Why not scent yourself straight away?" Sefoba protested.

Zipporah laughed tenderly. "Moses isn't here yet and I don't know what he has in mind. But, if need be, my hips and thighs will smell of amber for him."

FOR three days, Jethro's domain came alive with banquets, dances, and games. The air smelled of bindweed, coriander, and dill. Chirruping like flights of curlews, the young handmaids filled the big jars with bitter milk and beer, and mixed the wine with rosemary and date juice. The older handmaids took the gazelles that had been killed in the desert, stuffed them with almonds, pomegranates, and grapes, and skewered them on long pikes that were left to turn over low fires for a whole day. Ten more fires were lit to make honey cakes in leek and fennel mince, pies filled with dates, barley, and lambs' entrails, *kippu* broths, and crusty biscuits baked in sheep fat until golden.

Hobab, Sicheved, and the armorers were proud of how much they had sold. In Canaan and Edom, on the other side of the great deserts of the Negev and Shour, there was much fear of further raids by Pharaoh's soldiers, and the rich and powerful masters of the cities of Boçra, Kir, and Tamar had stocked up with arms and animals without quibbling over prices. Even Moses, who had set out with his meager flock, did not return empty-handed.

No sooner had he pitched his tent beneath the sycamore than he rushed to Jethro's domain. He found Zipporah outside her room, fussing over Gershom's cradle with the handmaids. The sight of the woman who was not his wife took his breath away.

Zipporah was again as slender as she had been before her son's birth. In addition, there was a calm about her, which seemed to give her body a stronger outline, her hips and breasts an extra fullness. Her thick hair was cut short, emphasizing the refinement of her features, the breadth of her temples, the elegant curve of her cheekbones. Everything in her testified to a new, serene strength. Even her lips, rounded in a tranquil smile, seemed shaped by all the words she had whispered to calm her child's fears.

She greeted Moses with a certain formality and ordered the handmaids to leave. She lifted Gershom out of his tiny bed and, for the first time, placed him in Moses' arms. Moses laughed, purred like a tamed beast, and at last brandished Gershom in his hands, surprised at the size of the little creature moving about in his huge palms.

"I seem to have been gone for so long, my son ought to be able to stand and say his father's name by now," he joked.

Zipporah nodded and withdrew to the doorway. They both felt awkward. They did not know what to do with their eyes or their bodies, and could not bring themselves to utter the words they had murmured to each other during their solitary wait. Moses tried to put his son back in the cradle. He was clumsy about it, and Zipporah went to help him. As she did so, she brushed against him with a little laugh that made them both tremble. Hurriedly, Moses searched in the canvas sack he was carrying over his shoulder and took out a long, narrow length of material, on which thick purple stripes alternated with thinner indigo stripes that shone like bronze.

"In the great cities of Canaan, like Guerar or Beersheba, the noblest women wear these around their heads. It suits them well enough, though to my taste their skins were too light. I immediately thought of you and bought one."

As he placed the cloth in Zipporah's hands, their fingers touched, and he immediately squeezed her fingers in his and raised them to his mouth. Zipporah had to use all her willpower to resist the desire to huddle in his arms, to demand his caresses and to smell on his neck the almost forgotten scent of love.

"Go to my father," she stammered, in a toneless voice. "He's dying to see you."

Moses tried to draw her to him, but she gently pulled away, taking advantage of a wail from Gershom. She leaned over the wicker cradle and began singing to him. She broke off to look up at Moses.

"Go to Jethro."

JETHRO was beside himself with joy at the return of his son and son-in-law. When Moses came to pay his respects, the old sage moved his scrawny body and stroked the arm of the man who was not his daughter's husband as if he wanted to make sure he was definitely alive. Moses placed a tall goblet of chiseled silver in front of him.

"You can either use it to make wine offerings to Horeb or to quench your own thirst," he said, with affectionate mockery.

"Both!" the old sage cried. "May Horeb protect you! Definitely both!"

"There's also a young she-camel outside my tent to replace the one you gave me when I arrived."

Much to the surprise of Hobab and Sicheved, Jethro accepted the she-camel unreservedly. His cheeks were turning red from the wine, and his eyes shone as he ran his fingers over the beautifully carved engravings on the outside of the goblet. Moses' behavior seemed to delight him more than anything in the world. "Did you meet any caravans coming from Egypt?" he asked, without any change of tone, after they had talked about the main events of the journey.

Hobab shook his head. "No. The merchants who trade with Egypt have stopped passing through Canaan, for fear of pillaging by Egyptian soldiers."

Jethro nodded. "That's why they passed this way while you were gone! It's a long way around Horeb's mountain, and you need good guides, but it seems to have become the surest route to reach the plains of the River Iterou."

He fell silent, and so did Hobab and Sicheved. They knew Jethro well enough to know that he had not questioned them only to arouse Moses' curiosity. But Moses simply rubbed his staff between his palms in a nonchalant gesture with which everyone was familiar by now. Jethro nodded and put down the silver goblet. He clicked his tongue and, in the tone he used for ceremonies, declared:

"This is what I've heard, my boy. According to the merchants, the land of the River Iterou is buzzing with rumors and plots. It's being whispered that the woman who used to be Pharaoh is not dead. According to some, she's confined to one of her palaces. Others think her ex-husband is keeping her in her father's tomb. Apparently, it isn't considered good to have been in the queen's affections, or even simply her servant. The merchants also say that the lives of the Hebrew slaves have become harder than ever, with all the bricks they're forced to produce, all the stones they're forced to carry, all the walls they're forced to build. Hundreds are dying every day, and still Pharoh's whip is not stayed."

Moses was already on his feet, his face ashen beneath the tan he had acquired on his long journey. Jethro did not take offense at his rudeness.

"I questioned these merchants as you would have done, my boy. I asked them if anyone in Egypt had mentioned a man named Moses. 'That's a name we never heard,' they replied. 'Even among the Hebrew slaves?' I asked. 'Who knows what names the slaves whisper to each other?' they replied. 'We're not really allowed to get close to them.'"

Moses had walked away.

"Moses," Jethro called in a loud voice. "Think of this: The woman who was your mother is alive, a victim of the same hatred that made you leave Egypt. If the Hebrews don't need you, she does. She has been humiliated by her own family for having made you a son of Pharaoh, and now she has but one hope left: to see your face before her eyes close. That much I know. She loved you; she gave you her name. You may not share ties of blood, but surely you are tied to her through the childhood caresses she gave you. And I also know that a man lives a better, freer life when he can say farewell to his own mother."

Moses had kept his back turned while Jethro was speaking. Now he wheeled around. "Nobody has the right to tell me what my duty is!" he screamed, brandishing his staff and pointing it at Horeb's mountain. "Not even those rocks and stones and sterile dust you take to be your god, Jethro!"

His tunic swaying as he moved, he strode to the other end of the courtyard and disappeared. His departure was followed by a shocked silence.

A stunned Sicheved made as if to stand up. "He can't say such things!"

Jethro calmly gestured to him to remain seated. "All that shouting is like the squeaking of a badly fitted door," he said, smiling tenderly. "He still refuses to understand that it's the whole building that won't stand up."

"But he's insulted Horeb," Sicheved insisted.

"Unless it's his proud way of imploring his help?"

"What upsets me," Hobab said, in a disappointed tone, "is that he refuses to speak to us. He never once talked about Egypt or Zipporah during the journey. And now here he is, running away like a thief."

"Because he thinks he is a thief!" Jethro cried. "He thinks he stole what he is. He's fighting his own shadow and his own heart."

He seemed quite unconcerned, and went back to admiring the goblet Moses had given him. Hobab and Sicheved still looked disapproving. The old sage rolled his eyes slyly and patted his son-in-law's thigh.

"Relax, son, and let time take its course. Horeb is big enough to respond to the insult himself if he feels the need. It's a good thing that Moses is angry with him. That means he's realized he himself lacks the power of eternity. Duty and shame are boiling away in his heart like barley soup that's been overheated. Now the herb of wrath has been added to the mixture. And Horeb knows all about wrath."

◆

ZIPPORAH crept out of Jethro's domain, carrying her son in a basket. Laughter and the music of flutes and drums could be heard from where the dancing continued. Zipporah had tied the cloth from Canaan around her head, and it gleamed in the light of the torches. There was no fire outside Moses' tent. He was sitting on a worn cushion, motionless. When he heard her steps, he turned and lifted his face to her, a face made hard by the moonlight. He watched her in silence as she put down the basket. The child's face was barely visible in the darkness.

Without a word, Zipporah took a few steps away. "Where are you going?" he asked.

"To find wood for the fire," she replied, over her shoulder.

By the time she returned, Gershom had woken up and was babbling merrily in Moses' unsteady arms.

Zipporah lit the fire with the flame of an oil lamp. Then she unfastened her tunic and gave the child her breast. Moses watched her like a man who has just awoken from a troubled sleep. The flames rose, revealing Zipporah's beauty, the coppery tones of her face as she held it tilted toward the child, the silky colors of the cloth from Canaan shining like a diadem on her brow.

When Moses finally spoke, it was in a low voice, as if he was afraid of scaring his son: "Your father said what he had to say."

Zipporah nodded. She took Gershom off her breast, deftly

refastened her tunic, and put the child on her shoulder. Like a little animal, he nestled his head against her neck. Gently, she swayed back and forth, humming quietly, so quietly that the vibration of her voice passed from her body to Gershom's.

Moses did not take his eyes off her. Although his face was still full of anxiety, he made a small gesture of approval. Time passed. He pointed to Jethro's domain, where the music and the sounds of merriment could still be heard. "Why didn't you stay and enjoy the celebration with them?" he asked.

Zipporah smiled, a beautiful smile that glowed in the firelight, and kissed the child's hand. "Because you're here."

"Does that mean you finally agree to be Moses' wife?"

She shook her head, still smiling. "No."

Moses closed his eyes and clenched his fists against his chest. Zipporah thought he was about to fly into a rage. When he opened his eyes again, he stared at the fire as if he wanted to throw himself into it.

They remained like that for some time, strangely patient and reserved, waiting for their child to fall asleep. Just once, Moses reached out his hand and put more wood on the fire. Sparks flew up into the branches of the sycamore. Gershom finally drifted into sleep. Carefully, Zipporah laid him in his basket. Then she came back, knelt by Moses, and embraced him.

"There hasn't been a single night that I haven't fallen asleep thinking about you," she said softly, her mouth close to his ear, "and there hasn't been a single day that Gershom hasn't opened his eyes without my whispering his father's name in his ear."

"So why are you still so stubborn? Anyone would think we were at war."

She put her hand over his mouth, pressed her lips to his neck, and began to run her fingers feverishly over his body. She stood and drew him up with her, kissing his chest through the

tunic. "Zipporah! Zipporah!" Moses muttered, as much in suppli-
cation as in protest. She kissed him with a fury that made them
both sway, and pushed him inside the tent. In no time at all, she
undressed him. When she took hold of his member, he made as
if to push her away.

"You did that to the handmaid Murti," she said. "Will you do
it to me?"

"You knew?"

"That morning, when she left your tent, I was standing outside."

She had stepped away. He took hold of her and now he, in
turn, undressed her, his hands and mouth aching for her. He fell to
his knees and pulled her down until she was lying beneath him.

Gasping for breath, Zipporah offered him the scent of amber
on her thighs and loins with just as much voracious impatience
as the people in her father's domain throwing themselves on the
feast.

LATER, they lay together, their bodies intertwined.

"You and your father are both wrong," Moses said. "Why should
I confront Pharaoh in order to see my mother, Hatshepsut? Perhaps, among thousands of slaves, my real mother is also alive. She's
the one I ought to be supporting, not the woman who stole her
child. But she's lost among the suffering multitude, like a grain of
sand in the desert. . . . Besides, Thutmose would be only too pleased
to capture me and use me to add to Hatshepsut's humiliation."

Zipporah listened without replying.

"In Edom, Moab, and Canaan," Moses went on, "they are
preparing for war with Pharaoh. They're being forced into it, and

they dread it. You have to realize, Zipporah: Whole nations tremble before the might of Pharaoh, and yet you and your father keep telling me to go to Thutmose and ask him to lessen the suffering of the Hebrews! It's absurd."

Still Zipporah said nothing. She listened out to make sure the child was sleeping. Her silence disconcerted Moses. He waited for a moment, then sat up.

"It isn't my death I fear," he said, in a louder voice, his irritation growing, "but the use Thutmose will make of it. What good will my corpse be to you and Gershom? I don't understand you! You are almost my wife; all it would take is one word. Why are you so determined not to say it?"

Zipporah lifted her hands and stroked his stomach and chest. "Because," she said in a very low voice, its gentleness softening the sharpness of her reproach, "you are not yet the man who is worthy to be my husband. The man I saw in my dream."

Moses sighed in exasperation and fell back on the bed. Zipporah sat down, smiling tenderly, and continued her caresses. "What you say is perfectly sensible. You're such a sensible man." She kissed his shoulders, chin, and eyes. "And you think that everything that isn't sensible must be madness, don't you? And yet, sensible as you are, you aren't at peace."

Aware of his desire rising, Moses tried to push her away. "The only reason I'm not at peace is because of you and Gershom. We are in sin. To everyone here in Midian, to everyone in your father's house, we are in sin!"

Zipporah sat astride him and drew him into her. "How do you know you're in sin, when you don't even believe in the wrath of Horeb and won't obey his will?"

LESS than a moon later, Zipporah announced to Moses that her blood had not come, and that for a second time he was going to be a father.

He opened his arms to welcome her, and clasped her to him. "We are in sin," he whispered in her ear.

Zipporah pressed her brow to his powerful neck. "My will is the will of Horeb. Listen to him!"

Moses gently pushed her away, and turned with a set expression on his face to Horeb's mountain, as if sizing up an enemy before a battle.

The next day, Sicheved came running and announced that Moses had taken down his tent and set off with his flock, his mule, and his two she-camels in the direction of the mountain.

Jethro greeted the news with a smile, but he was alone in doing so. The next day, Hobab himself returned from the western pastures. Jethro asked him if he had seen Moses on the way to the mountain.

"I was on my way back here yesterday when our paths crossed. I accompanied him until nightfall, trying to warn him about the dangers that awaited him. He didn't open his mouth, but he made it quite clear to me that he would have preferred to be alone."

"That's good," Jethro said. "That's good."

"How can you say it's good?" Hobab retorted, with a vigor that surprised Jethro. "The pastures on the mountain are wretched, and the slopes are dangerous for sheep and camels alike."

"He isn't going there to feed his flock," Jethro replied.

"Then you should have stopped him. It's madness to let him leave like that."

Jethro dismissed the protest with a flick of his sleeve.

"He doesn't know his way about the mountain," Hobab insisted. "He doesn't know where to find springs. He's sure to get lost . . ."

Jethro put his hand on his son's shoulder and pointed at the vaporous clouds swirling around the summit of Horeb. "Calm down. Horeb will take care of him. He'll find his way."

Hobab shrugged his shoulders gloomily, not convinced by his father's assurance.

A few days later, Moses had still not returned. Zipporah spent all her time with Gershom. Not once did she join Jethro when he made his offerings.

"Is Zipporah ill?" he asked Sefoba when she brought him his morning meal.

"If it's an illness to keep your mouth shut and hold back your tears simply out of pride, then yes, she's ill."

"But why?"

"Oh, Father, don't act surprised!" Sefoba said, angrily. "Moses has gone, she's pregnant again, and she still has no husband. Even the handmaids are starting to wonder what'll become of her. It's all because of your stubbornness."

"Hold on a minute!" Jethro cried. "Don't forget that when Moses came to ask me for her hand, she was the one who refused, not me."

"Oh, come on! I know the two of you. If you hadn't supported her and encouraged her in this madness, we would have broken bread at their wedding feast long before now."

Jethro contented himself with an indistinct mutter.

Days passed, and nights, and more days, and still Moses did not come back. Anxiety spread throughout the household. All eyes were on the mountain, and not a day passed when they did not fear that Horeb might give vent to his wrath.

Every morning, at first light, Zipporah went outside and looked up at the sky and the mass of sulfurous matter on the mountain, hoping it would not again come rolling down the slopes and set the air on fire. Her belly was growing, both gently and quickly, as if it were not only a token of the life that Moses had left within her, but also a relentless measure of the time that had passed since his departure.

One afternoon, as she was encouraging Gershom's first faltering steps, Sefoba joined her, all smiles. Zipporah got quickly to her feet, ready to receive the good news. But the words she heard were not those she had been hoping for. The reason for Sefoba's joy was something quite different: She, too, was pregnant at last.

"I've waited so long," she laughed. "And believe me, I haven't just waited. But nothing happened, while you . . ." Sefoba lifted Gershom and smothered him with kisses. "I don't mind telling you now, all this time I was afraid I was sterile, like Abraham's wife!"

She was jubilant, but Zipporah could not muster the strength to share her joy. Her own disappointment was too great. She clutched at Sefoba's shoulders like a drowning woman and burst into tears.

The next morning, as she was going out as usual to look at the summit of the mountain, Hobab came to her side. "The sky has never been so clear since Moses left," he remarked, in a puzzled tone.

They both remained silent for a moment.

"Where can he possibly be?" Hobab murmured. He pointed at the mountain, a thin smile on his lips, the same smile he had had when they had shared their chores and their games as children. "You watch the summit and I the slopes. If he ever makes a fire, we may be lucky enough to see the smoke."

"He won't make a fire," Zipporah replied, a haggard look on her face. "Even here, he never made one outside his tent if it wasn't made for him."

Hobab gave her a pained look, as if he resented the slightest criticism of Moses by Zipporah.

She turned to him, eyes bright and lips aquiver. "In any case, he didn't take anything with him for making a fire. No wood, and no stones either, I'm sure of that."

Hobab put his arm around her shoulders. "There are mouths of fire on the mountain," he said, calmly. "The fire comes out through faults in the rocks. You just have to throw shrubbery into them and you can keep warm when the nights get too cold."

The following morning, Hobab joined her again, and they stood watching the night slowly withdraw from the slopes. He took Zipporah's hand. "Why don't you go to our father at Horeb's altar and help him with the morning offerings?"

Zipporah assented with a pressure of her fingers.

Jethro was delighted to see her, but, despite his joy, he was unable to hide his anxiety. Moses had been far too long on the mountain.

◆

THE whole of spring went by. Summer came, but the heat was still bearable. Not once did Horeb's mountain rumble, and its summit remained serenely clear. The barley harvest was the best in many years, the flocks were not affected by illness, and the caravans, which now passed more regularly on the road to Epha, came back rich from their sales of incense in Egypt. The merchants bought everything the armorers had to sell without counting the cost.

Although—as they were to remember later—the sky over Midian had never been so radiant, it was as if a dark, invisible cloud pressed down over Jethro's domain. Laughter was rare, there were no more feasts, and everyone was grim-faced.

Jethro flew into a violent rage when he discovered that the oldest handmaids had begun to weave mourning garments. He immediately ordered them to be pulled to pieces and burned.

But he could not fight thoughts and silences. Who could sensibly believe that Moses was still alive?

"Would you be able to find his tracks on the mountain?" Zipporah asked Hobab one morning.

Hobab hesitated. He looked down at Zipporah's belly, already heavy with child, and sighed. "It would have been easier a while ago. But now? Who knows how far he climbed? He might be on the other side, where there are no springs."

"What if he's injured and unable to return? What if he's waiting for us to come to his rescue? I've spent days and nights imagining him like that."

Hobab looked at the mountain for a long time, as if it were an animal lying in his path. He knew what his Cushite sister did not dare say. If Moses had died, whether by accident, or through hunger or thirst, his body would have to be found before it was completely devoured by wild beasts. He nodded. "Yes. It's time we knew."

Seven days later, he returned. What he had to report was distressing.

At the western end of the mountain, he had found half of Moses' flock, wandering unattended. Then, over a distance of five hundred cubits, he had seen the faults and ravines strewn with the corpses of the rest of the sheep, eaten by wild animals and birds of prey.

"The flock must have scattered in all directions, scared and with nobody to stop them."

He had continued his ascent, calling Moses' name until he was hoarse. At twilight, barely halfway up, where the dusty slopes were full of stones, fallen rocks, and thornbushes, he had seen the tent.

"What remained of it, anyway. The poles were broken and the canvas had been torn to shreds by the wind."

Hobab had been unable to go on without risking his own life.

"Did you see his mule or camel?" Jethro asked.

"Neither of them." He knew what his father was thinking. "There's nothing up there, Father. Not a blade of grass to chew, not the slightest trickle of a spring."

Jethro glared at him. "Think again, son. There isn't nothing up there. There is Horeb!"

The sage of the kings of Midian could no longer tear himself away from Horeb's altar. Assisted most often by Zipporah, he performed all the rites scrupulously, making ever-richer offerings. He sacrificed ten of the finest sheep in his flock, two heifers, and a young calf. Hobab, seeing his father squander his wealth on a man who was neither a son nor a brother nor even a husband, did not protest once. Sicheved even gave his father-in-law animals from his own flock to be offered to Horeb in his name.

Soon, the courtyard and the surrounding pastures were covered with the thick, black, pestilential smoke of burning meat. They all had to go about holding their noses, but nobody complained. Then, in the hottest part of the day, Zipporah felt the first labor pains, and the linen and bricks were prepared.

The delivery was much quicker than it had been for Gershom. The sun had barely touched the horizon when she let out a final cry. Sefoba, who herself was already big with child, came out into the courtyard and announced that Zipporah had given birth to a boy. But, before the midwife had even cut the cord and placed the baby between Zipporah's breasts, there rose the sound of cries— cries so violent, so terrible, that all the handmaids who had assisted with the delivery trembled. Zipporah, her body still burning from the effort of labor, sat up with a groan. Sefoba opened the door.

"He's back!" a handmaid cried. "He's back!"

Zipporah fell back, the barely born child against her mouth. An icy wave went through her body, freezing the sweat on her skin.

"Moses is back!" Hobab, Sicheved, and the young shepherds yelled all together. "He's here. He's alive. Moses! Moses is here, he's alive."

"He came with you," Zipporah murmured against her child's little cheek. "Your father came with you."

◆

"HIS mule brought him back!" Hobab said, laughing. "It found its way all by itself with him lying on it. It's not in a much better state than he is—shivering with fever and thirst."

"He's breathing," Sicheved cried, "but he won't open his eyes! But it's unbelievable. How can he possibly be alive? How long is it since he last drank anything?"

Sefoba was weeping profusely. "You wouldn't recognize him," she muttered. "His tunic is in shreds. Oh, Zipporah, he looks as if he's made of dust! But he's alive."

Jethro's eyes were bright and his beard shook as he listened to everyone. "Horeb has brought him back to us," he kept repeating. "I told you."

Although her back was still painful from the labor, Zipporah wanted to go to the room where Moses had been laid, but the old handmaid forbade her.

"Your place is here," she ordered, putting the freshly swaddled baby down beside her. "Moses is alive. I'm going to see to him now. Trust me, be happy, and sleep. You can see your Moses tomorrow."

But when, soon after daybreak the next morning, Zipporah went with the child in her arms to see Moses, she had to bite her lips in order not to cry out. Moses had grown so thin that the bones of his temples seemed about to break through the skin. His torso was covered in scratches, his lips were swollen, and here and there his beard and hair had been burned away. There were dark scabs on his arms, and blood and pus oozed from his feet, soaking through the plasters and linen in which they were wrapped. When he breathed, it came out as a sharp, painful whistle, as if his throat were torn.

Zipporah knelt and placed her hands on his burning brow. Moses shivered. She thought his dark eyelids were about to open, but it was only an effect of the fever.

"The wounds on his feet and the scratches on his chest aren't as bad as they look," the old woman said. "They aren't deep, and the plasters will heal them soon. What worries me is his thirst. He must take little sips only. He has a bad fever that's burning his insides and whatever he drinks evaporates too quickly."

After a moment's thought, Zipporah asked for blankets to be brought, undressed, lay down next to Moses, and demanded her child. The old woman refused.

"Make a broth of herbs and meat," Zipporah ordered. "Pass it through a sieve and let it cool down."

"You're going to kill him! A man mustn't touch a woman who's just given birth!"

"I'm not going to kill him. My warmth and the warmth of his newborn son will burn away his fever." The old woman attempted to argue, but Zipporah cut her short. "Do as I say!" she scolded.

A moment later, the old woman returned with Jethro and Sefoba, grumbling about blasphemy and calling on all the members of the household who had gathered outside the door to be witnesses.

Jethro silenced her, and Hobab closed the door. In amazement, they looked at the curious spectacle of Zipporah, Moses, and their son forming a solid mass beneath the blankets. Jethro gave a dry little chuckle and narrowed his tired eyes. "Do as Zipporah asks," he ordered the old handmaid.

She left, cursing. Sefoba helped Zipporah to soak a clean

cloth in cold water from a pitcher, and Zipporah applied it to Moses' cracked lips. The water went into his mouth, and he swallowed with a little moan. At the same moment, the baby woke up and cried out for his milk. Sefoba wanted to pick him up, but Zipporah stopped her.

"Leave him. I'll give him what he wants."

Jethro burst out laughing. "Does my Cushite daughter plan to give birth to her husband after her child?"

IT took Moses four days and four nights to fight the fever and delirium and finally come back to life. In all that time Zipporah did not leave his side, feeding him at the same time as their child, quenching both his thirst and the fires of his memory.

In the middle of the second night, having dozed off, she was awoken by a pain in her hand. Moses was clutching it, his eyes wide open. An oil lamp was burning in the room, but its light was too weak for Zipporah to see if Moses had really regained consciousness. With her free hand, she made sure that her child had not awoken.

"They won't believe me!" Moses growled. "They won't listen! They'll say, 'How dare you speak the name of Yahweh?'" Leaning on his elbow, he pulled so hard on Zipporah's hand that she fell on top of him with a moan of pain. "They'd believe anyone else!"

The door creaked open. Zipporah made out the figure of Hobab.

"He's woken up! He's talking!" Hobab whispered, kneeling beside them. "Moses! Moses!"

But Moses had already released Zipporah's wrist and fallen back into his feverish sleep.

Hobab saw her rubbing herself and grimacing. "He's got his strength back, hasn't he?" he smiled.

Zipporah smiled back at him and gently stroked Moses's brow. He was breathing in rapid little gulps.

"Tomorrow, he'll be even better."

The child beside her wailed. Zipporah drew his cradle close to her. Hobab smiled again and went back to his place on the bed outside the door.

Zipporah was right. The next day, Moses was better. He woke fully during the night. Eyes wide open, half-frightened, half-relieved, trying hard to see in the dark, he discovered Zipporah beside him. "Zipporah?"

"Yes, Moses, it's me."

He touched her, pressed his dry lips to her neck, and embraced her. "I'm back, then!" he stammered.

Zipporah laughed, tears welling up in her eyes. "What was left of you came back on a mule."

"Oh!" He shivered, and Zipporah feared that the fever was returning. "He spoke to me," he said, gripping her shoulders. "He called me. He made me come to him!"

Zipporah did not need to ask who he was talking about. She tried to push him away slightly, but he would not let go.

"I must tell you. He made a fire come out of the mountain. 'Moses! Moses!' he called."

He was becoming agitated, his mouth and hands shaking. Zipporah placed her fingers on his lips. "Not now. Tell me tomorrow. You need more rest. You need to eat and drink to have the strength to tell me." To force him to be patient, she put the baby in his arms. "He came out of my womb just as the mule entered the domain with you on its back."

Moses finally seemed to calm down. He hesitated for a moment, then raised the child to his lips and nodded. "I'll give this one his name. He'll be called Eliezer—'God is my support.'"

Zipporah laughed, and relief spread through her body like a sudden intoxication. She hugged Moses and the child Eliezer.

"You were right," Moses whispered in her ear. "I have to go back to Egypt. I know that now."

THE next day was a day such as nobody in Jethro's household had ever known.

Zipporah finally left Moses' bed. His matting and tunic were changed, he was shaved and scented, and at last, just before the sun reached its zenith, everyone was given permission to come and listen to him.

Jethro was there, sitting on the cushion he had had carried into the room. Hobab and Sicheved were by his side, as was Sefoba, with Gershom on her knees, and Zipporah, cradling Eliezer. Sefoba squeezed Zipporah's hand. The others, the shepherds and hand-maids, both young and old, stood crowded in the doorway, in such a tightly packed group that daylight barely penetrated the room. Moses' voice was not very loud, and sometimes they had to listen very carefully.

"The flame appeared twenty paces from me. Real fire! I hadn't seen fire since the one Zipporah had lit for me beneath the sycamore! I had nothing at that point. My flock was gone, there was no milk left, no dates. I had nothing but the sandals on my feet. But there was the fire! I was so hungry that the only thing I thought of when I saw it was what I could roast on it. It was then that I realized that although the fire was real enough, the thorn-bush in front of it wasn't burning. How is this possible? I thought. Have I lost my mind? So I went closer. Yes, the flames were real flames, I saw that with my own eyes. But the bush was untouched.

The flames were blue and transparent, and they came directly out of the earth, with a soft rumbling noise."

Moses broke off, his eyes lowered. The only sound in the room was his breathing. He lifted his face again and touched his mouth, which still felt painful, with his thumb. His eyes came to rest on Zipporah, who did not flinch. Beside her, Jethro gave a slight nod, a sign of encouragement to continue.

"The flames were real flames, and I heard the voice. 'Moses! Moses! Here I am. Don't come too close! Take off your sandals. This earth is sacred! I am the God of your father, I am the God of Abraham, the God of Isaac, the God of Jacob!'"

Again, Moses fell silent, and this time he stared at those watching him as if the words he had just uttered might cause laughter or shouts. Jethro's beard shook, and he slapped his thigh with the palm of his hand.

"So what did you do?" a woman near the door asked impatiently.

"I covered my eyes," Moses replied, miming the action. "The flames may not have been burning the bush, but they were burning my eyes."

"Don't interrupt him!" Jethro grunted. "Let him tell his story. The next person who speaks will have to go."

They looked at Jethro reproachfully. But it was true that Moses still seemed quite weak. If his story was as long as his absence had been, he would have to marshal his strength, so they let him continue without further interruption.

He spoke of the anger that roared in the voice:

I have seen the whip falling on the shoulders of my people in Egypt. I have heard them cry out beneath the blows of the slave drivers! I have come down to deliver them. Go, Moses! I am sending you to Pharaoh. Bring my people out of the land of Pharaoh. Bring the children of Israel out of Egypt. I shall deliver them from the hands of the

Egyptians and lead them to a good, spacious land, a land flowing with milk and honey! Go, I am sending you to Pharaoh."

"If I go to the Hebrew slaves," a terrified Moses had replied, "and say to them, 'The God of your fathers has sent me to you,' they will ask, 'What is his name?' What shall I say?"

"*'Ehye asher ehye.* I am that I am,' the voice had replied."

"But I was still reluctant," Moses said. "'They won't believe me!' I protested. 'They won't listen! They'll say, "How dare you speak the name of Yahweh?"'"

"'Yet that is what you will say to the children of Israel,' the voice had replied."

Moses had again objected that he was no great speaker, that he was not very fluent in the language of the sons of Abraham, and that there were certainly Hebrews who were wiser, cleverer, and more confident than he was, and who would be more suited for such an important mission.

"Why me? Why me?" he had groaned, just as he had when Zipporah kept repeating, "You must return to Egypt, I've known it since I saw you in my dream!"

Then the voice had exploded with anger. "Who gave man a voice? Who makes him deaf or mute, sighted or blind? Who, if not I, Yahweh? Go, now! Go! I shall be your mouth. I shall teach you what you do not know."

And Yahweh had told Moses what would happen to him when he returned to Pharaoh Thutmose.

"'I know the king of Egypt,' the voice of Yahweh had said. 'I know how hard his heart is. He will not let you go unless I force him to do so! Then I will strike Egypt with all my wonders.'"

"I was even more terrified when I heard that," Moses said. "I gnashed my teeth. 'They won't believe me!' I begged. 'They won't listen!' 'Throw down the staff you have in your hand!' the voice said. So I did as I was told—like this."

And Moses took the staff that everyone knew, the staff he

had used to break the head of Houssenek's son, and threw it to
the floor, in front of the handmaids.

The result was pandemonium. There on the ground was no
longer a staff, but a snake. And what a snake! It was very long—
as long as the height of a man—and black all over. It lifted its
head, blinked with its slit eyes, put out its tongue and hissed.
They had all leaped to their feet: Zipporah with her baby in her
arms, Sefoba, Hobab, Sicheved. Everyone was standing, the
women were screaming, the children were shouting. Only Jethro
remained seated, laughing with his mouth wide open, his beard
shaking with pleasure, while the snake, frightened by all the
excitement, coiled like a whip, as if it might be about to strike or
to escape.

"Don't let it get away!" Moses cried. "Don't let it get away!
I have to pick it up by its tail!"

But he was much too weak to stand, and his arm could not
reach the snake. Sicheved had the idea of throwing a cushion at
the beast, which caused it to retreat with a sinister rustle, and
then Moses was finally able to get his hand on it. There was a
stunned "Oh," followed by a breathless silence.

In his hand, Moses was again holding his staff. No snake, just
his staff. There were more exclamations, more incredulous cries,
as, with a sigh, he put the miraculous staff down by his side. But
before they all went back to their places, hearts still pounding,
Moses raised his right hand for everyone to see and brought it
down violently on his torso.

"Yahweh also made me put my hand in my chest. Believe it
or not, it went right inside my body. When I took it out, it was
white with leprosy. 'Put it back in your breast!' he said to me, and
I did. When I took it out again, there was no more leprosy; it was
as you see it now. That's something I can't repeat, but it's the
truth."

In the stunned silence that followed, they heard Jethro

slapping his thigh. He took Zipporah's arm and forced her to resume her seat. "Sit down, sit down!" he ordered everyone. "Let Moses tell his story!"

This time, Moses had almost finished.

In response to Moses' continued reluctance, the wrath of Yahweh had flared up, setting both his beard and his mind aflame and knocking him back against the rocks. "Do as I command you!" Yahweh had thundered. "Take your staff and go to Egypt. You will not be alone. Your brother, Aaron the Levite, will come to meet you! If you need someone to speak, he can certainly speak! I shall be your mouth, and he will be your mouth if you want him, for you will be a god to him!"

Moses sighed, and shook his head. "How the mule brought me here, I don't know. Any more than I knew I had a brother named Aaron. I'm ashamed I tried so hard to flee Yahweh's will. I couldn't help it. You all knew that Horeb was up there, but how was I to know?"

He seized his staff, provoking more cries of terror. His tired face softened by a half smile, he put the staff back on his thighs. He looked in turn at Zipporah and Jethro.

"Now we must get our children ready to set off on the road to Egypt."

◇

THE days before their departure were so full of activity that nobody had time to think too much about the emotion of the imminent separation. Animals had to be chosen that would form Moses' and Zipporah's flock and provide them with milk and meat, be useful for trading, and make it seem that they were simply shepherds to any soldiers of Pharaoh they might meet on the way. The mules and camels had to be loaded with saddlebags full of grain, dates, jars of olives, linen, big gourds of water, and canvas and poles for tents.

Moses was so impatient that Hobab and Sicheved had only two days to make two cane baskets to be strapped to the backs of the camels. Strewn with cushions and covered with thick canopies, they offered good protection against the sun and would provide reasonable comfort for a long journey.

When Hobab showed his handiwork to Zipporah, he tried to convince her that he should go with her. "Moses is still very weak. He doesn't know the road. What will you do if you meet with brigands?"

"Your place is here," Zipporah replied. "Our father needs you more than we do. Who will lead his flocks to Edom and Moab if you leave? Stay here, support him, and find yourself a wife!"

Far from finding Zipporah's words amusing, Hobab became annoyed. "Sicheved can take my place here; he knows as much as I do. And Jethro will be happy to know I'm with you!"

But still Zipporah refused, gently but firmly. "We fear nothing, Hobab. Moses' god is protecting him. Do you think he's sending him to Pharoah only to let him perish on the way?"

Reluctantly, Hobab bowed to his sister's wishes: after all, the road to Egypt was no longer so unsafe since caravans of Akkadian merchants had started using it. But he sought out good guides to go with them, and had little difficulty in finding four young shepherds from among those who had followed Moses in previous winters.

Meanwhile, Murti and a half-dozen other handmaids came to see Zipporah. "Let us go with you. We'll be your handmaids. We'll take care of your sons. Moses will soon be a king, you'll need handmaids."

"Go and ask my father Jethro," Zipporah replied with a laugh. "It's he who'll decide."

Jethro granted them everything they wanted without even

tening to them. Handmaids wanting to follow Zipporah were the last thing on his mind. For the first time in his long existence, he was at a loss for words, unable to express the immense joy he felt inside him. He made Moses repeat over and over, for him alone, the words the voice had spoken. And, each time, he would clap his hands and kiss Moses, his old body vibrant with jubilation.

"He's come back to us! The Everlasting hasn't forgotten our covenant. His wrath is no longer upon us. Yahweh is again reaching out his hand to the sons of Abraham!"

But it was not long before his joy was tinged with sorrow. The day before departure, it suddenly came home to him that Zipporah was leaving. She would no longer serve him his morning meals, would no longer be by his side for the offerings, would no longer listen patiently to his endless learned chatter. All that day, he remained by her side, following her everywhere as she busied herself with the final preparations, watching her as if trying to imprint her face on his brain. His lips were frozen in a smile, but his beard shook and his eyes looked too bright. He kept wanting to touch her, and he would put his hand on her arm, or brush against her shoulder or the back of her neck. Once, like a young man, he seized her by the waist. Zipporah took hold of his fingers and kissed them with infinite tenderness.

"We'll meet again, Father. We'll meet again, I know. Your days will be tranquil now and at last you'll be able to become a very old man."

Jethro's childlike laughter echoed through the courtyard. "May Yahweh hear your words, may the Everlasting listen to you!" he exclaimed, happily rolling the words in his mouth.

At dawn on the day of departure, as she was breast-feeding Eliezer, two hands closed over Zipporah's eyes. She had no difficulty recognizing their cool scent. "Sefoba!"

Sefoba sat down beside her and covered the child and Zippo-rah's legs with a magnificent blanket on which colored stripes were interwoven with subtly drawn motifs.

"It's beautiful," Zipporah breathed, taking Eliezer off her breast so that she could feel the cloth.

The child screamed, and Sefoba happily took him and pressed him to her tear-dampened cheek. At this contact, Eliezer, sur-prised, fell silent.

Zipporah had spread out the blanket and was now able to clearly see the design that glittered in the morning light against a dark background. "The tree of life!"

"Do you remember that beautiful fabric that Reba gave Orma?" Sefoba asked, cradling Eliezer. "The one she tore the day after Moses arrived?"

Zipporah nodded, stroking with her fingertips the purple-and-gold birds, the ocher flowers, the indigo butterflies perching on the thin branches.

"I kept it for you under my bed," Sefoba sniffled, overcome with emotion. "I always knew that one day my Cushite sister would go away and leave me on my own."

For a long time, while the noise of the animals being formed into a caravan increased outside, Zipporah and Sefoba held each other in an embrace, into which they drew Eliezer and Gershom.

At last, everything was ready, and the caravan prepared to leave Jethro's domain. Moses was in one of the baskets, Zipporah and her children in the other. The whole household bade them a last farewell with much singing and shouting and the sound of flutes and drums. They headed off across the great dusty plain. The baskets disappeared last, swaying in rhythm to the steps of the camels, their canopies fluttering in the wind from the sea, a wind that seemed to spread over the whole of Midian a calm such as nobody had known for a very long time.

IT happened after four days on the road. The camels had been relieved of their saddlebags and the shepherds were pitching the tents. As was now his custom, Moses went off to erect an altar of stones to Yahweh, as Jethro had taught him. By the time he returned, the sun was very low, the shadows were long, and the light blinding. It seemed to Zipporah that there was something strange about the way he was walking, and she stood up to see better.

"Moses!" she cried.

At that moment, he stumbled and went down on one knee. If he had not been holding his staff, he would have fallen. He stood up again and resumed his unsteady walk. Zipporah ran to him and put her arms around him to stop him collapsing.

"What is it? What's the matter?"

He did not reply. His harsh breathing, his pale face, his closed eyes, his drawn lips—everything reminded Zipporah of the way he had been when he had come down from the mountain. The young shepherds came to her aid and together they laid Moses in the tent. Zipporah called for water and linen and put his head on her knees.

As she was cooling his brow, Moses opened his eyes. When he saw her bending over him, he grimaced. "Yahweh is taking my breath from me," he whispered. "My chest is burning."

He moaned and pressed his hands on his torso as if he wanted to tear out his lungs. Zipporah tore off the collar of his tunic in a single move. She stifled a cry. The wounds, which for several days had been no more than light, barely visible scars, were now spread, scarlet and swollen, over Moses' torso.

"Am I still in sin?" he groaned. "But what sin?"

Zipporah was so terrified, she could not think clearly. She

stroked Moses' face. "No, there is no sin, not now. I'll bandage your wounds."

She called for the oils and unguents that the old handmaids had wisely packed in leather bags before their departure. Moses grasped her hand. "How can we go to Egypt," he asked, gathering all his strength, "if Yahweh takes my life?"

Zipporah felt anger and fear well up inside her. "No, it cannot be!" she cried. "Yahweh has returned to bring goodness and justice. He cannot want you to die."

For a moment, Moses lay there with his mouth wide open, like an asphyxiated animal. Then breath returned to him. He gave a grimace that might have been a smile. "Yahweh can do whatever he wishes," he rasped.

"No!" Zipporah protested again. "I know he wants you alive to see Pharaoh! What good would Moses' death be to him now?"

She wanted to rise and beg the God of Moses, but the words she had spoken to Hobab came back to her: "The Everlasting is protecting him. Do you think He's sending him to Pharoah only to let him perish on the way?"

"Nothing has yet been accomplished," she said out loud. "It cannot be. I know you must live."

But why did some of Horeb's anger remain in Yahweh? She had to think carefully, look beyond the pain and the wounds. What had the two of them done wrong?

Oh, if only her father Jethro were here!

Moses shivered. "Yahweh punishes injustice," he moaned in a barely audible, almost delirious voice. "He's trying to remind us of his covenant."

Zipporah opened her eyes wide. "The covenant!" she cried, tears of joy mixing with her tears of terror. "Moses, remember what the Everlasting said: 'This will be the sign of my covenant between you and me.'"

But Moses no longer had the strength to listen and understand.

Zipporah rushed out of the tent. "Eliezer!" she shouted at the terrified handmaids. "Bring me my son Eliezer! And a flint, the thinnest
and sharpest you can find."

Barely able to breathe, Moses opened his eyes when she
returned, her son clasped in her arms.

"Pour mint and rosemary oil in this bowl!" she ordered. "Murti,
go and fetch me a flat stone. And you, bring boiling water, there's
some on the fire, I saw it. The flint needs to be dipped in it. And
linen, bring more linen, there isn't enough!"

As she spoke, she took the swaddling clothes off the child.
Eliezer's cries worried Moses even more than his own pain. "What
are you doing?" he moaned. "What are you doing?"

While the handmaids bustled around her, Zipporah placed
Eliezer's naked little body on the flat stone, by Moses' side.

"What are you doing?" Moses panted.

Zipporah showed him the cutting edge of the flint and tenderly pinched Eliezer's tiny member. "Your God said to Abraham: 'You will be circumcised as a sign of the covenant between
me and you. From generation to generation every child must be
circumcised when he is eight days old. My covenant will be in
your flesh, an everlasting covenant between me and you.' Your
son Eliezer is more than eight days old today, and neither you
nor my father has circumcised him. The Everlasting has called
you so that the covenant between your people and him may be
reborn. But how can that be if your son does not bear the sign of
it according to his will?"

With a steady, confident hand, as if she had been doing this
all her life, Zipporah dipped the flint in the herb-scented oil and
brought it down on her son's foreskin. The cry that Eliezer gave
was not much louder than those he was already making.

Without waiting, she picked up her son and raised him above
Moses. "Lord Yahweh, God of Abraham, God of Isaac and Jacob,
God of Moses! Oh Lord Yahweh, listen to Eliezer's cries. Your

covenant is in his flesh, an everlasting covenant. Look, Lord Yah-
weh, Moses' son, his second son, has been circumcised according
to your law. Oh Lord Yahweh, listen to the voice of Moses' wife,
Zipporah. I am only what I am, but receive my son, the son of
Moses, among your people. Lord Yahweh, may the blood of
Eliezer, may the cut foreskin of Moses' son, wipe out Moses' sin.
You need him, and I need him. I who am his wife by the blood of
Eliezer. Oh Lord Yahweh, I am your servant and, although my skin
is black, I am your people."

When she had finished, there was a curious silence that
surprised them all, until they realized that Eliezer had stopped
crying.

Then Moses' breathing was heard, as violent as a gust of
wind. It was as if life, in all its strength, were entering his chest.

Zipporah put Eliezer down near Moses' face. Moses' eyes were
shut, and he was taking large gulps of air. She pressed Eliezer's
face to his father's cheek. For a brief moment, they breathed
together. The child again let out a cry, then another. Zipporah
smiled. Murti and another handmaid, who was very young, burst
out laughing. Zipporah held out Eliezer to them. "Quick," she said.

They hurried off with him, to coat his wound with balm and
wrap him in linen.

Zipporah's fingers and palm were red with blood. She lifted
Moses' tunic, took hold of Moses' member as she had taken hold
of her son's, and smeared it with her son's blood. Moses sat up,
his chest rising and falling as his breath came faster now.

Zipporah did not give him time to ask any questions. "We have
not spoken our marriage vows, either," she murmured, continuing
her bloody caress. "But, as I promised you, today is our wedding
day. May the Everlasting see us and bless us, my beloved husband.
You are the man I want, the man I have chosen. You are the husband of my dream, the man who saves me and carries me off, the
man I have always wanted, the man I have waited for without

knowing his face. Oh Moses, you are the man you must be, and tonight will be our wedding night. I, Zipporah the Cushite, a stranger in every land, am from this moment on your bride of blood. The sin is no more. Gershom and Eliezer have a father and a mother. I am your bride of blood, oh my beloved husband."

Moses smiled and, with great effort, held out his arms to her. Zipporah fell into them, lay down by him, kissed his wounded chest, and put her mouth on his until their breath was one.

WHEN night fell, Zipporah saw, in the lamplight, that Moses' wounds had disappeared just as miraculously as they had appeared. She caressed him and kissed his chest greedily, but he did not wake or even make a noise. She laughed and fell asleep beside him, as exhausted as he was.

In the middle of the night, Moses woke her with his caresses. He had become Moses again, his desire reborn. "Oh my bride!" he whispered, hoarse with passion. "My bride of blood who gives me life over and over again. Wake up, this is our wedding night." He kissed her breasts and belly and thighs. "You are my garden, my myrrh and honey, my nightly tonic, my black dove. Oh Zipporah, you are my love and the words that save me."

Their nuptial hour lasted until dawn.

PART THREE

The Outcast Wife

Miriam and Aaron

T hese were happy days Zipporah was living through, days such as she had been dreaming of for a long time. She was on her way to Egypt by the side of her beloved husband, and it was no longer a dream that was impelling her onward, but her impatience to do what needed to be done in the land of Pharaoh. What did the monotony of the days matter, the endless swaying of the camels that made you feel seasick, the burning sun, the frozen nights? Each morning, when she looked at the grim plains stretching before her, she saw, rising on the horizon, the greatness of the mission Yahweh had entrusted to her husband. She had only to put her hand on Moses' wrist or chest or the back of his neck to be overwhelmed with joy. She had only to see her husband with her sons, or hear him moaning with pleasure in her arms, to be quite sure that he was like no other man. That everything about him, body and soul, represented hope.

And so the days passed, full of promise. But just as the

happiness of these days should have reached fulfillment, it came
to an abrupt end.

UNABLE to cross the Sea of Reeds with their flock, they had to
go around it. For five moons, they kept close to the desolate folds
of the mountains, a land of dust and stones, devoid of shade. They
moved ever westward, and still there was no sign of the River
Iterou.

Moses became restless. The slowness of the days and the
length of the nights made him irritable. His sons' laughter and
babbling no longer took the frown from his brow, no longer dis-
tracted him from his endless staring at the western horizon. Occasionally, Zipporah even sensed a certain weariness in his caresses.

Soon, not an evening went by without his being tormented
with anxiety. The shepherds had never gone as far as Egypt—
how could they be sure they were on the right road?

The shepherds would smile. "Have no fear, Moses. There's
only one route, and you could find it without us. You just have to
go toward the setting sun."

Then Moses would find other reasons to torment himself.
Would his brother, Aaron, come to meet him, as Yahweh had promised? How would he recognize him? How would they get to Waset,
the queen of cities? How would they get to see Pharaoh? Would
the children of Israel accept him? Would they even believe him?
Would the Lord Yahweh speak to him again?

"I build altars, as your father taught me," he would say to
Zipporah. "I call his name, I make offerings. But only the locusts
answer me!"

"Trust in your God," Zipporah would reply patiently. "What
have you to fear? Isn't the Everlasting the embodiment of will?"

Moses would nod, and laugh, and play with Gershom, drawing imaginary beasts for him in the sand. But his anxiety would soon return.

One day, he even threw down his staff, as he had done in Jethro's domain, and again it turned into a snake. The handmaids screamed in terror, the shepherds reacted with laughter, and Gershom was full of admiration for a father capable of such wonders.

Then, one day, as they came over the top of a hill similar to hundreds of hills they had left behind them, the shepherds stopped dead and pointed. "Egypt! Egypt!" they cried.

Zipporah and Moses had already got to their feet, gripping the handrails of their baskets. There at their feet, as far as the eye could see, a line of green stretched across the ocher and gray immensity to the horizon, linking earth and heaven. Moses picked Gershom up and placed him on his shoulders. When his camel knelt to let him down, he swept Zipporah up in his arms and danced with her, his cheeks wet with tears. That evening, his offering to Yahweh was a long one, and the fire of their celebration blazed all night.

After another day's walk, the River Iterou appeared, cutting across the green expanse like a snake without head or tail. Then they were on the plain, and there was more green than ever now, stretching from north to south. It was there, between the desert and the unimaginable opulence of the land of Pharaoh, that a group of men came out to meet their caravan in the early morning mist.

◇

THEY were wearing wide beige tunics that covered their whole bodies down to their feet. Their faces were wrapped in turbans that left only their eyes visible, and they all held staffs in their hands. They came to a standstill in the path of the flock. The shepherds whistled, and the whole caravan came to a halt.

The newcomers pushed the sheep aside and walked up to where the camels stood. A smile was already hovering on Moses' lips. Zipporah took Eliezer in her arms. Here at last is this unknown brother, she thought. She, too, was ready to smile, to share the joy that was about to overtake Moses. But a sudden twinge of fear made her hug Eliezer a little tighter and carefully adjust his colored turban before she forced her camel to kneel.

The newcomers walked briskly up to Moses' camel. Moses climbed out of the basket.

"Are you my brother, Moses?" Zipporah heard a man's voice ask. "Are you the one who has been sent back to us by the God of Abraham, the God of Jacob and Joseph?"

Moses was overcome. All he could do was open his arms and lift his staff.

"Yahweh, the God of the children of Israel, has visited me to announce this coming," the man went on.

The accent was unfamiliar to Zipporah. But in the ease and authority of the voice, she could sense that this was a man accustomed to words and their power. By contrast, Moses' tone was humble. "Yes, yes, of course," he stammered, almost inaudibly. "That's me! I'm Moses. How happy I am. A few days ago . . . Just a few days ago . . . Of course, I'm Moses!"

For a brief moment, they looked at each other, astonished as much by their respective appearances as by the reality of what was happening to them. The shepherds and handmaids who pressed around Zipporah peered at the strangers, searching for their eyes in the folds of their turbans. And the strangers stared back at them, uneasily, their hands gripping their staffs, as if still fearing a threat.

"And I am Aaron!" the man at last replied.

Aaron took hold of the end of his turban and skillfully unrolled it, revealing his face. It was a very thin but impressive face, with its dark, severe eyes, its red mouth, its thick beard. The brow was perhaps most like that of Moses, although it was higher and prematurely lined beneath the thick, curly hair. It was a face in which the flame of passion probably flared up quickly, a face that made Aaron seem older than Moses even though he was his junior by several years.

Moses at last gave full reign to his happiness and threw his arms around Aaron. The shepherds responded with cries of joy. Zipporah, with Eliezer resting against her chest, handed Gershom to Murti. But before they could reach Moses' side, one of Aaron's companions stepped forward and made the same movement as Aaron had made with his turban. A flood of heavy, silky hair was released. A woman! She seized Moses' hands. "Oh Moses, Moses!" she exclaimed excitedly. "What a happy day this is for me. I am your sister, Miriam!"

Moses stood rooted to the spot, incapable of responding to this impulsive show of affection. Zipporah was astonished to discover the reason for his silence.

Miriam had a face of great and terrible beauty. Full, perfect lips, eyes shining with emotion and intelligence, smooth, gentle brow, delicate nostrils—there was not a feature that lacked elegance or charm, and, unlike Aaron, she still seemed in the first flush of youth, even though she was perhaps fifteen or sixteen years older than Moses. But when the wind lifted her heavy hair, a horrible, disfiguring mark was revealed. Down the whole of one side of her face was a thick, shiny purple scar. It was irregular, with raised edges, and wider between the temple and the eye, as if it had been beaten flat.

"I have a sister," Moses stammered at last. "Miriam, my sister! I didn't know I had a sister." He burst into a great laugh, and pressed Miriam's hands to his cheeks. "Of course, not so long ago, I didn't know I had a brother, either!"

Zipporah was perhaps the only person present to sense how embarrassed Moses was beneath his effusiveness. Miriam and Aaron, though, were both beside themselves with happiness, and could not stop kissing him.

"It has come to pass, Moses, it has come to pass!" Aaron cried, raising his hands to heaven. "Yahweh came to me and said: 'Get up and go to meet your brother Moses! Support him, for he will deliver the children of Israel from the yoke of Pharaoh.' We abandoned everything and left. 'You will find him in the desert,' he said, 'on the road to Meidoum.' We came and waited for you on the edge of the desert on the road to Meidoum, and here you are!"

Moses laughed. "And I was so worried! I kept saying to myself: 'Will my brother come? Will I recognize him, when I don't even know his name?' How stupid I was to be afraid! Zipporah mocked me, and she was right again."

"Would you believe it?" Miriam cut in, as if she had not heard what he was saying. She could not stop looking at him. "Would you believe it? I used to carry you in my arms when you were a child!"

Moses laughed again, but he was surprised and somewhat disconcerted, and there was a serious glint in his eyes. "When I was a child?"

Aaron, meanwhile, had turned to the woman behind Moses. When he saw her and Eliezer, he frowned and looked at them with eyes like coals. "Zipporah?" he asked, before Miriam could answer Moses.

"Yes, Zipporah!" Moses echoed, fervently. "Zipporah, my beloved, my bride of blood, may she be blessed. I owe her everything, even my life. This is my firstborn son, Gershom. And this is my second son, whom I have called Eliezer, 'God is my support,' because he came to me at the same time as the voice of the Lord Yahweh."

Zipporah was smiling, but the only response was one of astonishment. Miriam, her gaze made even more penetrating by the terrible mark on her face, looked Zipporah up and down, as if able to see her naked under her clothes. Aaron blinked incredulously, and his mouth quivered. "Your wife?" he said, turning to Moses.

Miriam took a step forward and pointed in the direction of the handmaid Murti, as if she still hoped there was some mistake.

Moses laughed uneasily and put his arm around Zipporah and Eliezer. "The daughter of Jethro, sage and high priest of the kings of Midian. I owe him a lot, too. Everything you see here, brother—this flock, these mules and camels, even the tunic on my body and the sandals on my feet—I owe to Jethro's generosity. These shepherds are all from his household. But the greatest gift he has given me is his daughter. I tell you this: Without Zipporah and Jethro, Moses wouldn't be Moses!"

He had tried to put some warmth into this long speech, but the response from Aaron and Miriam was glacial. "So you were among the Midianites?" Aaron said. "And their priest is a Cushite?"

Moses laughed again, more openly this time, a laugh in which there was a touch of mockery as well as amusement.

Zipporah also laughed. "No, Aaron," she said, trying to make her voice both gentle and polite. "Have no fear. My father Jethro is like all the Midianites, a son of Abraham and Keturah."

Both brother and sister looked surprised, but they smiled politely at Zipporah. Their smiles forced her to lower her eyes, although she immediately regretted appearing too submissive.

Moses tightened his hand on her shoulder. In that pressure, she could sense his anxiety, the silent words that went from his body to hers: "Don't take offense; they don't know you yet. They have no idea. They're from Egypt and are accustomed to Pharaoh's whip. They'll soon forget their mistrust."

"It's a long story," he said out loud. "I'll tell you all about it.

But let's be off; I'm anxious to reach Waset. We'll talk more on the way. We have much to learn from each other."

Aaron acquiesced happily enough, but on Miriam's face, which had known such suffering, Zipporah saw disappointment and incomprehension. And a new suffering. The great joy of her reunion with her beloved brother, the brother she had been waiting for all these years, had already faded.

◇

FOR thirty days they walked southward, along damp, narrow paths away from the main roads. Zipporah had never seen landscape like this. A vast, green expanse of fields, gardens, and woods, and, running through it, an enormous river, dotted with islands of dense foliage and covered with countless boats, their sails gliding, like giant butterflies, on the strong current.

Some of the gardens and palm groves were so huge and luxuriant, they could have provided food for the whole of one of Midian's kingdoms. Zipporah discovered fruit, grains, and foliage she had never seen or tasted before. From time to time, between the cane hedges and the trunks of trees, figs and bays and palms loaded with dates, the walls of a city would appear. She would have liked to go closer, but each time Aaron and Miriam would move the caravan away in order not to arouse the curiosity of the inhabitants.

"There are spies everywhere," they explained. "They'll soon see you aren't from Egypt. They'll run and tell Pharaoh's soldiers."

More than once, Zipporah was tempted to say what she had been repeating throughout the journey: "Why be afraid, since you are acting according to the will of your God?" But she did not want to embarrass Moses, and so she remained silent. The fact was, she saw so little of her husband that to demand his attention might have exacerbated the already sensitive mood of his brother and sister.

Moses had told Aaron that they would have a lot to say to each other. In fact, they were inseparable. At first they spoke in the basket. But the swaying of the camel made Aaron feel sick, so then they rode side by side on mules, their voices droning from morning to night—especially Aaron's dry, clear voice, for, after a few days, Zipporah noticed that it was he who was doing all the talking. Moses would listen and nod his head.

Whenever they pitched camp for the night, they would go off together to sacrifice to Yahweh. Then they would eat separately from the others, Aaron still talking endlessly. Moses would not get back to his tent until the middle of the night, when Zipporah was already asleep. Aaron would wake them in the first light of dawn, anxious to perform the morning offerings with Moses as early as possible, for fear of being caught unawares by Pharaoh's soldiers or spies.

"Aaron is like your father," Moses had said to Zipporah in the first days. "He wants to know everything about Yahweh's appearance to me in the fire. I have to repeat to him a hundred times what he said to me. He also wants me to learn all about the history of the sons of Isaac and Jacob, especially what happened to Joseph. Yes, he's really like Jethro. But he's not as good a storyteller as you!"

He still found it amusing at that point. But soon, Zipporah detected an increasing sadness and anxiety.

"I thought I already knew something of our past," he said one day, "but I realize now that I know very little. I also thought I knew about the sufferings of the Hebrews in this land, and Pharaoh's wickedness and enmity, but I know nothing."

She refrained from asking him any questions, and he did not

ask for her help. In the evening, when the tents had been pitched, she would spend all her time with Gershom, Eliezer, and the handmaids. It was rare now for Moses to spare his sons so much as a glance. And, surprisingly, just as rare for his sister Miriam to take any notice of them.

Murti was the first to express surprise. "Isn't it strange that Moses' sister never comes to see your children? She did make an appearance the other day but since then she's kept her distance."

Zipporah remained impassive, pretending not to have heard.

"Is that typical of the women here?" Murti insisted, with a touch of resentment. "Keeping away from the children and the handmaids, even at night, and spending all day with her brothers and their companions, as if the rest us had the plague?"

Zipporah forced herself to smile. "We don't know each other. We're strangers. Don't forget, we've had Moses with us for a long time now. Miriam is greedy for her brother. She wants to have her fill."

"Well," Murti squealed, "she's certainly having that! If she could eat him, she would. I'm surprised she doesn't complain about him sleeping in your tent!"

"Talking of jealousy," Zipporah mocked, "could it be you're jealous yourself?"

"Oh no," Murti cried, sincerely. "I know I committed a sin, and you saved me from it, but now Moses is only my master and the man I admire. It's you I love."

"Things will be better soon," Zipporah said, stroking the back of her neck. "Aaron won't have so much to say, and Moses will spend a little more time with us."

"Do you think so?" Murti cried, skillfully turning Eliezer over in order to rub his buttocks with a fine chalk powder. "The day Aaron doesn't have much to say seems like a long way away."

Zipporah laughed, although her lips were trembling. What

was the point of revealing the pain gnawing at her heart before they even reached Waset? Murti's words were all too true.

One evening soon after they had set out together, Miriam had approached Zipporah's tent. With a veil concealing her right cheek, she had looked beautiful, although her smile was forced. Zipporah was just then unwrapping Eliezer's swaddling clothes. As she removed the last of them from the chubby little body, she had waited for Miriam's reaction and had seen a look of genuine terror on her sister-in-law's face.

Naked, Eliezer could not conceal his descent. Miriam had wanted to make sure that he was circumcised, but what she saw, more than anything else, was the color of his skin. In this respect, Eliezer, unlike Gershom, was more his mother's son than his father's. And the less he looked like a baby, the more his skin, although lighter than Zipporah's, acquired a soft, luminous blackness with a touch of brown. He looked just like a little loaf of bread stuffed with herbs, the tenderhearted handmaids would say, so crusty you could eat him all day.

But Miriam was not tenderhearted, and she had no desire to eat Eliezer.

She did not even try to conceal her repulsion and anger. Without a word, she walked away, leaving her bitterness hanging in the air behind her.

Zipporah, in fact, had no need of words to understand. Her whole life had taught her the aversion and rejection her skin could arouse. Miriam, totally imbued with the knowledge and tradition her brother Aaron loved to talk about, could not for one moment have imagined that Moses, this Moses she seemed already to worship as a god, as Yahweh had foreseen, could have a son who was so unlike his own people.

"WASET is five days' walk from here," Aaron announced one morning, as they were preparing to set off again. "From this point, we must go on foot, without our flocks, without camels or mules, and without shepherds or handmaids."

"Why is that, brother?" Moses said in surprise.

"If you approach the city of Pharaoh with this whole team, Moses, his soldiers will be upon us before nightfall. We are slaves. Slaves own nothing and don't have the right to own anything."

Moses looked at those who had made the long journey with him and were looking at him now, disbelief on their faces.

Aaron anticipated his protest. "They can go back downriver and wait in the place where we met. They'll run no risk."

"Wait for what?" one of the shepherds asked, with anger in his voice.

"Wait for Moses and me to talk to Pharaoh and lead our people out of Egypt."

"That could be a long time!" Murti squealed. "Now's the time my mistress and Moses' sons need their handmaids."

"Among the Hebrews," Miriam said, in a harsh voice, "wives and sons don't have handmaids. The wives take care of their children by themselves, without help."

Murti was about to answer, but Zipporah silenced her with a gesture. Moses threw her an embarrassed look, but also said nothing.

Zipporah smiled at Miriam and Aaron. "Moses isn't a slave," she said, calmly, "nor is his wife. He hasn't come to see Pharaoh so that he can lead the life of a slave, but in order to bring that life to an end."

A curious silence ensued. Aaron and Miriam stared at Zipporah with as much astonishment as if they were seeing her for the first time.

Moses bent down and took Gershom in his arms. This simple

gesture encouraged Zipporah to finally say what she had been keeping silent about for days. "The Everlasting wants Moses to appear before Pharaoh. Do you think a pair of camels, a few mules, and a flock of sheep will go against his wishes? Isn't it better for Moses to arrive among your people as he is—a free man who does not fear Pharaoh's power, nor his hatred, nor his whims? Do the Hebrew people think that the man who will free them is timid and submissive?"

Miriam and Aaron quivered with indignation.

"Daughter of Jethro!" Aaron cried, raising his eyebrows. "We know our people, and we know what they expect. It is presumptuous for a daughter of Midian to speak of the will of Yahweh."

"Aaron, Miriam," Moses intervened, with a smile on his lips but not in his eyes. "I understand your anxiety. It is perfectly sensible, and I am grateful to you for it. Don't forget, though, that I myself know Thutmose quite well. I know his roads and I know his power."

"Of course! Of course!" Aaron agreed, already less sure of his ground.

Moses placed his son in Zipporah's arms and again smiled coldly at his sister and brother. "I don't doubt your great wisdom, Aaron, my brother. But the reason I'm here among you is that I listened to Zipporah. She is wise and knowledgeable as I cannot be. I've said it before and I'll say it again. Without Zipporah, Moses wouldn't be Moses. Her thoughts are my thoughts. That's why she became my wife."

There was embarrassment on every face. Even Aaron lowered his head as a sign of humility. Only Miriam, her eyelid deformed by the throbbing of her scar, continued to look at Zipporah with all the severity she could muster.

"Let's all go together to the slaves' village," Moses said, in a conciliatory tone, "and see if we're welcome there."

That night, Moses came back to the tent earlier than usual

and took Zipporah in his arms. They lay for a time in silence, savoring this moment of simple tenderness.

"Don't be angry with them," Moses murmured. "Aaron knows perfectly well who you are, but they still need a little more time to accept . . ." He hesitated.

Zipporah finished the sentence for him. "Accept his wife even though she's a stranger."

Moses laughed, and kissed Zipporah's temples and eyes. "And of course Aaron has no great love for the Midianites. He's quite prejudiced against them, for learned reasons. He's convinced they sold our ancestor Joseph to Pharaoh."

They both laughed, but then, abruptly, Moses turned serious. "Things are getting complicated," he sighed. "These are the people for whose sake I came. They have suffered, and suffering has molded their minds. But they're strong and they're sincere. Give them time, and they'll learn to love you and judge you by the good you do for them."

Zipporah thought of the way Miriam had looked at Eliezer and her. "You mustn't fear my impatience," she replied, as lightly as she could, kissing Moses' neck as she liked to do. "You mustn't fear anything! Not Aaron, not Miriam, not even Pharaoh. You are Moses. Your God has said to you, 'Go, I shall be with you.' How could I wish for any other joy than to be with you and our sons?"

Two Mothers

For two days, they followed the river, which was still dense with boats. Along the banks were brick houses with whitewashed walls and flat, square roofs, often with an upper floor. They had many windows, which were wider than the doors of bedchambers in Midian. The spacious gardens were adorned with colonnaded monuments, planted with vines, palms, pomegranate trees, fig trees, and sycamores, and surrounded by walls of beautifully stacked bricks, ten to fifteen cubits high.

The walls ran along wide, straight roads that led to other gardens, even larger and overflowing with fruit and vegetables. Everywhere, men, women, and children bustled. The men were beardless and bare-chested. The women were dressed in short tunics held in below the breasts, their long, smooth, flowing black hair sometimes covered with straw hats. Slow-moving old men led heavily laden donkeys, while young men carried nets full of freshly caught fish.

Farther on, as they came closer to the queen of cities, the road parted company with the riverbank, and they found themselves facing a vast expanse of palm groves between the river and the hills and ocher cliffs, beyond which the desert began. And there, finally, rising into the blue sky, were the temples of Pharaoh.

There were about ten of them, the largest surrounded by smaller ones, as if they had given birth to them. Seeming to grow out of the rock, the tops reaching up into the sky, they beggared belief, so fantastically huge that beside them, even the cliffs seemed mere hillocks. Their faces shimmered in the heat like oil against the transparent sky. The neatly laid brick road leading to them burned in the sun.

Zipporah remembered Moses' words about the splendor of Pharaoh's temples, but their hugeness surpassed anything she could have imagined. Nothing here was on a human scale. Not even the stone monsters with the heads of men and the bodies of lions that stood guard before them.

Farther on, beneath great pyramids, they could see vast building sites. Colonnades and needles of white limestone and walls carved and painted with thousands of figures rose on the fronts of palaces hollowed out of the cliffs. There were unfinished monsters without wings, and statues without heads. In places, the roads became mere dirt paths, with bricks piled at the sides. And everywhere, the slaves swarmed, working, carrying, hammering, creating a din that rose into the heat of the day and was carried on the air from the farthest reaches of the building sites.

Moses, who was familiar with the spectacle, remained impassive. But Zipporah was no more able than the shepherds and the handmaids to hold back an exclamation of admiration. Aaron, who had no doubt been expecting this reaction, pulled on the reins of his mule, turned, and raised his emaciated face to them.

He seemed even older than before. He dismounted and waved his hand furiously in the direction of Pharaoh's temples.

"All this, all these things that are Pharaoh's, all these things you admire, we built!" he cried. "We, the children of Israel, the slaves. Pharaoh takes pride in what he has been building with our blood for generations and generations. But look . . ."

He ran to pick up two old bricks that had been left by the side of the road and vigorously rubbed them together. They crumbled, giving off a fine dust, as if they were melting in Aaron's hands.

"Pharaoh builds, but what he builds is only dust," he proclaimed.

With a cry that might have been a laugh, he threw down what remained of the bricks, which shattered at the camels' feet.

"One breath from the Lord Yahweh will be enough to sweep away everything you think so prodigious," Aaron concluded, scornfully.

All those who, a moment earlier, had been contemplating Pharaoh's extravagance with childlike amazement lowered their eyes. Zipporah glanced at Moses. He was looking at his brother with fervent admiration. As the Everlasting had said, if Moses needed someone to speak, Aaron could certainly speak.

◇

THE slaves' village sprawled at the bottom of a disused quarry. It was a maze of long, narrow alleys, surrounded by a wall three cubits thick and five cubits high. The houses were shanties of rough brick, built back-to-back. They all looked the same, each with a door and a hole in the roof through which the smoke escaped from the hearth.

Moses ordered the shepherds to pitch their tents on one of the slopes of the quarry, where a caravan of merchants had already camped. Only Murti and two other handmaids followed Zipporah as she set off behind her husband along a dirt path. Miriam watched them, but said nothing. Aaron was walking proudly at the head of their little band. Moses was surprised that there was no sign of Pharaoh's soldiers.

"No, they almost never come here anymore," Aaron said. "What's the point? They know very well we have nowhere else to go apart from these hovels. They simply come every two or three moons to count the pregnant woman and the babies."

Aaron and Miriam hurried along a dusty street that seemed to run through the middle of the village, then turned into a warren of alleys filled with rubbish. They finally came out into a square, in the middle of which was a deep well with a cane roof. Children sat by the well, the little girls washing clothes, the boys weaving mats out of straw. They looked up as the newcomers appeared and, recognizing Miriam and Aaron, immediately leaped to their feet.

"They're here! Mother Yokeved, Aaron and Miriam are back!"

Alerted by the cries, a crowd filled the little square. There were shouts of joy. An old woman advanced toward Miriam, who smiled at her and seized her hand. "Mother . . ."

But Yokeved walked past her and stopped a few paces from Moses.

Despite her age and the tribulations that had turned her thick hair white, she still retained the beauty her daughter had inherited. Beneath the lines caused by exhaustion and suffering, there was an elegance about her features, and her eyes had a mixture of power and gentleness, a serenity that overwhelmed Zipporah. She stood there, short of breath, lips half open, hands shaking, but with a dignity that ensured her emotion did not come across as excessive. In a very low voice, she spoke Moses' name. Only his name: "Moses."

It was not a cry, not a question, not an expression of doubt. Zipporah sensed that this woman, this mother, was savoring the extraordinary joy of uttering the name again after such a long, long time!

"Moses!"

Moses had understood her joy before even savoring his own. He smiled, and nodded hesitantly. "Yes, Mother, I am Moses."

Still without a tear in her eyes, she returned his smile. "My name is Yokeved," she murmured.

Only then did the two of them cross the distance that separated them and embrace. Now, at last, huddled in Moses' arms, eyes closed on a sorrow that went beyond age, Yokeved let out a sob. "Oh my son, my firstborn son!"

Zipporah trembled, realized she was clasping Eliezer a little too tightly to her chest, and loosened her embrace with a nervous laugh.

All around, the villagers pressed, filling the narrow space with a great clamor of voices. Moses took Yokeved by the hand and led her to Zipporah. Yokeved looked at her with rapture. "My daughter!" she exclaimed. "You are my daughter!"

Her eyes grew even larger at the sight of Gershom and Eliezer, and her gentle laugh was like a blessing. "And here are my grandchildren!" she cried, opening her arms. "My daughter and my grandchildren. May the Everlasting be praised!"

These words, for which Zipporah had so long been waiting, warmed her chest like fire. Lacking Yokeved's restraint, she found it impossible to hold back the flood of tears. Almost dropping Eliezer, she clasped the shoulders of Moses' mother as she had never been able to clasp her own mother.

THERE followed ten days full of joy and hope.

Moses sacrificed half the flock that had been brought from Midian. The women ground the grain that had not been consumed during the journey. The air was filled with the smells of cooking, and makeshift tables were set up in the night, while men posted themselves on the road to give the alert in case there was a visit by Pharaoh's soldiers. Sitting by the fires, Moses told his story. Whenever his voice became blurred with exhaustion, Aaron would continue, vigorously and with a greater profusion of details. When dawn rose, those who had to return to the building sites became slaves again, despite having had only a few hours of rest.

But the next night, other men, women, and children would slip into the village and the little square in front of Yokeved's house. They, too, wanted to see and hear the man who had received that extraordinary promise from the Everlasting: "I shall deliver them from the hands of the Egyptians and lead them to a good, spacious land, a land flowing with milk and honey!"

The news spread through the building sites like the scent of flowers in spring. The faces, too, were like spring flowers, as if exhaustion no longer had any hold over them.

As the days passed, Zipporah hardly saw Moses, who was always being detained by one group or another and rarely snatched more than a few hours' sleep. She herself spent her time in the company of Yokeved, taking care of her sons and doing women's chores. Miriam spent little time with the two women. On the few occasions that she did, she would remain distant and silent. Most often, she would busy herself with the village women or the newcomers, who treated her with great respect and asked for her counsel.

Yokeved, whose one happiness was to look after Gershom and Eliezer, was unaware of Miriam's coldness toward Zipporah. She did not notice the severity of her gaze, the way she pursed her lips whenever she, Yokeved, with much laughter, kissed and stroked Eliezer's black skin. Not once did Zipporah's own black skin stop Yokeved from tenderly calling her "my daughter."

And Zipporah would laugh to hear it. She could not get enough of these marvelous words: "Come now, my daughter." "Zipporah, my daughter, where are you, my child?"

Words that flowed into her like honey, as if the promise of a gentler, more just world that had been made to Moses were already coming true.

◇

SOON, a number of venerable old men arrived in the village. They were received with great consideration, and a family gave up its house to provide them with somewhere to stay. Zipporah realized that some of them had come a long distance, from the farthest building sites in Waset, both north and south. Moses' name had spread there, too, like a seed carried on the wind. She was delighted at first: Everything was happening as the God of Moses had announced.

But one morning, while he was sharing his meal with Moses as usual, Aaron said something that surprised Zipporah. "They'll all be here soon, Moses. They'll listen to you, and give their opinion on the best way to see Pharaoh. Then we can decide what to do."

His features drawn, dark shadows beneath his eyes, Moses had barely listened. "Decide what to do?" he asked, after a moment's pause. "What do you mean?"

"Decide on the best moment to approach Pharaoh. How to get to him. Many of those around him will try to stop us. We also need to think about what to say to him."

Moses seemed surprised. "Aren't there too many of the elders? How will they ever reach agreement?"

Aaron took offense at this, and assured Moses that this was the only way to proceed. "Our elders have always done this, and we must follow their example. Assemble the elders, listen to their counsels, and apply them. That's the way things have always been done. It is our law. Nothing is greater than the mission that awaits us, and we must carry it out according to custom. The elders will decide."

Zipporah froze when she heard this. She could not believe her ears. Had Aaron forgotten the words of his God, which he himself had been repeating endlessly? Hadn't the Lord Yahweh said to Moses, "You will go, you and the elders of Israel, to the king of Egypt"? Hadn't he said, "I shall be your mouth, I will instruct you on what you must do, and to your brother Aaron you will be a god"? Weren't those the very words of the voice on the mountain of Horeb?

Hadn't everything already been decided? What was the point, then, of further decisions? As for the difficulty of approaching Thutmose, which so worried Aaron, wasn't Moses Moses? He simply had to appear outside Pharaoh's palace, Zipporah was sure, and the guards would make themselves the instrument of the Lord Yahweh's will.

She was about to give vent to her irritation, but she bit her lips and held back. She hoped that Moses would look at her, but he merely approved Aaron's words resignedly.

At that moment, Zipporah realized how exhausted her husband was by what had happened so far and how much Aaron's constant interventions were wearing down his spirit and his will.

Remorse gripped her heart. Thinking that Moses did not need his wife, given all the acclaim with which he was surrounded, all the outpouring of hope, she had been happy to surrender to Yokeved's gentle care. But now, seeing Moses again plagued by torment and doubt, she realized her mistake: She had abandoned Moses to

Aaron's intransigence, his self-belief, and his lust for power, which were eating away at the self-confidence and authority Moses had acquired during the journey.

Wanting to avoid a confrontation with Aaron, Zipporah said nothing, thinking that she would soon find an opportunity to talk to Moses alone. But events were to overtake her.

IN the middle of the afternoon, while Moses was asleep, children came running. "One of Pharaoh's spies!" they cried. "They've caught one of Pharaoh's spies!"

The square filled with people. A short, middle-aged man with thick eyebrows was dragged before Aaron. He was dressed in the tunic common to the Hebrews, but his hair, his mouth, and, above all, his cheeks, with the merest shadow of a beard, clearly indicated that he was an Egyptian. Zipporah, who had approached with Yokeved, saw a touch of fear in his deep, dark eyes. Those who held him were handling him roughly. Then Aaron asked him who he was, and he rose to his full height and looked straight at Aaron. It was clear to everyone that this was a man who had once been accustomed to being obeyed.

"Senemiah, guardian of the corridor to the mighty Hatshepsut," he replied without any attempt at evasion, and with the barest trace of an accent.

These words, and the composure with which they were uttered, silenced those who had been shouting a moment earlier. Even Aaron seemed impressed. He sought the support of Miriam, who was just then approaching. She was taller than the Egyptian. She looked him up and down, and coolly lifted her hair to reveal her scar, as if she wanted the man to get a good, hard look at her. She gave a brief laugh, a laugh that mixed indignation with contempt. "You seem to have lost your way, then, spy. Your queen is no more."

"No, she lives!" Senemiah protested. "Her death is only a rumor spread by Thutmose. She lives, I swear it, by Amon!"

"Don't swear on the name of your filthy god here!" Aaron thundered.

Senemiah waved his hands as if to erase the words. "Forgive me! Hatshepsut wishes you no harm."

Miriam laughed again. "I know Hatshepsut, and I know what she wishes for us—if she still lives, as you claim."

Senemiah looked at her in surprise—as did Zipporah and some of the others present. "I'm not here to spy on you," he said, turning to Aaron. "I've come to see Moses."

A murmur of astonishment went through the square. Zipporah felt Yokeved's hand grip her arm. She turned to the old woman and saw that her face was distorted with fear. But before she could react, Moses' voice rang out, full of gaiety and warmth: "Senemiah! Senemiah! My friend!"

Eyes still puffy from his interrupted sleep, Moses came hurrying out of the house and, heedless of the others, ran to the newcomer. Everyone stood rooted to the spot, watching the unthinkable: Moses greeting the Egyptian, taking him in his arms, kissing him, clasping him to his chest with cries of joy and affection.

Moses became aware of the heavy silence around him. He looked at the faces, the mouths wide with astonishment, and smiled, hesitantly at first, then with more open amusement. "Have no fear," he said. "Have no fear; Senemiah is a friend. He was my master when I was a child. He taught me many things. He scolded and chastised me, as a good teacher should." Moses laughed again and squeezed Senemiah's shoulder. "Most important of all," he said, in a more serious voice, "Senemiah risked his own life to help me flee from Thutmose."

His words did nothing to lessen the general embarrassment. His eyes sought Zipporah's. Gently, she removed her arm from Yokeved's grip and approached him.

"Moses," Miriam said, "we have no friends among the Egyptians. They pretend to help us one day and betray us the next."

"And why is he wearing Hebrew garments?" Aaron asked, with a grimace of mistrust.

"Because I'm fleeing Thutmose and his spies," Senemiah replied curtly, all his fear gone now. "And because it was the only way I could get to see Moses."

"And what do you want with Moses?" Miriam asked. "Why should Moses make you brave enough to slip in among us like an eel?"

There were laughs and jeers in support of Miriam's sarcasm.

Moses raised his hand, his face set hard. "I have said that Senemiah is my friend! Show him some respect and let him speak."

Miriam closed her eyes, as if Moses had slapped her. Zipporah, fascinated, could not take her eyes off that terrible, severe, inscrutable face, on which the scar seemed to grow darker, seemed to become a living, menacing thing.

The elders had moved to surround Aaron, forming a majestic halo of white beards around his severe figure.

"Hatshepsut is alive," Senemiah said to Moses, his urgent voice insistent. "She's waiting for you. She wants to see you."

Moses stifled a cry.

"It's a trap set by Pharaoh," Miriam said, pointing at Senemiah. "How do you know he isn't lying?"

Moses did not appear to hear her, any more than he felt Zipporah slip her hand into his. "So it's true!" he murmured. "She's alive?"

"Thutmose is keeping her prisoner in her palace. But she's alive. At least for a few more days. She wants to see you before she dies, Moses."

The silence was now heavier than ever. Zipporah, still holding Moses' hand, felt his body shaking. He seemed indifferent to the mood of the crowd. He gave a start when Miriam said, "You can't go there; it's impossible."

The elders nodded and murmured their approval of Miriam's words.

"Now is not the time," Aaron said. "It's over, Moses; you're not an Egyptian anymore."

Zipporah saw horror and incomprehension on the faces of the elders, of Aaron and Miriam, and of the villagers. How could Moses hesitate? How could Moses pay any attention to what the Egyptian said?

But Moses looked at Senemiah. "So she knows I came back?"

Senemiah nodded. "She's known for more than a moon," he said, in an urgent voice. "It's what's keeping her alive. But we must leave without delay. Arrangements have been made for you to get into the villa tonight. Tomorrow, it'll be too late."

"Moses! Moses!" Miriam cried. "Why should you care about the woman who stole you from your mother? The woman who stole your life and will be punished by Yahweh tomorrow?"

Moses recoiled from the violence of her words. He became aware of Zipporah's hand in his and gripped it hard.

Aaron stepped forward, his arm raised. "Miriam is right, Moses! Are you forgetting your duty? What does the woman who was Pharaoh matter to you? It's over. Your place is no longer there."

Around Aaron the old men muttered their agreement. "It would be an insult to all of us," one of them declared.

"An insult?" Moses retorted, his voice as heavy as stone. "An insult for me to see the woman who rescued me and kept me alive when I was a baby?" He raised his hand, with Zipporah's hand still in it, and shook it angrily. "Didn't my mother, Yokeved, reject the death foreseen by Pharaoh so that I could live? And didn't it take the love of another mother to save me? Where is the insult in so much love, venerable elders?"

The only answer was an icy silence. Miriam, her eyes aflame, put her fists together as if about to bring them down like a hammer. Yokeved placed her hand over Miriam's, then turned to Aaron and the elders.

"Listen to the word of Moses. What he says is right. I entrusted my firstborn to the river and prayed for a woman to find him. I prayed for her to love him as I loved him. Remember, Miriam! Calm your anger, my child; you prayed just as I did. Listen to Moses. Hatshepsut is going to meet her god, and she wants to have Moses' face in her eyes when she goes. There is nothing wrong in that. It is only fair."

"Nothing wrong?" one of the elders thundered. "What are you thinking of, woman? The Egyptian woman is going to meet her god, you say? But her god is nothing but lies and darkness, and an insult to Yahweh!"

Moses was about to fly into another rage, but it was Zipporah's anger, so long held back, that now exploded.

"Are you all incapable of trust? You roll the names of Moses and the Lord Yahweh around in your mouths, but you might as well be drinking milk diluted with stagnant water! For days and days, you've been getting drunk on Moses' words and the words Yahweh spoke to him. Oh yes! You're all drunk, but you're all deaf, too! Do you think there is now one gesture Moses makes, one word he speaks, that hasn't been willed by the Lord Yahweh? The Everlasting said to Moses: 'Go, I am sending you to Pharaoh. You will not be alone. I shall be your mouth. . . .' Do you think those are idle words, mere chatter on which you can endlessly give your opinions? For days, Moses has been telling you the Lord Yahweh's will. But you continue to act as if his words were merely words! Don't you understand that what must take place started a long time ago, even before Moses reached the land of Midian? And that nothing, nothing can prevent it? You must have trust! If the Everlasting did not want Moses to go to Hatshepsut, would she still be alive? Or don't you believe your God has that power?"

These last words were greeted with astonishment, exasperation, and anger.

"How dare you speak to us like that, you who are not of our people?" cried Miriam, with unrestrained fury. "Do you think you can teach us anything, stranger? Don't you know that the people of your race bow down to Pharaoh and bear arms for him when he orders it?"

"Miriam!" Moses roared. "Be careful what you say."

"For too long, you have let yourself be swayed by the dreams of Midian, brother," Miriam retorted, clearly with no intention of keeping silent. "They may indeed have been sweet dreams. But now you are back among your people, and it is your people you must hear. Open your eyes, Moses, listen to the elders, free yourself of the errors you have been taught. The people of Midian weren't Joseph's people, and they are not yours now."

Zipporah could see how easily Moses might be swayed by his sister's sophistry and stepped in. "Don't let yourself be blinded, Moses. They always trot out these old stories. Do you really think the man who is to be a god to his brother Aaron could have taken a wife the Lord Yahweh did not want him to take? When the Lord Yahweh turns his eyes on me, does he look right through me, like the breeze blowing through a leafless tree? Am I, the wife of Moses, the mother of his sons, the woman who circumcised Eliezer, merely a shadow ignored by the Everlasting?"

They all lowered their eyes. Only Miriam sustained her gaze, but this time she said nothing.

Moses turned to Senemiah. "Take me to Hatshepsut. I'll follow you."

He was still holding Zipporah's hand in his.

ZIPPORAH smelled the strange smell while they were still on the river, huddled in the bottom of the boat. It was a peppery, carnal, animal smell, which aroused in her a strange mixture of attraction and repulsion.

It was dark. The reflections of hundreds of torches and bowls of burning pitch undulated on the surface of the river. By their light, the walls and roofs of huge palaces could be seen, with gates and landing stages and, at regular intervals, sculptures with painted faces and wide-open eyes that seemed to withstand the night.

Senemiah murmured a few words in the Egyptian language. The two oarsmen responded in unison and pointed the stem of the boat toward an area where no light shone.

"We're nearly there," Moses whispered in Zipporah's ear. "Don't worry, it'll be all right."

In the darkness, Zipporah replied with a smile in which there was no anxiety.

"Watch out!" Senemiah suddenly whispered. "A sail!"

Moses and Zipporah moved further down into the bottom of the boat. The two oarsmen did not slow down as a felucca glided past along the other bank, going toward the southern part of the city. Peering over the rail of the boat, Zipporah saw figures dancing on the deck of the felucca in the light of torches. Laughter, the sound of flutes, and the beating of drums echoed on the water.

A moment later, their own boat entered the dark area and the oarsmen rowed faster. Like a shadow within a shadow, the boat glided alongside a landing. An animal yelped somewhere. Two figures loomed up and brought the boat to a standstill. Senemiah jumped out. "Quick, quick."

Moses lifted Zipporah and set her down on the landing. By the time he joined her, the boat was already moving away. Zipporah felt Moses' hands on the small of her back. They broke into a run, their sandals echoing on the flagstones. She looked back to see the boat enter the blurred halo of the torches. The strange smell, more intense and pungent than ever, caught her by the throat. A door closed soundlessly behind them.

"Wait," Senemiah whispered. "I'm going to make sure everything's all right."

He vanished into the blackness. Her eyes accustomed now to the dark, Zipporah realized that they were in a vast garden. The murmuring of a fountain could be heard, and the rustling of foliage in the light breeze. Zipporah had to stop herself from coughing. Her throat was inflamed by the smell, which here left a taste of dust in the mouth.

"Frankincense!" Moses whispered. He guessed that Zipporah was looking up at him. "What you smell is frankincense," he said, softly, with amused tenderness. "My mother Hatshepsut has always sworn by it! It's obtained from trees in this garden—thirty of them. Apparently, Thutmose hasn't had the courage to remove them."

Zipporah had no time to ask him the question that came to her lips. Footsteps approached, and a small lantern swayed before them.

"Come!" Senemiah whispered. "All is well."

The garden was so large, they could easily have got lost in it if Senemiah had not been guiding them. They went through a door into an antechamber. It was a dark room, lit only by lanterns held by two young handmaids, who bowed low to Moses and whispered words that Zipporah did not understand. Ahead, Senemiah was already opening another door, which was twice as high and had gold corners. They went through it into another antechamber, better lit this time, full of draperies and low columns supporting painted wooden sculptures of men and women wearing transparent tunics and necklaces of blue stones, their raised arms reaching up to the dark ceiling.

The smell here was stronger than ever, and the air was thick with blue smoke, but neither Senemiah nor the handmaids seemed to mind. He stepped across the purple rugs, went behind the columns, and pulled on a drape. Light flooded across the floor. Senemiah bowed low and remained in that position.

Moses, his arm now shaking, led Zipporah into the next room. Once there, Zipporah had to press her hands to her mouth to stop herself from crying out.

◇

IN the middle of a huge, bare room, Hatshepsut lay on a half-raised slab of green granite. She was naked, except for a gold plate over her pubis. Her body glistened with a thick film of frankincense oil the color of amber, which covered every inch of her flesh.

In the harsh glow of the torches, she looked as if she were made of bronze. Her body showed all the ravages of old age, while her face, which she was straining to turn toward Moses and Zipporah, was surprisingly young. Her almond-shaped eyes, each with a thick black line under it, were so perfect, her brow—beneath a headdress of blue and red tufts and an ostrich tassel—so smooth, her chin so round and soft, that Zipporah thought at first it was only a mask. But the eyelids lowered, the mouth opened, and a sigh emerged from her throat, to indicate that there was still a little life left there.

Opposite the woman who had been Pharaoh, as if in a mirror, on a slab identical to the one beneath her, lay a sculpture of painted wood, as naked as she was, but with a youthful body and, on its head, a leather cap adorned with the long, twisting horns of a ram and two ostrich feathers. Around Hatshepsut, a few paces behind her, between the bowls of burning frankincense, a dozen handmaids stood with their heads bowed, motionless despite the overpowering smell.

Hatshepsut sighed again, then made a soft sound that vibrated in the air like a cry. Moses nodded and stepped forward. Zipporah, overwhelmed by everything around her, remained rooted to the spot.

Moses stopped a few paces from the old woman's glistening body. "Yes, it's me, Mother Hatshepsut," he said. "It's Moses."

Hatshepsut's mouth fell open. Zipporah thought she was going to cry out. But no sound emerged, and her mouth slowly closed. Zipporah realized, aghast, that Hatshepsut had just laughed.

For a time, with her eyes fixed on Moses, the old woman's face again became a mask, although her chest continued to rise and fall violently, shimmering in the light of the torches, and her curiously short fingers moved against her hips. Zipporah wondered what she was feeling at that moment: pain or pleasure. Then the queen's throat quivered, and words emerged from between her half-open lips. "Amon is great, my son. He has given me your light so that I can join him."

Moses gave a forced smile in agreement.

Hatshepsut regained her breath. "Did you meet her?" she asked, her voice clearer now.

"Yes," Moses replied, without hesitation.

"How lucky she is."

Zipporah realized that they were talking about Yokeved.

Moses inclined his body a little. "I'm happy to see you, Mother Hatshepsut."

Her face, which seemed not to belong to her body, briefly quivered with denial. "I would have liked to be beautiful for you, son of my heart. But even frankincense cannot help Hatshepsut now." She paused for breath. "You, too, are different."

Moses nodded, with a little smile. "I am Moses the Hebrew."

Again, Hatshepsut made one of the grimaces that served as her smiles. Zipporah was suddenly aware of the extraordinary complicity between Moses and the old queen, so evident in the way they looked at each other.

"Thutmose is cruel and cunning," Hatshepsut whispered.

"I know."

"More than you know. He won't yield."

"He'll have to."

"He hates you."

"He'll be weak."

"May your God hear you." Again she had to stop for breath. The only sound in the room was the sputtering of the incense. Suddenly, Hatshepsut fluttered her eyelids and looked at Zipporah. "Approach, daughter of Cush," she said, in a clear voice.

Moses was as startled as Zipporah. He turned to her and held out his hand. Hesitantly, Zipporah stepped forward. She avoided looking at the queen's body, but it was her eyes and mouth she feared.

"Here is my wife," Moses said.

Hatshepsut's eyelids flickered as a sign of comprehension. She raised her hands a little, and the thick oil on her fingers shimmered. "Wife of Moses, the frankincense comes from Cush! Hatshepsut has been living on frankincense for a long time! Frankincense is Amon's gift to Hatshepsut. You are Amon's gift to Moses! But he no longer cares about Amon." Running out of breath, she opened her mouth wide, and grimaced her silent laugh.

Horrified by what she was witnessing, nauseous from the smell, her temples throbbing, Zipporah could feel her legs give way beneath her. Stifling a moan, she gripped Moses' tunic.

Hatshepsut closed her eyes for a moment to gather her strength. When she opened them again, she looked at Moses. "I know you have returned. Thutmose knows it, too. Go now."

Moses nodded. After a brief hesitation, he said a few words in Egyptian. Hatshepsut's eyes had lost their glimmer of life and seemed identical to those of the statue opposite her.

AS quickly as he had helped them to enter the palace, Senemiah hurried them out. Lantern in hand, he led them back into the garden.

Still shaken by the sight of Hatshepsut, her mouth thick from inhaling the fumes of frankincense, Zipporah was relieved to feel the coolness of the night. As Senemiah and Moses walked off into the darkness, she stopped for a brief moment to catch her breath.

In the blackness, she made out Moses turning to her and heard him whisper: "Zipporah!"

She rushed to follow him, but Senemiah's lantern was already too far to light her steps. Forced to advance with caution, to avoid bumping into the bushes and getting the ends of her tunic snagged, she was soon left behind. Rather than getting closer, in a few seconds the halo of light from the lantern had moved farther away, appearing and disappearing between what she imagined to be trees, a vague reference point that confused her more than it guided her. Worried now, she put her hands out in front of her to avoid obstacles. "Moses!" she called in a low voice.

Moses did not hear her. She touched what she guessed to be a rough tree trunk, moved away from it, and called out in a louder voice. At that moment, much closer than she had imagined, the door leading to the river and the landing opened with a very slight creak. She heard cries. By the light of torches, she saw Moses raising his staff as if ready to fight. Men in leather helmets, armed with spears, surrounded him, hiding him from Zipporah's view. Senemiah's voice rose, covering the others. Zipporah heard herself screaming: "Moses! Moses!" Her cry pulled her from the stupor into which the sudden ambush had plunged her.

She rushed to the door of the garden. She was only a few steps from it when a figure loomed up. She was stopped by a powerful arm, and a hand went over her mouth. She could feel the hardness of the muscles that held her tight against a man's chest, still soaking with river water. The stranger pulled her unceremoniously into the darkest part of the garden. From the landing came more cries, and torches were waved, casting crazy shadows on the door. Suddenly, the door was closed.

The garden was again shrouded in darkness. Zipporah, as angry as she was scared, took hold of her attacker's damp tunic and swung her other hand at him, scratching his shoulder and arm. For what seemed to her a long time, she twisted in vain until she was out of breath and was forced to stop her pointless struggle.

"Soft now, Zipporah, soft now!" she heard the man whisper in her ear. "I mean you no harm. I'm Joshua. A friend of Aaron. Soft now, calm down!"

She let go of the tunic, and the stranger loosened his grip and took his hand away from her mouth. "Have no fear, I'm here to help you."

She could not see his face and could barely make out his figure, but the voice and the way he had struggled told her that the man must be young. From the other side of the garden wall came cries and the noise of weapons. Orange lights crossed the sky. Joshua took Zipporah by the elbow and tried to pull her away.

"We have to help Moses and Senemiah," she protested.

Joshua again put his hand over her mouth, this time gently, even a little shyly. "Shh! Don't shout! Follow me . . ."

He drew her to the wall and led her around to the side of the garden opposite the door. There, he took her hand and put it on what felt like a round step. "This is the base of a statue," he whispered. "The arms of the statue are solid enough to lean on." As she placed her foot on the pedestal, he added, "Before you get to the top of the wall, there's a ledge you can hold on to."

Groping her way, Zipporah climbed, vaguely aware that Joshua was climbing up the other side of the statue. When her eyes came level with the top of the wall, she was unable to restrain an exclamation.

Four large ships formed a semicircle in front of Hatshepsut's palace, their bows and sterns lit by naphtha torches that glittered on the river. She saw Moses being pushed into a smaller boat by soldiers. When the boat moved off from the landing stage, Moses remained standing.

Zipporah thought of Hatshepsut's last words: "I know you have returned. Thutmose knows it, too."

Beside her, Joshua groaned, although it could have been a stifled laugh. "That's Pharaoh's way of summoning Moses to his palace. At least he knows Moses is a great man. He's sent four ships and a hundred soldiers to get him."

Zipporah turned to him, surprised at how calm he was. In the reflected light of the naphtha flames, she saw his face properly for the first time. He was younger than she was, with candid eyes that had the same coppery glints as his short beard, and a pointed, determined chin. He responded to Zipporah's surprised look by raising his eyebrows, which made him look even younger.

"Didn't you yourself say that Moses has nothing to fear? The Lord Yahweh wants him to appear before Pharaoh."

With his chin, Joshua indicated a number of small boats full of soldiers that were escorting the boat in which Moses stood as it headed toward the ships. "That's all show. Pharaoh's only trying to impress him."

Zipporah did not reply, her eyes drawn by a dark form lying motionless and abandoned on the landing. "Senemiah!"

There was enough light for the bloodstain on his tunic to be visible.

"Not so loud. Voices carry on the river."

"They've killed him."

"They had to kill someone," Joshua replied, without emotion. "Better it should be the Egyptian."

"He was Moses' friend!" Zipporah said, indignantly, shocked by his cynicism.

Joshua grimaced with embarrassment. "I'm sorry! What I meant was that if the soldiers had got their hands on you, they might have killed you. Pharaoh can't touch a hair of Moses' head. But killing his wife would have been a good way to undermine him before he appeared."

Zipporah watched the boat in which Moses stood, firmly gripping his staff, as it came alongside one of the ships. With a pang in her heart, Zipporah saw Moses grip the rope ladder hanging against the hull. Whatever Joshua said and whatever she herself asserted, she could not help thinking at that moment that this might be the last time she saw her husband.

"Look who's there," Joshua breathed.

As the soldiers pulled Moses on board, a familiar figure appeared on deck. "Aaron!"

He walked up to Moses and threw his arms around him, before the soldiers separated them.

"The soldiers came to the village at nightfall," Joshua explained. "They went straight to Yokeved's house and asked for Aaron. Not Moses—Aaron. They tied his wrists and took him away. I followed them."

Orders rang out on the ships. They heard the noise of the

heavy oars sliding through the tenons. There was a drumbeat and another cry, and hundreds of oars lifted in unison and plunged into the dark water. Slowly at first, but soon building up momentum, the ships moved out into the middle of the river and headed south. Moses and Aaron were soon out of sight. With the naphtha torches gone, Hatshepsut's palace was again plunged into darkness.

"What a strange smell there is here," Joshua said, wrinkling his nose as if he had just noticed it. "What a strange place it is, too. Is this Hatshepsut's palace?"

Zipporah said nothing, unable to take her eyes off the ships.

"Can you swim?" Joshua asked, taking her hand to make sure of her attention.

"Yes."

"That's good. I have a little cane boat over there, downstream of the landing. When I saw the soldiers push Aaron into a boat, I didn't hesitate. I had to come upstream, but this time it'll be easier, we just have to follow. There's no risk—cane boats are so small that at night people think they're drifting tree trunks. Or crocodiles."

"Crocodiles?"

Joshua gave a little laugh. "Have no fear. There aren't any around here. Not at this season."

"You seem quite merry! Moses is in the hands of Pharaoh's soldiers and you joke."

"Thanks to you," Joshua replied, with all the enthusiasm of youth. "I listened to you in the village, and I liked what you said. I liked the fact that you showed us how much you trust Moses. And I believe you. Yes, I think you're right. Moses will accomplish the mission for which Yahweh sent him among us. As for us, our duty is to help him as best we can, not to fear our own shadows. That's what the old men find hard to understand. But they'll come around."

With a few words and a luminous smile, Joshua had dispelled the sadness and the doubts that had troubled Zipporah since she had seen Moses among Pharaoh's soldiers. Even Moses' difficult farewell to Hatshepsut already seemed far away. "Thank you."

"Oh, don't mention it!" Joshua replied, with a little laugh. "What could be better than to know that the world will soon be less unjust?" Already he was squatting on the top of the wall and sliding down the other side. "Come on, we must run now."

When they reached the cane boat, Joshua put his hand on Zipporah's shoulder. "I should tell you," he said, very seriously this time, "that not everyone in the village thinks like me. Especially as the soldiers took the opportunity to ransack a few houses. One thing you can be sure of—Miriam will be furious."

The Scar

Joshua was right. Miriam's anger was indeed terrible, as if she hoped single-handedly to equal the wrath of Horeb.

Zipporah and Joshua reached the village soon after dawn. As they advanced into the warren of alleys, they were greeted by silent, averted faces. When they reached the little square, Zipporah found the elders crouching on mats outside the houses, their lips pursed. Lifting their staffs in their blotched and bony hands, they looked up threateningly when they saw Zipporah and Joshua.

If Joshua had not given her a friendly push to urge her forward, Zipporah might not have had the courage to go as far as Yokeved's door. Fortunately, Yokeved greeted her with her usual inexhaustible tenderness.

"Zipporah, my daughter! You're back at last. How happy I am!" She kissed her, her laughter tinged with tears. "I have not feared for my sons. But for you, yes. Pharaoh's soldiers hate the people of Cush. I said to Joshua, 'Go and see if Zipporah needs you.' Nobody is more capable and devoted than him—and such a handsome boy!"

Yokeved was all smiles. She hugged Joshua, making him blush like a red pepper. Then, before even asking what had become of Aaron and Moses, she urged Zipporah to go to her children.

"Gershom has been as well behaved as a star of the Everlasting. Not a laugh, not a grimace. But Eliezer is asking for you. The poor little prince can't live without you."

As Zipporah was comforting Eliezer, cuddling him and kissing away his tears and laughter, Miriam burst into the room. "Well, daughter of Jethro," she thundered, "are you happy?"

Zipporah was so surprised that she sat up abruptly, almost dropping her child.

"Are you satisfied now?" Miriam went on, the venom of her words reflected in her eyes. "My brothers are in Pharaoh's jail."

The sharpness of the rebuke inflamed Zipporah. She placed Eliezer in Yokeved's hands. Yokeved gave her a little sign of encouragement, as if to say: "Stay calm, my daughter, stay calm. It's fear that's making her talk like this."

Although she did not think she was capable of such moderation, Zipporah made an effort to be calm. "You know what I think, Miriam," she replied, curtly. "Why quarrel about it?"

"Oh, it's so easy for you! We are imprisoned, slaughtered, our houses destroyed, but you . . . ." Miriam addressed a malicious smile to Joshua, who lowered his eyes. "There's always some kind soul ready to help you."

Zipporah sustained her gaze, but refused to reply.

"Miriam," Yokeved intervened, gently, "anxiety is making you unjust, and injustice heals no wounds."

Miriam glared at her and seemed about to retort. But she contained herself and merely shrugged her shoulders. Behind her, Zipporah noticed now that the elders had got up from their mats and were standing in the doorway of the room, listening.

"My husband and Aaron will be back tonight," she said. "They aren't in jail; they're appearing before Pharaoh!"

"What do you know about it? The Egyptian betrayed them, as I told you he would. You made sure Moses walked into the trap. But you always claim to know more than us!"

"The Egyptian didn't betray them, Miriam. He died at the hands of Pharaoh's soldiers."

"It's true," Joshua confirmed, his voice almost steady.

Miriam's exasperation grew. Her scar throbbed with the strength of an animal. She was so beautiful and so terrible at that moment that Zipporah could not help turning away.

Clearly, Miriam misunderstood this gesture. Zipporah heard her cry of annoyance, and the rubbing of her sandals on the ground as she rushed out of the room. Zipporah ran after her as far as the doorway of the house.

"Miriam! Miriam!" she cried out, so angrily that the elders recoiled. "When you see me, Zipporah the Cushite, the adopted daughter of Jethro, you see a stranger. A black woman who isn't the daughter of Abraham, or Jacob, or Joseph. All of that is true. But I'm not a creature of Pharaoh. I'm not your enemy. I'm your brother's wife!"

◈

AT twilight, there rose a great hubbub of voices: Moses and Aaron were back, and the whole village came out to acclaim them. It was quite a while before Moses, half carried by the crowd, reached Yokeved's house and was able to clasp Zipporah in his arms.

"I was so afraid for you!" he whispered in her ear, amid the general hubbub.

"Joshua's here. He took care of me. But Senemiah . . ."

"I know. Without hesitating, he threw himself in front of the soldiers' spears. There was no need. He didn't understand I wasn't afraid."

"Pharaoh would have killed him anyway."

"Alas, Thutmose has turned cruel. He has no remorse. He's worse than his ancestors."

Moses clasped her tighter. By the way his chest heaved, Zipporah grasped that the encounter with Pharaoh had been a failure.

"It's terrible," he murmured, knowing that she had already guessed. "Terrible! What am I going to say to them? They won't understand. Already Aaron doesn't understand."

Zipporah did not have time to respond with a kiss or a gesture of encouragement. The old and the young, the women and children, the men returning from the building sites, with hollow cheeks and muddy hands and feet, their bodies caked in places with dried blood where the ropes of the hoists and winches, the stakes, and the stones had torn their skin—everyone was there, anxious to hear Moses. They tore him from her arms. "Tell us, Moses, tell us what Pharaoh said!"

Moses looked at them, his eyes bright, and they, too, knew that the news was bad. The cries faded away.

"Aaron will tell us," Moses said. "It was he who spoke to Pharaoh."

Aaron told the story, and told it well, without omitting any detail—how they had been dragged before Thutmose's golden throne, how he, Aaron, had announced the will of Yahweh, and how Pharaoh had replied: "Who is this Yahweh, that I should listen to his voice and release my slaves? I know no king of that name. Nobody can give me orders!"

He had cried that Moses would be glad to see the Hebrew rabble completely idle. Moses had lost his temper and had threatened Pharaoh with the wrath of Yahweh, the Everlasting, who would punish him with plague and sword if he persisted in his refusal to free the children of Israel.

Pharaoh had laughed. "I know you, Moses! I know you very well. You were almost my brother. Even when that madwoman Hatshepsut dressed you in gold and called you her son, you were as timid as a sheep. And now you come to me in a slave's tunic and threaten me? I could die laughing."

Much to the outrage of those present—the viziers, the princes, the veiled girls—Moses had climbed the steps to Pharaoh's throne, seized Thutmose's wrist, and lifted it above his head.

"In that case, Thutmose," he had thundered, "if you don't fear me, kill me. Raise your whip to me, the whip that has taken so many Hebrew lives! Come, brave Thutmose, wipe me from the surface of the world, since you are its god."

Pharaoh had laughed again, with a forced laugh, and ordered his guards to pull Moses away, but forbade them to hurt him. "It suits me to let you live. That way you'll see the results of the law I shall pass on your people. From tomorrow, those who make bricks will no longer be given straw. Let them go and find it themselves! If they have feet to tread the mud, they also have hands to gather straw. Why can't they use them? But I want the same number of bricks as yesterday and the day before yester-day. Not one less, or the whip will crack."

When Aaron came to the end of his story, the only response was silence and terrified looks.

THAT night, Moses did not get to bed until late. Zipporah was waiting for him. She took him in her arms and caressed him for a long time. For the first time in her life as a woman, she felt her husband's tears on her chest.

"Remember," she murmured, "remember the words of Yah-weh on the mountain of Horeb: 'I know Pharaoh. He won't let you go, unless forced by my strong hand. I will stretch out my hand and strike Egypt with all my wonders. And Pharaoh's heart will harden.'"

"I haven't forgotten," Moses murmured, after a long pause. "But who will believe these words after tonight? Who will believe tomorrow, when they have to go and search for straw? 'Oh, Moses, how well you have freed us from the yoke of Pharaoh!' That's what you'll hear, Zipporah. And what shall I answer?"

Moses was right. What had been hope turned the next day to despair and resentment. The work became harder, Pharaoh's whip sharper. The most exhausted returned in the evening, while the others had to continue to press bricks all night. Moses was dispirited, and felt as if he were going round in circles.

"We should have consulted the elders about the best way to approach Pharaoh," Aaron said.

"Why did you go and see that old madwoman, Hatshepsut?" Miriam said. "Pharaoh hates you all the more for it, and he will never listen to you again."

"It isn't me he has to listen to," Moses retorted, matching her anger. "Don't you see? It's the voice of Yahweh he has to hear through my mouth and Aaron's. That's how things must come to pass. And it's Yahweh's will to harden Pharaoh's heart against us."

"That's what your wife says," Miriam replied. "That's her way of seeing things, but she isn't one of us. How can you listen to such nonsense? Who could possibly believe that the Lord Yahweh wants to increase our burden? How could he, if he wants us to be free?"

It was then that a rumor sprang up in the village, and was spread by the elders: It was the fault of Moses' wife that Pharaoh hardened his heart and refused to listen to Moses. For how could Moses be the man chosen by the Everlasting, how could he be His mouth and His guide, if he had a daughter of Cush as a wife—the daughter of a people on whom Yahweh, as everyone knew, had not turned his eyes and with whom he had made no covenant.

When the rumor reached him, Moses waved his staff and threatened anyone who dared utter this lie to his face. "She gave me life when I was only a fugitive; she led me to the voice of Yahweh. She circumcised my son Eliezer when I myself had forgotten and Yahweh was taking my breath as a punishment. And is this how you repay her?"

But behind his back, the elders muttered that Moses did not know enough of the history of his people to be certain where his duty lay. What was the value, in truth, of sons whose mother was not a daughter of Israel? Miriam no longer hid her disdain for Zipporah.

"Don't listen to them, my love," Moses would implore Zipporah when they lay together at night. "Don't pay them any heed. They are lost. They no longer know what they're saying, and I don't know how to fulfill the promise I made them."

"Yes, we must listen to them," Zipporah would whisper, returning his caresses. "They don't love me. They're disappointed with your choice; I'm not the wife they would have wished for Moses. And it may be that Miriam is right—she and the elders, and all of them. The Moses they need must belong to them more than he belongs to his wife."

❖

"DON'T blame Miriam, Zipporah, my child," Yokeved said tenderly to Zipporah one morning. "Moses owes her a lot, too. When I entrusted him to the river to protect him from the killing of the firstborn, Miriam was a young handmaid in Hatshepsut's palace.

Hatshepsut didn't share her father's hate for the Hebrews. It was Miriam who pointed out to her the basket in which I had laid Moses. Everyone knew the queen had a weak husband who couldn't give her a son. When she saw my Moses, she didn't hesitate for long." Yokeved was strong enough to laugh at this memory. But then her face turned somber. "Alas, Hatshepsut grew old, and her power diminished. The lords of the palace tore each other apart. Thutmose remembered Moses' impossible birth. He sought out all of Hatshepsut's old handmaids—"

"And found me." Miriam's voice made them both jump. "You're right, Mother, to tell my brother's wife the story. She thinks she's so clever, but she has no idea what it means to belong to the people of the Lord Yahweh under the yoke of Pharaoh." Holding herself erect, Miriam walked up to Zipporah, her eyes burning and her voice like lava. "Thutmose suspected that Moses had not come out of his sister's womb. Everyone suspected it. And he found me. The soldiers took me to the cellars of the palace. For twenty days, they interrogated me about the man they called Moses. At first, I replied: 'I don't know. Who's Moses?' The questions became blows. Then the blows became something else. After each time, they asked: 'Who is Moses? Whose womb bore him?' And I would say: 'What Moses? Who's called Moses?' Then they brought irons and braziers." Miriam raised a trembling hand to her scar. "They thought that would be enough. But I said: 'What Moses? Why should I know that name?'"

Miriam unfastened her tunic and opened it, revealing her naked body to the two women. Zipporah gasped in horror and covered her mouth with her hand.

On Miriam's chest, belly, and thighs were some ten purple scars as horrible as the one on her face. They cut across her right breast, forming folds like old leather that disfigured it.

"This is what it means to belong to the people of Yahweh

under the hand of Pharaoh," Miriam roared. "Take a good look, daughter of Cush! Look at the mark of the slave! Do you understand now? You are only Moses' wife, and you must be content with that position and not crow about it, for there are those among us who will never know kisses and caresses like those my brother lavishes on you."

PART FOUR

Zipporah's Words

I had had a dream, and it had come true.

But, faced with Miriam's body, it faded.

I had called the god of my father Jethro: "Who will be my god if not you?" Moses' God had replied: "I am here, I am Yahweh, he who is."

And now, faced with Miriam's tortured body, Moses' God was forbidden to me. Faced with Miriam's stomach and breasts, faced with her ruined beauty, her violated flesh, my own flesh, intact, made for love, cast me back into the darkness of women with no ancestors.

Zipporah the stranger; Zipporah the wife, who counted for nothing.

There was no need for Miriam to repeat the lesson; I had understood. Moses' wife could not raise her voice along with those who suffered the hatred of Pharaoh, because they belonged to the people of Moses and Yahweh. Moses' wife was of no people, whether loathed or glorious. She was like the chaff that has been separated from the wheat.

Yahweh had appeared to Moses in order to make himself heard by his people, and now Moses belonged to that people, just as Miriam's wounds spoke for all the wounds endured by the children of Israel under the Egyptian yoke.

How insignificant was Zipporah in this struggle!

How severe were Miriam's words, forbidding me to receive my husband's love, or even to support him other than by keeping silent and taking my black body as far away as possible!

And I moaned, still unaware of the days of blood and turmoil that awaited me. Unaware of the terrible loss I would suffer, a loss that is killing me now just as surely as the blood flowing from my gashed belly, from the wound that is gaping as much as Miriam's.

The Return

t took me many words and caresses to convince Moses that the wisest course for me would be to return to Jethro's domain. His rage echoed through Yokeved's house and the streets of the village.

"Yahweh speaks for you as much as for the others!" he roared.

"Stay with me," he implored. "I'll never do anything good without you."

He went to the elders and cried: "Would the Everlasting be the Everlasting if he only supported those who have the same color of skin as us? Do you think he will turn away from my sons because their mother is from Cush?"

But the elders did not relent. "You are forgetting the covenant, Moses," they replied, confident in their own knowledge. "The Everlasting holds out his hand to those he has elected to his covenant, not to the others."

That merely increased Moses' irritation. "You were quite happy to forget the covenant and its duties in the days when Joseph was sold into the hands of Pharaoh."

So violent was his rage, it made clear how certain he was that I would go. Then he turned his pain against me:

"Is that how you show your love for me? By running away? You, my bride of blood? Leaving me here to face the multitude, even weaker than I was in the desert, when you gave me back my life?"

I had to calm him with kisses and caresses, intoxicating myself with them as if savoring honey that would soon be finished. I had to calm myself, too, to overcome my desire to grant him what he asked and say, "Yes, yes, of course I'll stay with you."

But Miriam was there, before my eyes. The sight of her was enough to bring me back to my senses.

Finally, one evening, after a day when the whip of Pharaoh had decimated a whole group of men for being exhausted and unable to supply all the bricks demanded by the foremen, those returning to the village attacked Moses.

"Look, Moses! Look at these corpses! Men turned into mincemeat. Oh, may Yahweh see what you have done, you and your brother. You have made Pharaoh and his princes despise us even more. You have given them a sword with which to slay us. And you bleat because you have to lose your wife?"

Moses spent the following night standing on the ridge of the quarry overlooking the village. Fearing for him, Joshua and I had followed him. Crouching behind a rock, we heard him calling Yahweh at the top of his voice.

"Why did you send me? Since I came to Pharaoh to speak in your name, he has been mistreating your people and you have not delivered them. Why force me to go on, if all I do is make things worse?"

He was shouting so loudly, he could be heard down below in

the village. What could not be heard, either by the villagers or by Moses, was Yahweh's answer.

When dawn broke, Joshua came to me and told me what Aaron and the elders were saying: "The Everlasting won't answer Moses. He is impure because of the Cushite woman. Yahweh won't appear to him until he's resolved this problem."

I could not wait any longer. I ordered my handmaid Murti to rouse the shepherds.

"Tell them to prepare my camels and what we need for the journey. Tomorrow at dawn, we set out for Midian."

Moses did not protest. In fact, he did not even dare look at me.

He took his sons in his arms and held them for a long time, much to their surprise.

His caresses that night were different from those I had known. It was I who was leaving, yet Moses was already distancing himself from me, like a man who is about to leave on a long journey.

When the time came to say farewell, only Yokeved and Joshua had tears in their eyes.

For two whole days, I did not open my mouth. If I could have stopped breathing, I would have. If my skin had been light, everyone would have seen my face flush red with humiliation. I had become Zipporah the outcast wife.

Two terrible days.

Then, as we were going north along the River Iterou, I heard my name being called. There were so many boats on the river, I didn't see him at first. It was Joshua! Joshua waving his arms excitedly and laughing.

A moment later, he stood before me. "I hoped I'd catch up with you! I jumped into a boat as soon as I could. Boats are much quicker than horses and mules!"

"Why jump into a boat? Are you planning to flee Egypt and get to know Midian?"

My voice was sharper and more mocking than I had intended. But Joshua took no notice. He laughed and kneaded my hands.

"Yahweh has answered Moses! Yesterday. Yahweh spoke to him! He said: 'You will see what I am going to do to Pharaoh! The king of Egypt may endure, but my hand will prevail! He will surrender, he will expel my people, he will not want to hear their name spoken! I will lead you to the land over which I have raised my hand, the land I gave to Abraham, Isaac, and Jacob! You will see, I will harden Pharaoh's heart and I will multiply my signs and wonders!'"

Joshua was shaking with joy. Was he aware that to me, his words were like a slap in the face?

Of course, I could not help but rejoice. At least the Lord Yahweh was not leaving Moses in torment!

But how heavy my heart felt as I listened to him! No sooner had I turned my back than Yahweh spoke to my husband! Was he teaching me a lesson because I had not been absolutely convinced that my departure was a good thing? Did he want to show me that Miriam was right?

Was he, too, saying, "Let's rid ourselves of this Cushite"?

My eyes filled with tears. Joshua guessed what was tormenting me. "No, no! You're wrong. I'm sure of it." He kissed me, took me in his arms, tried his best to fire me with his enthusiasm. "Moses will lead us. The elders won't doubt him anymore. And you will see him again. I know it. We, too, shall see each other again. I know it as well as if it were written in those clouds." He pointed to a long line of vapor hanging over the northern horizon.

I tried to laugh with him. "Can you actually read?"

"Of course! I can read and write! Almost as well as Aaron. And not the writings of Pharaoh; rather, the writings of our elders."

"Be a valued friend to Moses, then," I murmured, giving him

one last kiss. "Watch over him, love him, and don't let Aaron be
the only one to instruct him."

◇

THE winter rains had only just begun when I saw again the low,
whitewashed walls of the well of Irmna.

Throughout the journey from Egypt I had been brooding on
my woes, but now, just the sight of the rough bricks surrounding
my father's domain was like a caress. The joy of returning home
soothed me. I clasped Eliezer and Gershom to me and whispered, "We're back!"

Gershom, who was starting to put names to things, recognized the great sycamore on the road to Epha and laughed, and
Eliezer clapped his hands when he saw the pen full of mules,
kids, and rams.

Of course, it was all a far cry from the splendor of Egypt.
Here, the green of the oases was merely a patch in the immensity of the desert, whereas the green banks of the River Iterou
filled the horizon from one end of the earth to the other. But
here, the bricks that had been used to build the walls and houses
had been made with joy, the joy of constructing and harboring
the simple delights of peace, affection, and justice.

My heart was beating in advance at the thought of the cries
of joy that would greet me, I knew, as soon as my children and I
had passed through the heavy door with its bronze fittings. And
that was exactly what happened.

Sefoba came running with a little girl in her arms, shouting
as loudly as though the roofs were on fire. My brother, Hobab,
lifted me off the ground as if I were still a child. My father Jethro,
shaking from head to foot, raised his arms to heaven and blessed

the Everlasting for letting him see his daughter Zipporah again. The handmaids made so much noise with their screams of joy that they frightened Gershom and Eliezer. There was much kissing and hugging, much laughter, many tears, and a banquet like those I had known in the old days when I had helped prepare them for my father's guests.

It was only then, sitting beneath his canopy on comfortable cushions, that Jethro, in his usual gentle manner, asked me: "And why have you returned, daughter? Is Moses well?"

It took me all that evening, all the next day, and beyond to tell him everything that had happened in the land of Pharaoh.

Jethro, as was his custom, listened attentively and then asked a thousand questions: Why had Moses done this? How had Aaron said that? Were the slaves' houses real houses? What was the correct name for the resin Queen Hatshepsut smeared on her body?

"Oh, may Yahweh bless me, what horror, what horror!" he would exclaim after each answer.

That was the only judgment he made, although he questioned me again and again about Miriam and the elders.

He also sent for Eliezer, to see with his own eyes the circumcision his daughter had performed. He stroked his grandson's member tenderly, then gripped my hand and, with fingers that were now twisted with age, squeezed it until it hurt.

"May the Everlasting bless you, daughter!" he cried, merrily. "May he bless you to the end of time. What an extraordinary thing! Quite extraordinary, I tell you, and something we'll always remember."

When I finally told him about my departure, how Joshua had caught up with me, and the advice I had given him, my father clapped his hands happily. "That's my Zipporah! I'm proud of you, daughter of Jethro. For this and for everything else you've told me, I'm proud of you."

That was his only comment.

For the next two or three days, I reacquainted myself with life in the domain. Sefoba and the handmaids wanted to know everything I could tell them about the strange things I had seen in the land of Pharaoh. Then, exactly as he used to do whenever he wanted to tell me something important, Jethro asked me to serve him his first meal of the day.

As I was putting down the pitcher of milk, he pointed to the cushions. "Sit next to me, daughter."

With a little wink of his crumpled eyelids, he indicated the summit of Horeb's mountain. "Up there, there hasn't been a single rumble since you and Moses left. Not the slightest rumble since the great row with your sister and Moses." He chuckled, then clicked his tongue. "Do you know she's a queen now? Lady Orma, they call her. Lady Orma, wife of Reba, the king of Sheba. Still as beautiful, still as scatterbrained, and just as much a creature of whim. She loves power. She loves it so much, she terrifies all who come near her. Even the armorers fear her. Who would believe she is Jethro's daughter? She may come and visit you. Or she may not. She still bears you a grudge, you know—a big one, apparently. On the other hand, she might be happy to hear that you've left Moses, and then she won't be able to resist coming here and showing off her wealth and her handmaids to you . . ."

The look he gave me told me that all that was of no importance and that he had something quite different to tell me. He drank his milk slowly before resuming.

"Moses is on the right road, the road that Yahweh has shown him. He is committed to it. Things aren't over yet. Quite the contrary. He is performing the task he came here to find." My father made a gesture that encompassed his domain and Horeb's mountain. "I know what you're thinking, daughter. This Aaron and Miriam, the brother and sister, rejected you unceremoniously.

Your Cushite skin has become the banner of their jealousy. The elders of Moses' people have rejected you. It's possible that even the Everlasting has rejected you. That's what you're thinking."

He shook his head and raised an eyebrow, just as he used to in the old days when he reprimanded me for making a mistake in writing.

"Zipporah, you are finer and stronger than the resentment you feel. Don't let the appearance of things and the pain in your heart make you believe that it is night when the sun has already risen. Look at it this way. What are the children of Israel today? Poor suffering devils, who for years have been regarded by Pharaoh as nothing more than pairs of feet and pairs of hands. They have no idea how much they know! Their hearts have been hardened by suffering. They go from one misfortune to another, like flies trapped in a pitcher who have no idea the neck of the pitcher is wide open. They see a strange woman and cry: 'Oh, how horrible, she isn't like us! Her skin is black, the Lord Yahweh has covered her with darkness, let's stay away from her!' It's as if they saw an unknown flower and the first question they asked was 'What's its poison?' Zipporah, my child, don't forget that they have lost their way because Pharaoh's whip and the hard labor they are condemned to perform killed the innocence they once had when they were in Yahweh's heart. Miriam is right. The only reason some of them are still standing, still holding their heads high as men and women should, is because they cling to their own wounds, like a climber clinging to the rocks on Horeb's mountain." He paused to regain his breath, and put his hand on my thigh.

"Slaves are slaves in their hearts as much as in their bodies. Just as it will take them time to escape Pharaoh's whip, it will take them time to get away from the knots he has tied in their minds. But the Everlasting knows all about time. They are on the march behind Moses. Do not doubt it, daughter, do not doubt it!

And that young man, that Joshua, is right. You will see your husband again. Have faith, Zipporah, my sweet. Let Yahweh's time give birth to life."

◇

I LISTENED to my father Jethro's wisdom and I let time take its course. A strange time.

At first, all I could do was wait. Moons passed, and I watched Gershom and Eliezer grow. Hundreds of dawns when the name of Moses was on my lips, and my anxiety about him was in my offerings to the Lord Yahweh. And just as many nights when my desire for him, my hunger for him, would wake me in tears.

A year went by without any news from Egypt.

"Have the Akkadian merchants disappeared?" my father would grumble.

"The caravans have started going through Moab and Edom again," my brother, Hobab, explained. "Those lands are more prosperous than ever. That's the place to buy and sell."

Nevertheless, at the height of summer, a caravan leader came to ask permission to draw water from the well of Irmna. Jethro lost no time in questioning him about his journey and his business. The man raised his arms to heaven and cried that he had just come from Egypt, where he had lost almost all his goods because of the chaos that reigned there.

"Oh!" my father exclaimed, with a big smile. "Tell us all about it."

And so it was that we learned about the wonders the Lord Yahweh had brought to the land of Pharaoh through the hand of Moses.

"One minute, the River Iterou turns to blood," the merchant said, rolling his eyes. "And then when it turns to water again, the fish are dead. Can you believe that? It's the truth, though. And the truth stinks. Oh yes! What a stench! Even the sand of the desert stank of it! But that's not all. No sooner is that pestilence over than the whole land is covered in frogs. They swell in the sun and explode with this terrible farting noise. Then it stinks again, really stinks! Wait, it's not over! Gnats, hail, locusts—each new season brings another calamity down on Pharaoh's head. How can anyone trade in such a land? When I ran away with what I had left, you couldn't see the sun anymore. For three days, the whole country was covered with clouds. Three days of darkness! Can you believe it? If I hadn't seen it with my own eyes, I wouldn't believe it myself!"

Jethro laughed. A laugh so big and so joyful that the merchant took offense.

When he caught his breath again, my father threw me a look, as if to say: "You see, daughter! I was right, wasn't I?" As for me, I had to hold my hands tightly together to stop them from shaking.

Once again serious, Jethro turned back to the merchant. "What is Pharaoh doing to overcome these misfortunes?" he asked.

"Oh, nothing! As far as anyone knows, nothing at all. He's told the people these things will pass. They're just magic tricks and his priests will deal with them."

"Oh!" Jethro said in surprise, with a sardonic grin, and winked at me, his beard shaking.

"Yes, I think like you," the merchant snorted. "Maybe these magic tricks will pass, but the way things are going, Pharaoh is in danger of passing with them!"

"And does anyone know why these things are happening? There's a reason for ordinary things. There must also be a reason for extraordinary ones."

"Oh, you hear all kinds of theories. Some say it's because

Pharaoh's god, Amon, is angry at him for rising up against the former Pharaoh, his wife and aunt, who was protected by Amon. Others say it's because of the slaves. But, I ask you, how could slaves perform such wonders? All the slaves do is stamp mud to make bricks."

The next day, Jethro summoned the household beneath his canopy and told them of the wonders taking place in Egypt. Moses' name was again on everyone's lips, and I was the center of attention.

"Oh, how proud and happy you must be to be Moses' wife and the mother of his sons!"

I was, yes, I was. And all the sadder to be separated from him by such a long distance.

Other caravans came. Now the merchants were fleeing Egypt, and each one who passed rolled his eyes in terror and told of new wonders.

"The slaves have found themselves a leader who's almost a god. His name is Moses, and he's the one who's inflicting these wounds on Pharaoh, because he wants to lead all the children of Israel out of Egypt."

All over Midian, people were starting to remember that this Moses had been welcomed to Jethro's house and had become his son-in-law, the husband of Jethro's Cushite daughter. Visitors flocked to hear news of Egypt from Jethro's own mouth. Each time, my father sent for Gershom and Eliezer and made them sit on the cushions beside him.

"These are my grandchildren, the sons of Moses and my daughter Zipporah. It is good for them to hear and learn what their father is accomplishing over there beyond the sea."

And he would launch again into the story of the river of blood, the gnats, the hail, the boils, the darkness . . . He would take his own staff, brandish it, and bring it down between the cushions.

"Your father, Moses, is hearing the voice of Yahweh. And this is what it says: 'Go to Pharaoh and tell him: Be just, king of Egypt. Free the slaves from their labor, allow them to leave your land.' Pharaoh laughs. His beardless mouth curls wickedly. He sits on his gold throne, with snakes on his head, his eyes dark with scorn. 'No!' he says to Moses. 'Make bricks for me, you slave rabble.' Then Moses points his staff, like this, at the dust. And suddenly, the wind rises. Without warning. In the north, in the south, whoosh! A great, icy, rasping wind! Pharaoh runs out onto the terrace of his magnificent garden and sees the clouds massing. The thunder crashes. Huge lightning flashes split the sky, and the hail falls and falls until it covers the whole of Pharaoh's green land."

"What's hail, Grandfather?" my son Gershom would ask, delighted to be scared.

And we would all laugh and feel happy. Like Eliezer and Gershom, we all wanted to be told over and over again about the wonders my husband was performing.

"Soon," everyone said to me, "you will be a queen just like Orma. Greater even than her."

To which I would reply: "Moses is neither a king nor a prince. To his people, Moses is the voice of their God. And I am here."

One day, however, Eliezer, who was beginning to know how to use words, asked: "What's my father, Moses, like? Is he all old and white like you, Grandfather? Or is he like Mummy, all black and with no beard?"

The handmaids laughed until they cried. I cried without laughing.

Jethro had been right. Yahweh's time was doing its work. Moses was accomplishing his task. But the time was passing slowly. Moses had been gone so long, my son had forgotten his face.

With all the wonders Moses was performing, there was one I

did not think would ever come to pass: that we would finally be reunited. That I would once again kiss his neck as I had loved to do. That I would see him clasp his sons to his breast.

AT the end of the following winter, a piece of news reached us that was more remarkable than any that had gone before.

The slaves had finally set out from Egypt. They had left the marshes and the villages. Thousands and thousands of them. Men and women of all ages, the strong and the weak, all the children of Israel! The other slaves, too, those captured in wars of conquest. Pharaoh's building sites were now as silent as if time had stood still.

Moses had led these thousands of people to the Sea of Reeds, and Thutmose had set off in pursuit with his army. By the time they had reached the shore, a storm was gathering and the spears of Pharaoh's soldiers could already be seen in the valleys leading to the sea. Moses had plunged his staff into the waves.

The waters had opened before him. The Sea of Reeds had split in two, that's what had happened! The waves stopped, and the seabed became a path to the opposite shore!

The thousands and thousands of slaves who were following Moses rushed in. When they reached the other side, they saw the waves join again and engulf Pharaoh's war chariots. They were free!

For the first time in many years, I thought of my dream. I saw the water opening before me, the boat plunging between the huge liquid walls. I saw the cliffs of water threatening to join together, like the edges of a wound, and swallow me up.

And there, on the dried-up seabed, I saw a man holding out his arms to me and giving me back the breath that the waves were trying to take from me. Moses, although I did not yet know it was Moses.

The man the Lord Yahweh would appoint to give back the breath of freedom to his people.

My father Jethro was watching me. He saw the look in my eyes, my trembling body, my hands kneading my sons' shoulders. He guessed my thoughts.

"Didn't I tell you?" he said softly. "They're on their way. Yahweh is moving time on. We'll have more news soon. A new story is beginning."

Tears welled from his eyes, rolled down through his wrinkles, and disappeared in his beard.

"Tomorrow," he said, "we'll go to the sea. I want to see if anything about it has changed."

But before reaching the cliffs, where I had so many memories, we saw a man wrapped in a heavy woolen coat made even thicker by dust, his face masked by a hood pulled down over his brow, sitting on an exhausted ass that he was kicking to make it move. He looked like a forlorn brigand. But when he saw me with Gershom and Eliezer, the man jumped down from the ass and rushed to me.

"Zipporah!" His hood fell back. "Zipporah!"

He was shouting and waving his arms. I recognized the voice before the face, which had grown thin, the beard matted with dust and sea spray.

"Joshua! Joshua!"

He laughed and hugged me. It was like an anticipation of Moses' body, and it made me tremble.

The Days of Blood and Turmoil

A nd so began the days of blood and turmoil.

Joshua told us that Moses and his multitude had pitched their tents in a desert plain called Rephidim, just five days' walk from Jethro's domain.

"Less, if you run," he said, pointing to the folds in Horeb's mountain, which were almost white in the mist that shrouded the west.

I had imagined Moses a long way away and yet he was so close!

"I've come to fetch you," Joshua went on. "Zipporah and you, too, Jethro. Moses needs you. His mother, Yokeved, is dead. He's at the end of his tether. They're all out of their minds. Nothing's going right: They quarrel, they grumble, they're hungry and thirsty, they have no pasture for the animals . . . If it isn't hunger and thirst they complain about, then it's the fact that they're tired of putting up and taking down the tents. The desert is too empty for them, the rocks too hot, and the land of milk and honey too far! It's as if they've brought the chaos of Egypt along with then. The other day, one man even complained they were no longer under the whip of Pharaoh. 'At least there, we had food and drink and shade!' he said. If I hadn't held him back, Moses would have cracked the man's skull with his staff. 'What shall I do with all of you? I lead you out of Egypt, and now you all look as if you want to stone me to death!' He was shouting so much, you could have heard him from here. Apart from that, Aaron and Miriam want to be in charge of everything. Yahweh speaks to Moses and counsels him. But Aaron tells him that he doesn't understand the meaning of these counsels. He quarrels with everything and about everything. This confusion only increases everyone's discontent. And now it seems the Amalekites are sending an army against us! And we have no weapons. Moses said to me: 'Run to Jethro. He'll take you to see the armorers.'"

Jethro nodded. His mind was made up, I knew.

"We'll leave at dawn. Get some rest, Joshua. My son, Hobab, will go to the armorers. Their leader, Ewi-Tsour, will supply you with iron swords." He winked at me. "Anything Zipporah asks him, he'll supply double if he can. Meanwhile, Sicheved will divide my flocks in two. He'll keep half here, and take care of my house, and the other half we'll take to Moses."

If I could, I would have set off immediately.

I spoke to Gershom and Eliezer. "We're going to see your father, Moses, again."

"Will he do wonders for us with his staff?"

Laughing with happiness, I assured them he would.

MAY the Everlasting forgive me, but Joshua was right: His people had brought the chaos of Egypt with them when they crossed the Sea of Reeds!

There were tents as far as the eye could see, and smoke, and a constant din, and rubbish stinking in the sun, and a swarming multitude of people and animals, thousands of faces—somber old men, sad children, anxious women, people dying, others being born. A multitude, yes—a multitude that covered the fields of dry grass on the edge of the desert and seemed lost somewhere between yesterday and tomorrow. By the time we arrived, the noise, already shattering to our ears, had been made even louder by the battle with the Amalekites, which had begun the day before on the northern edge of the camp.

It was there that I saw Moses again. I was so astonished, I remained rooted to the spot. Astonished and perhaps even terrified.

He was standing on a big, flat rock overlooking the fray. The shields and spears of the Amalekites glinted in the sun. The only weapons we could see in the hands of Yahweh's fighters were sticks and stones. The ground was strewn with corpses. Moses, up there on his rock, was raising his arms to heaven and brandishing his staff.

As I stood there speechless, Jethro pointed him out to the children. "Look, there's your father. The man over there, with his arms in the air, that's Moses."

Eliezer, frightened by everything he saw around him, gripped Gershom's arm with both hands.

"Why does he have his hands in the air like that?" Gershom asked.

We were to find out later: Whenever Moses put his arms down, the Amalekites were victorious; whenever he kept them up, the Amalekites were routed.

"Look at Hobab and Joshua!" Gershom cried.

They were descending the slope toward the battle, followed by Ewi-Tsour and his armorers, who had consented to come with us. We heard the cries that greeted them. The mules were unloaded in a trice, and the iron swords shone in the hands of the Hebrews.

I saw Aaron climb onto the rock to support Moses' right arm. Another man, whom I didn't know, did the same with his left arm.

The battle went on until evening.

So it was that on the day of my return I did not get a chance to see my husband.

By the time night fell, Joshua was victorious, and when he returned to the camp, he was acclaimed with songs.

Scented with amber and adorned with jewels, I dressed in my most beautiful tunic. Holding my two sons close, I waited for Moses outside the newly pitched tent. My heart was pounding so loudly, I was afraid everyone could hear it.

As Moses was late, busy thanking Yahweh along with Aaron, hundreds passed before us. They wanted to make sure of the rumor that had already spread from one end of the camp to the other, even more swiftly than the announcement of the victory over the Amalekites: Moses' wife was back.

And yes, there was a stranger, as black of skin as they had said. A daughter of Cush.

At last we heard cries, trumpets, ram's horns, drums, singing. My sons knew what that meant. "Here's our father, Moses!" they cried, leaping up and down. "Here he is!"

A serried mass of people was climbing toward us. The crowd parted.

Lord Yahweh, what had you done to my husband?

He was walking forward, tottering like an old man. Older, it seemed, than my father Jethro. Supported by Aaron and Miriam, both of them upright and strong, the gleam of victory in their eyes.

Gershom and Eliezer were stunned. I felt a clamminess in my throat, and a shiver went down my back.

My husband, my beloved. My Moses.

He looked so tired, so exhausted.

"What have they done to you?" I murmured. "What have they done to you? How is this possible?"

"Is that my father?" Gershom said.

His voice reached Moses, who opened his eyes wide. With all his remaining strength, he rose to his full height.

Regally, Aaron and Miriam moved aside a little to let him greet us.

All around, the multitude of the people of Yahweh watched us. They saw Eliezer, with his half-breed skin, in his father's arms, which shook so much that it was hard for him to carry the boy. Zipporah, her black cheeks glistening with the tears that streamed down them. Gershom, clinging to my husband's waist and burying his face in his stomach. That's what they saw. The whole of Moses' family.

"You're here!" Moses moaned. "You're finally here!"

His voice was weak, but everyone heard him. In the camp, the din had died down. No more noise. No more singing. No more drums, horns, or cheers. Silence.

Silence in recognition of the fact that Moses' family was once again together.

Then Jethro, in his old voice, let out a cry. "Moses, Moses, my son. Glory to you, glory to Yahweh! May he be praised for all eternity, and you, too!"

Joshua blew his trumpet, and the noise of the camp resumed.

My father Jethro kissed Moses. "I've brought enough for a victory feast! Tonight, those who fought can eat their fill."

Moses was still holding my hand. He laughed, with a laugh I finally recognized. "Let's go to the great council tent," he said. "You can meet the elders."

I walked by his side, leading my sons by the hand.

Miriam stepped out in front of me, barring the way. "No! You can't go in the council tent. It's forbidden to women, let alone foreign women. You'll have to learn. It's not like the land of Pharaoh here, still less like Midian. Women have to know their place. They don't get involved in the affairs of men. If your husband wants to see you, he'll go to your house."

HE came.

He arrived in the middle of the night, supported by Joshua. I laid him on my bed.

Like a blind man, he touched my face and brow and lips with his fingertips. "At last you came," he said, with a smile in his voice. "My bride of blood, my beloved Cushite."

I was glad that it was dark and he couldn't see my despair.

He fell asleep before I could answer him. So quickly, so suddenly, that I took fright. I felt as if I had a corpse beside me. I almost cried out, almost called for help. At last, he let out a sigh, and his chest rose and fell beneath my hand.

He was sighing in his sleep. The sigh of a man who dreams despite all his fatigue.

I lay down next to him, weeping. "Moses!" I cried, holding him close. "Moses!"

This was the end of Zipporah the strong. At that moment I knew it.

Now and forever, I was Zipporah the weak. The weakest of the weak.

I didn't yet know quite how weak I was, how incapable of sustaining and nurturing life. But I knew how powerless I was. I would have had to be Moses to resist the madness of this multitude. The madness of their Exodus and their hope. I would have had to be Miriam, Aaron, Joshua. To be one of the people of

Yahweh. To have endured the yoke of Pharaoh for generations
and generations, and bear the marks on my body and in my
heart.

Later, feeling calmer, I studied my husband's face by the light
of the lantern.

There were so many lines on it, it was almost unrecognizable.
Long, hard lines on the brow, disappearing beneath the hair,
deeper over the eyebrows. Lines on the temples, meeting at the
corners of the eyes like rivers flowing into the sea. Lines on the
nose, the lips, the eyelids, the chin . . . As if Moses, my beloved,
had to have as many lines on his face as there were men, women,
and children in the unruly people he was leading.

BEFORE dawn, he woke abruptly. He was surprised to see me
there. I kissed his eyelids and his thousands of lines. I kissed his
neck. And then, gently, he pushed me away.

"I have to get up. They're waiting for me."

"Who?"

"All of them. They're waiting for me there, outside the tent."

I didn't understand. I went with him, and I saw.

There they were, long columns of them. Two hundred, three
hundred? A thousand? Who could have counted them? There
they were, waiting, all wanting to pass in front of Moses with
their complaints.

"My tent mate has moved his goat. It's right under my nose,
and it stinks. Order him to tether it somewhere else."

"They stole the stone my wife uses for grinding barley. It was
a good stone, the best. Here, there's nothing but dust and the
stones are no good. What can we do?"

"Moses, the tents of the tribes are scattered all over the camp, and nobody knows where anybody is. We can't do anything in this chaos!"

"Moses, the women are giving birth without midwives because there aren't enough of them. Children are being born without anyone knowing when to cut the cord. What should we do?"

"Someone stole the cushion I brought with me from Egypt. I know who it was. What can you say to him, Moses, to make him give it back?"

I understood now why Moses was so exhausted. It wasn't from keeping his arms in the air during the battle against the Amalekites.

I ran to Jethro. "Go and see Moses, Father! Go and see him and counsel him!"

That evening, in the council tent, Jethro cried: "Have you gone mad, Moses? Do you want to lose everything? They're going to tire you out for good, and themselves with you. They wait whole days in the sun for you to answer them!"

Aaron intervened. "Who else but Moses can judge sins, separate good from evil, show the path each person must take? Only he can do it. Only he, through the voice of Yahweh."

"Do you need the voice of Yahweh to find a stolen cushion or sweep away a goat's droppings? Let's be reasonable about this. You're dealing with a multitude. Moses can't manage on his own. Let him indicate the way and the rules, and let him appoint those who are capable of applying them. Is Moses the only one in all this mass of people who has an upright heart and a bit of common sense?"

"Could you do better? Everyone knows the Midianites are sly. They were the ones who sold Joseph to Pharaoh."

"And, by doing that, kept him alive, whereas his brothers would have preferred poor Joseph to die in the hole where they'd put him. Come now, Aaron! Let's not argue about the past; we'd both be old and toothless before we got to the end of it. Aaron, sage of the people of Yahweh, what matters is today and tomorrow. Lighten Moses' burden; appoint men to help him. Leaders of tens, leaders of hundreds, leaders of thousands. The petty thefts, the jealous quarrels, and the arguments about goats' dung, they can settle for themselves. Moses will decide about the things that concern everyone. That's my suggestion."

But the next day, Joshua came to Zipporah. "The camp is up in arms about Jethro. Aaron and his followers are stirring everyone up, saying that Moses takes too much notice of your father, that the Midianites are thieves by nature. All that old nonsense. They're afraid of losing control, that's the truth of it."

"Let them complain! Isn't that the reason you came for us?"

"Yes, of course! And Moses will follow your father's counsel. All the more reason—if Jethro still wants to help Moses, it's better that he doesn't stay here."

Before saying farewell, my father and Moses spent some time together in my tent, away from prying eyes and ears.

"Did you feel the earth shake yesterday?" Jethro asked Moses.

"No. I'm so tired these days, the only things I can feel shaking now are my knees. But I heard about it."

"Remember the wrath of Horeb, then, my son. The wrath you experienced when you were in my domain. This is what is going to happen. Tomorrow, the mountain of Horeb will rumble. In three days, four at the most, it will be covered in clouds and spitting fire."

Moses took fright.

Jethro smiled. "Have no fear. Yahweh is coming to your rescue. You must make all those ears outside listen. Tomorrow or some time soon, at the first rumble from Yahweh, order fasting, purification, and sacrifices. Order them to strike their tents and walk to the foot of Horeb. When they are there, leave them and climb the mountain, as you did once before, that time when we thought we had lost you."

"Climb for what reason?"

"To make yourself heard when you return. Today, you sit outside your tent and say, 'This is our law.' And you set a hundred tongues wagging, asking for the law to be less strict, while a thousand others want it to be stricter! Such confusion! How do you plan to establish the justice of free men among these people, if all they understand is fear and the whip? Don't forget, Moses, they were born and grew up in slavery, and in their hearts they are still as much slaves as children of Israel."

"But the clouds, the ash, the fire! They will die."

"Trust in the Lord Yahweh. Nobody will perish in the ash. It is time for this people to receive its laws and open its ears to hear them. Your voice alone will not suffice. But the terror of ashes and darkness should make them a little more receptive."

MY father was right, and Moses was wrong to fear for his people. It was I who had to fear.

Moses said: "The Lord Yahweh will come down to the summit of the mountain. He wants me to go up there and hear his commandments. Anyone who tries to follow me will die. Wait for me, and when I return, we shall have our rules and our laws, which will make us a people free for all eternity."

Like everyone else, I saw him disappear into the clouds amid the rumblings of Horeb.

Like everyone else, I waited. My sons and I were well used to waiting by now!

But not Aaron, not Miriam, not the multitude. They could not bear waiting.

Moses was still on the mountain when Joshua came to see me. "When is Moses coming back? The camp is noisier than the mountain. The clouds may not be killing them, but they're making them as drunk as if they were guzzling wine from morning to night."

All it took was one person to assert, "Moses won't come back! He died up there!" and everyone believed it.

I began to run through the camp, begging: "Wait! Keep waiting! The mountain is high, give him time, he'll be back. My husband isn't dead, I know it. Moses can't die—he's with the Lord Yahweh."

To which they laughed and replied: "What do you know? You're a Cushite! How dare you speak about the Lord Yahweh? Since when has he been the God of strangers?"

Miriam took me by the arm and led me back to my tent. "We don't want to hear you anymore! Your voice is a blemish to our ears and your presence a blemish on our land! Know your place once and for all."

When Moses still did not come down, they went to Aaron, first in hundreds, then in thousands. "Moses has gone! We have nobody to lead us. Make us gods we can see and touch."

Then I saw them, these thousands of women and girls, these husbands and lovers, these fathers. I saw them bring out their gold, although they said they had nothing, and melt it in a clay mold made by Aaron. I saw them laugh and rejoice as the golden calf took shape, I saw Miriam's brow streaming with sweat and joy, I saw her scar throbbing with happiness when Aaron said to the multitude, "Here are your gods, Israel!"

Oh yes, I saw them dance, rejoicing over Moses' death. I saw them, their faces and bodies gleaming like the gold they had just melted, dancing naked in the night, singing and kissing each other, giving in to the fire in their bellies and the promptings of their fear, and prostrating themselves before Aaron and his golden calf as they had prostrated themselves in terror before Pharaoh.

My voice was too weak to cry out, my hands incapable of holding back my sons, who were laughing to see such a great fire, such a great celebration, and were desperate to join in.

"Let Moses come down!" I begged the Lord Yahweh. "Let Moses come down!"

Joshua was as appalled as I was. "I'll go up there and find him. I don't care what happens to me!"

He did not have to go far. Moses had sniffed the stench of sin and was coming down. I saw him, emerging from the cloud, walking down the path nobody had trodden for moons. I saw him stop at the sight of his people's madness, the golden calf enthroned on the altar. I heard the roar of his voice—or was it the rumbling of Horeb? I called Gershom and Eliezer and pointed. "Moses is here! Your father is here!"

The children leaped up and down. "Our father, Moses, is back!" They ran to the path to join him and plunged into the crowd, laughing. "Our father, Moses, has come down from the mountain!"

The people heard them and swallowed them up. They did not part as the sea had parted before Moses' staff. They swallowed them up. They did not part as the waters had parted before the stem of the canoe in my dream. They formed a dense, dark, raging swell. They heard Moses roar in anger and took fright, crushing my little children. They heard the wrath of Yahweh and panicked, trampling my sons. I ran to them, calling: "Gershom! Eliezer!"

Up on the mountain, Moses broke in pieces the very thing he had gone to his God to find. Down here, the earth opened and caught fire. The people ran over my sons' bodies, fleeing in terror as the earth opened and swallowed the golden calf. They ran, trampling on the sons of Moses.

Nothing was left of them now but two little bloodstained bodies. I clutched them to my chest and screamed.

Gershom and Eliezer.

◇

AND now Moses wept and raged, wanting to slaughter his people for the killing of his sons.

He did it. He put the armorers' weapons in the hands of Aaron's descendants, the sons of Levi, and ordered: "Kill them. Kill your brothers, your companions, your neighbors. Kill!"

The camp was wet with blood, as if my sons' blood were covering it with one huge wound.

Moses wept in my arms, he wept against my chest, which was still bloody from holding the bodies of Gershom and Eliezer. It was the second time my husband had wept against me, the second time I had marked him with his sons' blood.

"Go back up the mountain," I said. "Go back to your God and don't come back empty-handed. Your wife is the weakest of the weak. She wasn't even able to defend her own sons. She is weaker than the slaves you are leading. She needs the laws of your God in order to breathe and give birth in peace. I need the laws of your God to stop Miriam from shouting me down. The stranger needs laws to be considered more than a stranger. Go back, Moses. Go back for your sons' sakes. Go back for my sake. Go back, oh my husband, to ensure that the weak man is not naked before the strong."

"If I go back, what new madness will they perpetrate?"

"None. There's enough blood in the camp to turn their stomachs for generations to come."

◇

MOSES took up his staff, and again disappeared into the clouds.

"I'm leaving," I said to Joshua. "I can't stay here any longer."

"Where will you go?"

"To Midian, to my father's domain. There is no other place for me. When I'm there, I'll ask for food, grain, and animals for you. At least your people will have enough to eat and won't have to nourish themselves with violence."

"I'll go with you to bring everything back. Ewi-Tsour and his armorers will go with us. Hobab will stay here to help Moses when he comes down."

◇

I WAS wrong. There was no place for me now in Midian, or in Jethro's domain.

When we reached the well of Irmna, a group of men were waiting for us.

"Look!" Ewi-Tsour cried. "It's Elchem. He's come to meet us."

He was smiling. I recognized Elchem's burned and disfigured face, which reminded me of Miriam's. I, too, had a scar now, but it was invisible.

But Elchem did not smile back at Ewi-Tsour. From among the group of armorers he was leading rose a voice I recognized.

"Where are you going? Who gave you permission to approach this well?"

"Orma!"

My sister Orma had stepped forward. She was as beautiful as ever—perhaps even more so—her eyes as black, her mouth as scornful.

"I'm on my way back to our father's house," I said. "I'm also looking for food for Moses' people. They're dying of hunger in the desert."

"Jethro is dead. It is I, the wife of Reba and queen of Sheba, who gives the orders here now. It is out of the question for the multitude led by your Moses to descend like locusts on what belongs to us."

"Orma, my sister!"

"I'm not your sister and my father, Jethro, was not your father!"

"Orma, they're hungry! My sons died because hunger drove them mad!"

"Who was it who wanted at all costs to be Moses' wife?"

She simply had to smile, and Elchem and his men unsheathed their swords and threw themselves on us.

When Elchem plunged his superb blade into my belly, I again saw his scar throb, as Miriam's had throbbed at the sight of the golden calf.

But what did it matter? I was already dead. I had left my life behind in my son's bodies.

EPILOGUE

Joshua returned to the tents of Israel.

Moses came down from the mountain. His face was so radiant that none dared approach him. None except Joshua, who told him of Zipporah's death.

Moses did not fly into a rage, did not curse Orma and the people of Midian. But, for the first time, those who had followed him out of Egypt saw tears in his eyes.

He whispered Zipporah's name. He called her name, as if calling for something lost in the darkess: "Zipporah, Zipporah, Zipporah!"

Softly, not wanting the syllables to be lost on the wind.

Then he uttered the names of his sons, Gershom and Eliezer. "May they not be forgotten, they who were trampled by the madness of the crowd!"

Moses showed Joshua the tablets of the Law. "Look," he said. "I have not come down empty-handed from the mountain. From this day on, Zipporah is here." He touched some of the words lightly with the tips of his fingers. "Yahweh heard my wife, the woman of Midian. He heard her, Joshua!"

Joshua saw that it was true. On the stone, these words were engraved: "If you receive a stranger, do not ill-treat him. May the stranger in your house be as one of your own. Love him as yourself, for you too were strangers in the land of Egypt. I am Yahweh your God, and no injustice shall be done in my name!"

The next day, the breath of Yahweh descended on the camp. Showing his wrath, he punished Miriam with seven days of leprosy for her harsh treatment of Zipporah, Moses' black wife.

But, as time has shown, men are fools, and slow to learn. Aaron's son came to see Moses. "We must march on Midian," he declared, waving his arms. "We must avenge the murder of your wife."

"I want no part of your vengeance," Moses replied. "Nor was vengeance ever in Zipporah's heart. My wife wouldn't have wanted her memory tarnished with the blood of Midian. She wouldn't have wanted any blood, any wars. She loved only trust, respect, and peace. She said that all men were equal before the Everlasting, and that no man should lift his hand against another.

"Zipporah," he went on, "wanted caresses from me to honor the lovely blackness of her skin. But how long was it since I'd last given them to her? If you want vengeance, kill me, for I too killed her."

Men are fools, and slow to learn. Aaron's son did not heed Moses' words. He persuaded those who would listen to him, and they set off to wage war on Midian.

Moses had more deaths to mourn. Deaths that Zipporah had wanted to avoid.

"We are not milk and honey," he said to the people. "I freed you from slavery thanks to the strong hand of the Everlasting, but in your hearts you are still slaves. In your hearts, you are in the desert. And in the desert you will die."

"What do you mean?" the people answered, in surprise. "What have we done wrong?"

"The word of the Almighty is addressed to free men," he explained. "Freedom is like water at the bottom of a well. We must learn to bring it out into the light of day, and then we must learn to drink it. You are not capable of that. Your children and your grandchildren, who have never known slavery—they and not you will enter Canaan and discover the Promised Land!"

And so it came to pass that the people whom Moses had led out of Egypt wandered in the desert for forty years, until all Pharaoh's former slaves had died and their bodies had become dust in the dust of the desert.

It was a new people that reached the banks of the Jordan. Old and worn by now, Moses still mourned his wife, Zipporah, the black woman. He missed her voice, he missed her eyes, he missed her wise counsels. Not a day went by that he did not miss everything about Zipporah!

When he reached the borders of Canaan, he climbed Mount Nebo to gaze upon the land of which the Everlasting had spoken.

At the sight of this land of milk and honey, his heart was filled with doubt. Was he not like all the others, unworthy of setting foot in the promised land? Hadn't he hesitated to accept the will of the Almighty? Without Zipporah, would he have had the courage to confront Pharaoh or even to listen to Yahweh? Without Zipporah, would he have known the beauty of a black woman, a stranger? Would he have known the breath that unites all hearts?

But Zipporah was no longer there to teach him what he still did not know.

So Moses gave the stones of the Law to Joshua. "It is you and not I who will enter Canaan," he said. "It is you who will lead the people. I shall stay here. Mount Nebo will be my tomb."

And he died, it is said, with a kiss from the Everlasting.

In accordance with his wishes, there was no stone monument, no sacred cave for his bones. Yahweh did not want any idolatry. Moses was not a god, merely a man of flesh and blood who had died with his dream before his eyes. A man who will remain forever in the vast mausoleum of words and memories.

Who, though, will remember Zipporah the black woman, the Cushite? Who will remember what she accomplished? Who will still speak her name?

◈

MAY this book serve as her humble tomb.

About the Author

MAREK HALTER was born in Poland in 1936. During
World War II, he and his parents narrowly escaped the
Warsaw Ghetto. After a time in Russia and Uzbekistan,
they emigrated to France in 1950. There Halter studied
pantomime with Marcel Marceau and embarked on a
career as a painter that led to several international exhibi-
tions. In 1967, he founded the International Committee
for a Negotiated Peace Agreement in the Near East, and
played a crucial role in the organization of the first official
meetings between Palestinians and Israelis.

In the 1970s, Marek Halter turned to writing. He first
published *The Madman and the Kings*, which was awarded
the Prix Aujourd'hui in 1976. He is also the author of several internationally acclaimed, bestselling historical novels,
including *The Messiah*, *The Mysteries of Jerusalem*, and *The
Book of Abraham*, which won the Prix du Livre Inter. The
third volume of the Canaan Trilogy, *Lilah*, will be published in 2006. Marek Halter lives in Paris.

ZIPPORAH, *Wife of Moses*

MAREK HALTER

◆

A Reader's Guide

ZIPPORAH, *Wife of Moses*, is bestselling novelist Marek Halter's latest portrait of a noteworthy woman of the Bible. In a spectacular feat of imagination, Halter has breathed new life into this little-known, though influential, Old Testament figure. Orphaned as an infant, Zipporah is adopted by Jethro, high priest and sage of the Hebrew Midianites, who raises her as his own, despite her black skin. Although she is accepted and adored by his family, as a woman her color keeps the Midianite men at bay. She feels forever an outsider—until one day she meets Moses, himself a fugitive from Pharaoh's Egypt. Their connection is immediate, and before long, Moses asks Zipporah to be his wife. But her innate wisdom, and the sense of justice instilled by Jethro, are stronger even than her passion for the love of her life: Zipporah refuses to marry Moses until he fulfills his destiny and frees his people from Pharaoh's brutal slavery.

Bold, independent, and a true survivor, Zipporah is a fascinating heroine, and her world of desert oases, temples, and ancient wonders is a fitting backdrop to an epic tale.

"Marek Halter has not only written a passionate epic, but also revealed the fundamental role that a black woman played in the destiny of the Jewish people . . . Truly captivating." —PARIS MATCH

This guide is designed to help direct your reading group's discussion of Marek Halter's powerful novel.

FOR DISCUSSION

1. Before reading this novel, how much—or how little—did you know of Zipporah's story? Read the portions of Exodus pertaining to Zipporah's story. How has the novel changed your understanding of her importance? Of Moses' actions?

2. If you haven't already, read the beautiful excerpt from *Song of Solomon* on page v. What did this make you expect from the book? What about the other biblical quotations on page v?

3. Discuss how the novel changes your perspective on race relations: How have they changed since biblical times, if at all? Would Zipporah's experience be any different today?

4. On page 1, Zipporah says, "I have had a dream." Considering that this is the story of Moses and the Jews' exodus from slavery, does this strike you as an intentional reference to the famous speech by Dr. Martin Luther King, Jr.? Do you see any other King allusions in the novel, for example to the Promised Land?

5. What is the significance of Zipporah's dream? In what ways did it come true, and in what ways did its accuracy fail? On page 73, Jethro says to Zipporah, "Live your dream in sleep, but do not let your life become a sleep." Lacking Zipporah's influence, do you believe Moses might have done just that?

6. On page 36, Zipporah watches Moses catching fish and sees "a vast shimmer on the sea, much more intense than any of the others, like a wind spreading light as far as the shore." Several pages later we read, "In the days, weeks, and years that followed, Zipporah was often to remember that moment, a moment she was sure was neither as brief nor as supernatural as it had seemed to her at the time." In the end, what did this moment mean?

7. When Moses confesses that he has killed a man on page 64, instead of turning him away or being afraid, Jethro invites Moses to tell his story. At this point, Jethro knows virtually nothing about him. What makes Jethro react this way? Is it Zipporah's influence?

8. Both Moses and Zipporah are adopted by powerful families. Do you believe this shaped their destinies, or were the adoptions themselves preordained?

9. Throughout the novel, various characters are portrayed as storytellers. Do you believe this is how the stories of the Bible were shared initially? Was this how Moses' story was passed down? If so, how might that explain Zipporah's minor role in the recorded bible?

10. It seems on pages 120–121 that Moses would be quite content to be a shepherd in Midian with Zipporah as his wife, but Zipporah sees something more in his destiny. She says, "I know you must put on your gold bracelets and go among those who are your people. You must hold back the whip that strikes them." How does she know this? What gives her the strength to refuse him, even after bearing his children?

11. Why did Jethro allow both Zipporah and Orma to refuse to marry suitable men? If he weren't a powerful man, would he have been so willing? Discuss the role of women in Midian society and contrast it to Hebrew and Egyptian life.

12. How did Marek Halter's depiction of the burning bush deepen your understanding of the story?

13. When Moses and Zipporah meet Moses' family, Miriam's response to Zipporah is immediately negative, while Yokeved's is the exact opposite. Why do you think there is such a difference between the sister and the mother?

14. On page 229, Zipporah says, "The Moses they [the Hebrews] need must belong to them more than he belongs to his wife." Why does she feel this way? Does the same hold true for the wives of today's leaders?

15. When Miriam shows her scarred body to Zipporah, it changes radically the way Zipporah feels about her own place in the world. Was she right?

16. In his efforts to strengthen Zipporah's resolve, Jethro says, "The only reason some of [the Hebrews] are still standing, still holding their heads high as men and women should, is because they cling to their own wounds, like a climber clinging to the rocks on Horeb's mountain." Are there any groups that you believe are behaving this way today?

17. In Halter's depiction, Aaron and Miriam turn out to be somewhat treacherous. Is it purely jealousy, or something deeper? How does this jibe with your knowledge of the biblical characters?

18. After Zipporah's murder, Moses refuses the suggestion of retribution against the Midianites. "What good would that do? What she wanted was trust, respect, and love. Not war. She wanted caresses to beautify the blackness of her skin. How long is it since I last gave them to her? I, too, killed her." What does Moses mean by this? What has he learned?

19. Reread the last lines of the novel: "Who, though, will remember Zipporah the black woman, the Cushite? Who will remember what she accomplished? Who will still speak her name?" How would you answer those questions? Discuss Zipporah's legacy.

PROLOGUE

Antinoes is coming back.

My heart trembles.

My hand trembles. I hold the stylus tight between my fingers to make sure that the words the camphor ink is laying down on the papyrus are legible.

Antinoes, my beloved, is coming back!

Last night, a messenger in dusty tunic and sandals brought me a wax tablet.

I immediately recognized my beloved's writing.

A sleepless night followed. Tossing and turning on my bed, I pressed the tablet to my breast as if to stamp the words into my flesh.

Lilah, my sweet, my lover, in three days and three nights I shall be with you again. Count the shadows of the sun. I am returning nobler and more victorious! And yet, until I have you in my arms, until my lips have sated themselves on the scent of your skin, I will have achieved nothing in two years of separation.

My heart is beating faster than it does before a battle. Soon, by the will of your God of heaven and that of the

mighty Ahura Mazda, god of the Persians, we will at last be
man and wife.

All night long, my heart has been drinking in Antinoes' words.

If I close my eyes, I read them within me. If I try to forget them, I hear my beloved's voice whispering them in my ear.

That is my madness. And if I tremble, it is also with fear.

This ought to be the hour of peace. The darkness is receding. All is silent in the house. The handmaids have not yet risen, the fires are not yet lit. The light of dawn is as white as the milk that they say conceals deadly poison at banquets given by the King of Kings.

Man and wife, that was our promise. Antinoes and Lilah!

A children's promise, a lovers' promise!

I remember the time when we were like the fingers of one hand. Antinoes, Ezra, and Lilah. To see one was to see the others. Two boys and one girl, always together. The fact that one was the son of a lord who attended the meals of the Great King and the others the children of exiled Jews mattered little.

The roofs of the upper town of Susa echoed to our laughter. Whenever our mother called us, we heard a single cry: Antinoes, Ezra, and Lilah!

Then my mother's voice fell silent.

My father's voice fell silent.

A deadly disease spread through Susa. It spread through the fields along the River Shaour, it spread as far as Babylon, striking rich and poor alike, not only in Persia, but also in Zion, Lydia, and Media.

I remember the day when Ezra and I, our bodies drained of tears, stood before our mother and father, asleep in death.

We held hands with Antinoes. Our grief was also his. We stood shoulder to shoulder. The three of us had become one, like some strange animal whose limbs had become inextricably entwined.

I remember the scorching summer's day when Antinoes led us into his magnificent home and presented us to his father.

"Father, this is my sister, Lilah, and this is my brother, Ezra. Whatever they eat, I eat. Whatever they dream, I dream. Father, let them come to our house as often as they wish. If you refuse, then I will have no other roof over my head than that of their uncle Mordecai, who has taken them in now that they have neither father nor mother."

Antinoes' father laughed until he could laugh no more. He called the handmaids and told them to bring fruit and cow's milk. When our stomachs were full, we hurled ourselves into the great pools of the house to cool ourselves down. Children are greedy for happiness.

Our days were again carefree. "My brother, Antinoes!" Ezra would cry, and Antinoes would answer, "My brother, Ezra!" Together, they forged swords and bows and javelins in Uncle Mordecai's workshop.

Oh, Yahweh, why must we stop being children?

I remember the day when the games ceased and the laughter trembled at the touch of a caress.

Antinoes, Ezra, and Lilah. Two men and a woman. A new expression in their eyes, an unaccustomed silence on their lips. The beauty of nights on the roofs of Susa, the beauty of embraces, the pleasure of bodies catching fire like lamp oil too long heated.

The three of us becoming one: that was over now. Now it was Lilah and Antinoes. Lilah and Ezra. Antinoes and Ezra. Lovers and siblings, rage and jealousy.

I remember it well; it churns in my memory like the dark waters of the Shaour in the rainy season.

The handmaids have arisen now. The fires are lit. Soon there will be cries and laughter. It may turn out a fine day, alive with hope and promise.

As I write, my face is reflected in the silver mirror above the writing desk. Antinoes says it is a beautiful face. That my youth is the scent of springtime.

Antinoes loves me and desires me, is generous with words that speak of his love and his desire.

But all I see in the mirror is a furrowed brow and anxious eyes. Is this the face—this sad, preoccupied beauty—that will welcome my beloved when he returns?

Oh, Yahweh, hear the plea of Lilah, daughter of Serayah and Achazya, I who have no other God than the God of my father.

Antinoes is not a child of Israel, but he is loyal to his promise. He wants me for himself alone, as a husband must want his bride.

Ezra will say to me, "Ah, so now you are abandoning me!"

Yahweh, is it not your will that our bodies should grow beyond childhood? That we should become men and women, each with his own breath, his own strength, the joy of his own senses? Is it not your will that man's caress should delight a woman? Is it not your law that a sister should find other eyes to love than those of her brother, another voice to hear and admire than that of her brother? Is it not your teaching that a woman should choose a husband according to her heart, as Sarah did, and Rachel and Zipporah, the wives of Abraham, Jacob, and Moses?

Whichever I am faithful to, the other's pain will be just as strong.

Why must I cause pain when my brother and my lover have an equal place in my heart?

Oh, Yahweh, God of heaven, God of my father, give me the strength to find the words to appease Ezra! Give him the strength to hear them.

Also by Marek Halter

THE CANAAN TRILOGY
BEGINS WITH THE OLD TESTAMENT'S MOST
UNFORGETTABLE MATRIARCH

1-4000-5278-5 · $12.95 paper

In the Sumerian city-state of Ur, Sarah, the daughter of a power-ful lord, finds herself drawn to an exotic stranger named Abram. When she gives up her exalted life to join Abram's tribe and fol-low the one true God, it is then that her journey truly begins. From the great ziggurat of Ishtar to the fertile valleys of Canaan to the bedchamber of the mighty Pharaoh himself, Sarah's story reveals an ancient world full of beauty, intrigue, and miracles.

THREE RIVERS PRESS · NEW YORK

Available from Three Rivers Press wherever books are sold
www.crownpublishing.com